Terese laid a gentle hand on Lachlan's. "You truly are a hero."

Her warm palm made his flesh tingle, but then her innocent touches always did. She sparked something inside him that he could not deny.

While he loved the pleasure of her touch, he knew it was wrong.

"I am no hero," Lachlan told her.

"I would say you are modest, but I know better."

He laughed. "You have gotten to know me well in the short time I have been here."

"You have made it easy for me to get to know you."

"How so?"

"Our talks. When two people spend time talking they are bound to get to know each other."

"And become friends?"

"And become friends."

He was glad she thought of him as a friend, but he wished there could be more between them. He berated himself for such sinful thoughts. He had to forget how her lips were perfect for kissing, how he itched to take hold of her slim waist and roam his han

Romances by **Donna Fletcher**

THE ANGEL AND THE HIGHLANDER
UNDER THE HIGHLANDER'S SPELL
RETURN OF THE ROGUE
THE HIGHLANDER'S BRIDE
TAKEN BY STORM
THE BEWITCHING TWIN
THE DARING TWIN
DARK WARRIOR
LEGENDARY WARRIOR

DONNA FLETCHER

THE
ANGEL
AND THE
HIGHLANDER

A V O N

An Imprint of HarperCollinsPublishers

This is a work of fiction. Names, characters, places, and incidents are drawn from the author's imagination or are used fictitiously and are not to be construed as real. Any resemblance to actual events, locales, organizations, or persons, living or dead, is entirely coincidental.

AVON BOOKS
An Imprint of HarperCollins*Publishers*
10 East 53rd Street
New York, New York 10022-5299

First Avon Books paperback printing: May 2009

Avon Trademark Reg. U.S. Pat. Off. and in Other Countries, Marca Registrada, Hecho en U.S.A.
HarperCollins® is a registered trademark of HarperCollins Publishers.

Printed in the U.S.A.

10 9 8 7 6 5 4 3 2 1

Chapter 1

"I'm not going. She's a shrew, and from what I've heard an ugly one at that. There's not a man alive who can deal with her. Why do you think her father stuck her in a convent?" Lachlan shook his head adamantly all the while knowing that no matter how hard he protested, he would have no choice. He would have to go and escort Alyce, daughter of Angus of the clan Bunnock, the laird of the largest and most powerful clan in the whole north of Scotland.

"By now she'll have learned to behave," Cavan said bluntly.

Lachlan bit his tongue. It wasn't because Cavan was his oldest brother, but rather that Cavan was laird of the clan Sinclare and was due respect and obedience. Lachlan would have given it to his brother regardless. Cavan was a man of tremendous courage and conviction and he lead the clan with honor. He couldn't disrespect him just because he didn't like the task at hand.

Besides," Cavan said with a glint of a smile, "there isn't a woman I haven't seen you able to charm. I'm confident that you can handle a shrew."

Lachlan grinned and nodded. "You're right. There isn't a woman I can't handle, nor one who's impervious to my charm."

"Then the mission should prove simple and successful. Go retrieve Alyce Bunnock so that she may wed the man of her father's choosing."

Lachlan was about to ask the obvious question when Cavan held up his hand.

"It doesn't matter if she objects. She has a duty to her father and clan. Tie her to the horse if you have to, but get her here."

"That's all I wanted to know," Lachlan said, satisfied his hands weren't tied if she should give him trouble.

"You leave tomorrow at first light. Take a strong contingent of warriors with you. Angus Bunnock informed me that the area is mostly pagan, the reason why the church sent the nuns to establish the convent five years ago. On top of that a band of mercenaries has been plundering the region. To what extent or how strong their group, I do not know."

"Ten Highlander warriors should do against a ragtag band of misfits."

"Don't ever underestimate your opponents. Some of those misfits have probably fought more battles than you."

"I will be sure to stay alert," Lachlan said.

"Be sure you stay alive," Cavan commanded.

Lachlan finished recalling the meeting he had with his brother Cavan prior to his departure three weeks ago. So far it had been an uneventful journey, but they weren't far now from the convent. They were deep in pagan territory and there were signs of another group inhabiting the area, probably the mercenaries he had been warned about.

The horses were skittish over unfamiliar sounds that followed them. The forest was the thickest Lachlan had ever seen, making it more difficult to find or blaze a sufficient trail. Then there was the strange mist that could be counted on to confound since there was no rhythm or reason to its arrival or departure.

The men voiced their concerns in whispers, afraid of insulting the forest spirits. Though new beliefs proliferated, old beliefs died hard and it didn't hurt to pay homage to the old ones now and again.

Lachlan led his men with confidence and caution. They were in unfamiliar territory and it wouldn't do to be careless. He had chosen good, experienced men, though Boyd and Andrew had volunteered. He shared much in common with the two. They craved adventure, women, and were close in age to his twenty-six years.

Boyd rode up alongside him. He sat tall in his saddle, though his height fell several inches short of Lachlan's not quite six feet. He was broad and thick with muscle and had long dark red hair and a boyish face the lassies loved.

"The few farms we've passed looked to be prosperous." Boyd shook his head. "I hadn't expected to see that with talk of mercenaries in the area."

"I thought the same myself," Lachlan said. "They usually take what they want in the way of food and women."

"Yet in the last two days it appears as if we've crossed

a border of sorts where every farm and its people are flourishing and happy."

"We are not far from the convent; perhaps the nuns have had a beneficial affect on the land and its people."

"Not if Alyce Bunnock had anything to do with it," Boyd said.

Lachlan cringed. "Don't remind me. I've heard more horrid tales about the—" He stopped himself from referring to her as a lady, which gave Boyd time to throw in his own descriptions.

"Shrew, witch, ogre, hellion—"

"Come, she can't be that bad," Andrew said, joining them, his sharp smile, craggy features, and jet black, straight shoulder-length hair in sharp contrast to Boyd's boyish appeal, his height nearer to Lachlan's.

"Then you deal with her," Lachlan and Boyd said in unison.

Andrew laughed, though he grew silent when the shrill cry of a bird pierced the air.

Lachlan and Boyd did the same. Another cry followed as if in answer then a cacophony of cries and the men relaxed, the chorus letting them know it was no signal.

"I'll be glad to get our task done and be home," Boyd said, his eyes sharp on his surroundings.

Lachlan understood his men's concerns. The forest shadows and unpredictable mist added to the unease, and it didn't help that they were placing themselves in harm's way to retrieve a sharp-tongued woman. "We'll be gone from here fast enough."

Evan, the warrior sent to scout ahead emerged from the shadows of the trees. Sweat poured from his pale brow even though the start of spring retained a bite of winter.

"There's a cropping of buildings ahead with freshly turned ground. It doesn't look like any convent I've seen. It resembles more a farm, though a large cross at the entrance of one building catches the eye as do the women who tend the place." He shook his head. "There's not a man in sight."

"How about an ugly shrew?" Boyd asked.

Evan cocked a brow. "None that I saw."

"We are closer to being done with this chore," Lachlan said, feeling a sense of relief. He'd soon have Alyce Bunnock in his grasp and they would be on their way home within a day or two.

With a command to his troop, all his warriors sat firm in their saddles and with a steady gait they proceeded over the pitted terrain, past the dense foliage, combating the creeping mist to arrive at the convent just before the sun settled in a gray sky.

Lachlan halted his men on the outskirts to what appeared to be the convent, though as Evan had informed him it more resembled a farm. The large crude cross fashioned from stripped tree limbs was the only indicator that the place was one of worship. It stood tall in front of the smallest dwellings, which he assumed designated the chapel.

There were two cottage-like dwellings past that and a short distance beyond was a thatched-roof compound that boasted two chimneys and several windows whose thick white wood shutters were closed tight. The door was also white and centered on it was a cross made of twigs.

A small field, its earth turned and ready for planting, didn't sit far from the compound and a pathway of pine needles directed visitors straight to the white door as if welcoming all who took it.

There wasn't a single person in sight, but then it was growing darker by the minute and more than likely the women were huddled inside the safety of the compound for the night.

"You are welcome to rest here."

Lachlan and his men were quick to clamp their hands on the hilts of their swords so startled were they all at the unexpected voice, but upon seeing who spoke they immediately relaxed their grips.

"I am Sister Megan and this is Everagis Abbey." She laughed lightly. "It may appear a farm to outsiders; however, to the sisters who share it with me, it is the grandest of abbeys."

Lachlan saw how his men glared besotted at the petite, dark-haired beauty. Her skin was pale and flawless, her voice like soft musical chimes, and her radiant green eyes intoxicating. And then there was her perfectly proportioned body, large breasts, narrow waist and round hips. She certainly looked nothing like a nun.

She demurely lowered her glance. "Does my peasant attire offend you, sir?"

"No. No," Lachlan assured her, though he did wonder whatever would make her shed her robes. She quickly settled his curiosity.

"Our daily chores favor the peasant's dress rather than our cumbersome robes."

"A wise choice," Lachlan agreed while catching the agreeable nods of his men out of the corner of his eye.

"We can offer you sustenance and a place to camp for the night if you wish," she said.

"Actually, I was sent here," Lachlan said.

She cocked her head.

"I am Lachlan of the clan Sinclare and Angus Bunnock has sent me to collect his daughter Alyce."

"I see," Megan said. "It is best you come and speak with—"

"The abbess," Lachlan finished, wanting her to realize his business was with the woman in charge.

"I will take you to the one you need to speak with."

Megan hurried ahead of him looking more like she floated along the ground at a remarkable gait, and arrived at the compound well ahead of him and his men.

Lachlan waved Evan up alongside him. "This Megan appeared out of nowhere, not the least bit surprised by our arrival and offering us shelter. It's as if she expected us."

"I thought the same myself," Evan said. "Yet when I scouted the area I detected not a soul in sight."

"Someone had to have spotted you."

"Perhaps someone who keeps watch over the nuns," Evan suggested.

"Find out," Lachlan ordered.

Evan nodded and retreated to his position.

Once at the compound Lachlan ordered his men to

dismount and wait while he went inside to speak with the abbess. The door opened before he reached it and two women came out carrying pitchers and tankards. They were dressed similarly to Megan though both were taller, one reed slim and the other fuller in figure though shapely. Where the slim one had a pretty face, the fuller one had a lovely face and both wore generous smiles, which added to their appeal.

"I am Hester," the slimmer one said, and with a nod toward the other woman she introduced her: "This is Rowena and we have ale for your men, for they surely must be parched."

"Thank you. We appreciate your generosity," Lachlan said, giving permission to serve his men and wondering how they could have been prepared so soon to quench the thirst of ten visitors. Again it appeared they had been expected.

Suddenly out of nowhere a whirlwind of dirt and debris swirled from around the end of the compound and when it settled a wiry young woman, her red hair piled wildly on her head appeared. Her pretty face was streaked with dirt, her dark green wool skirt and tan linen blouse dusted with it.

"Haven't missed supper, have I?" she asked anxiously, turning wide-eyed when her eyes fell on the men.

"No, Piper, but supper will wait until we see to our visitors," Hester said, handing her a pitcher.

The young woman nodded obediently and followed the other two helping to fill tankards of ale for all the men.

Lachlan wondered where Alyce was, for none of these women appeared a shrew. They were much too accommodating and attractive to be Alyce Bunnock. And thinking of the information he had been given, there should be at least ten nuns besides the abbess. So far he had met four, though not one of them resembled or acted like a woman dedicated to the church.

Megan appeared at the open door. "Please come in. You are most welcome here."

Lachlan almost took a deep breath in anticipation of the confrontation with the harridan, who he was certain would object to returning home to wed a stranger. However, he let a heavy breath ripple through his body and instead planted a smile on his face ready to charm the abbess, and hopefully tame the shrew enough to get her home for her wedding.

He stepped over the threshold and entered a large room. A stone fireplace covered one wall and two black cauldrons hung over the roaring fire, the contents bubbling and a delicious scent permeating the air. He had to fight not to lick his lips in anticipation of the appetizing taste.

A long table with five chairs at each side and one at each end sat in the middle of the room while a plethora of candles throughout provided the area with more than sufficient light. A soft blue wool curtain hung in a doorway that he assumed led to the nuns' sleeping quarters.

Not seeing anyone, he was about to ask about the abbess when a woman slowly emerged from the corner shadows. He had expected to see an older woman garbed in robes of one of authority. He didn't, though what he did see had his eyes popping wide and his loins tightening uncomfortably, not to mention the guilt that weighed heavily on him for finding a nun so damn appealing.

She was at least eight inches over five feet, her body full and curvaceous. While her face was round it was also sculpted, her soft yet defining features making her a rare beauty. Add to that sky blue eyes and wheat blond hair severely drawn back into a long braid that fell over her large bosoms and came to rest at her waist.

This couldn't be the abbess, though she did appear a woman in charge. Her blue eyes were sharp, her head high, and her stance solid. He admired her mix of beauty and strength.

He silently chastised himself for his lusty thoughts and with a respectable bow of his head said, "Good evening, Mother Abbess."

"I am not the abbess."

That couldn't be the voice of a nun. It was too deep and sultry. He nearly muttered oaths beneath his breath at his outrageous thought but caught himself only to wonder, or was it hope, that perhaps the beauty wasn't a nun at all.

"I am Sister Terese."

Was that a punch of disappointment to the gut he felt? Mind your thoughts, he warned himself silently, and ordered firmly, "I need to speak with the abbess."

"I'm afraid that won't be possible," Sister Terese said just as decisively.

Lachlan had enough. He wanted to speak with the abbess and now. He wanted to get Alyce into his custody and ready for the return trip home, leave by first light and finish this task he never wanted part of in the first place.

"I must insist," he said, locking his dark eyes with her blue ones, and damn if the color didn't remind him of the sky on a hot summer's day, and he felt like melting into them. He cleared his head with a quick shake and spoke forcefully. "Now! I will see the abbess now!"

Sister Terese kept her hard gaze locked with his, then blinked softly several times, closing her eyes, lowering her head, then raising it after a moment and opening tear-filled eyes. "The mother abbess is dead."

Lachlan didn't hide his shock. He nearly choked when he asked, "What happened?"

"Mother Abbess succumbed to an illness shortly after our arrival here."

"I am so sorry to hear that. Have you taken over her duties?"

Sister Terese nodded. "I have."

While the loss was certainly tragic, it didn't change his plans and he wanted to see to them immediately. "Then it is you I need to inform that I have come for Alyce Bunnock at the request of her father. I am to return her home so that she may wed."

Sister Terese rolled her eyes and shook her head slowly.

Lachlan assumed she expected a problem from Alyce and sought to assure her. "There is no need to concern yourself with the situation. I will handle Alyce Bunnock."

"I'm afraid not—"

Lachlan didn't let her finish. "Believe me, Sister Terese, whether Alyce wishes to go with me or not, will make no difference. She *will* return home with me. Now, please, take me to her so I can deliver the news and be done with it."

Sister Terese stared at him for a moment and then gave a sharp nod. "Follow me."

Lachlan was surprised when they left the compound, a torch in her hand as she led him down the pine-strewn path. They looked to be headed in the direction of the small cottages, and he immediately wondered if Alyce was so difficult to get along with that they had given her separate quarters.

His curiosity took over when they left the pine path and passed the two cottages. Had they confined Alyce to some remote dwelling to be rid of her?

They finally came to a stop in an area devoid of any dwellings and Sister Terese pointed to a spot just beyond her.

Lachlan glanced at her as if she were crazy. There was nothing there—until the woman raised the torch she carried, the flicking light casting a broader glow across the area.

Lachlan froze when he saw several crosses stuck

in the ground, some tilted oddly while a few stood straight.

Sister Terese glared at him. "Not only did Mother Abbess and several of our sisters die, but so did Alyce Bunnock."

Chapter 2

L achlan stared at the tilted cross with crudely carved letters, the last squeezed in tightly to finish the name Alyce. It took a moment to comprehend that the grave marked the end of his mission.

"Were you with her when she died?" Lachlan asked. "Her father will want to know that . . ." He didn't finish, for he didn't know how Angus Bunnock would react to the news. Would he cry over the loss of his daughter or would he be relieved that a troublesome daughter was gone?

"I understand," Sister Terese said softly. "You can tell him that she didn't suffer and she truly is at peace."

He nodded, not knowing if it would be enough to assuage Bunnock's loss, but at least it would be something.

"Please let me offer you and your men food, shelter and rest," Sister Terese said, "before you begin your long journey home tomorrow."

She turned and holding the torch high to light their way retraced her steps to the compound. As he followed, he wondered if it would be wise to leave the five vulnerable women unprotected.

He hastened his steps toward her thinking to discuss the matter with her before they reached the door. He halted abruptly when he suddenly found himself too close to her. He tempered his steps to keep an appropriate distance from her, silently admonishing himself for allowing his eyes to fall on her swaying hips and rounded backside.

Looking at her as a desirable woman instead of a nun wasn't proper, but damn if she didn't have an attractive backside. It was just the kind he liked, squeezable, especially so when the woman was riding him.

You're going to rot in hell, Lachlan, for such lascivious thoughts.

His silent warning did little good, since he couldn't help but think of how her long blond hair would fall over him and tantalize his naked body as she rode him.

Burn! You're going to burn forever in hell.

His second warning should have been like a cold splash in the face. However, with his loins lusting he'd need more than a splash. He'd need a good dunking in a freezing cold lake.

He jumped at the soft touch to his shoulder.

"Forgive me," Sister Terese apologized. "I called your name several times but you didn't answer. The news has obviously disturbed you, and how insensitive of me not to have offered my condolences."

Damn, but if he wasn't going to suffer never-ending damnation.

He let her think what she would and mumbled what he hoped passed for a thank you, but was really a plea for forgiveness. After all, he didn't want to rot, burn, or suffer never-ending damnation.

"Food and rest will have you feeling better," Sister Terese offered and extinguished the torch in a bucket near the door before opening it.

For a brief moment the half-moon cast a soft glow over her face and he near gasped. He had thought he had known beauty, but seeing her face kissed by the moonlight he realized he had never known it until this very moment.

The splash of light from the open door was what he needed to clear his head and his lust. He entered the common shelter glad for the chatter, delicious scents, and the company of his men.

He quickly joined them at the long table; the nuns busy filling tankards with mead and heaping more food on the platters in the center. His men were enjoying the generous fare of meat, fish, potatoes with wild onions, and bread.

Silence fell around the table when Lachlan informed his men that Alyce Bunnock was dead.

Boyd broke the silence. "We'll be leaving then at first light?"

"No," Lachlan said shaking his head. "With signs of mercenaries in the area, I don't think it would be wise to leave the nuns unprotected."

Sister Terese stepped forward. "No one bothers us. We do fine here and we are needed here."

"That may be but I can't leave you here," Lachlan said.

"The people need us," Sister Rowena argued, her smile firm.

"We cannot desert them," Sister Hester added

Sister Megan hugged the pitcher of mead she held. "This is our home."

"I don't mean to upset you, but I believe the church would want to know your circumstances," Lachlan clarified.

"The church does," Sister Terese said. "It was our mission to establish a convent to help convert the pagans. Slowly, we are accomplishing what we were sent to do. Only the church has the authority to order us to abandon our post. So you see, we cannot, nor will we leave here."

He admired her dedication, and it was obvious she would remain tenacious about her decision, leaving him only one choice.

"I will contact the church," he said.

Sister Terese shook her head. "That isn't necessary. We are doing as the church ordered."

"But with far less help and much more vulnerability than expected," Lachlan corrected. "I would feel more comfortable notifying the church."

"That will be fine," Sister Terese agreed, though obviously with reluctance. "We will await the decision. Now eat and rest. We will make sure you have plenty of food to take when you leave tomorrow."

"You misunderstand," Lachlan said. "We're not

going anywhere. I will send two of my men to see to the task while the rest of us remain here."

"That isn't necessary," Sister Terese repeated adamantly. "You would be stuck here two months at least, or more if the church takes time to respond."

"We could use a respite, and you our help," he said resting back in his chair with a smile.

"That's asking too much of you and your men," she persisted.

"Not at all." Lachlan glanced around the table at his men. "Do any of you object?"

Every man shook his head.

"Your men have no say. They have to obey you," Sister Piper objected strenuously, surprising everyone, though Evan grinned.

Lachlan watched as with a firm nod Sister Terese silenced Sister Piper, her mouth shutting with a petulant pout.

"They serve him as we serve the church," Sister Terese reminded.

"Then you agree," Lachlan confirmed. "We will remain here until we hear from the church."

"I truly do not wish to impose—"

"Nonsense," Lachlan interrupted another of her attempts to object. "I would feel remiss in my duty if we did not remain here and see you safe until the church determines your fate."

Sister Terese nodded. "It would seem there is no changing your mind."

Lachlan stood and bowed gallantly. "I and my men are at your service, Sister Terese."

"I appreciate your offer, but you will find we are self-sufficient here."

"As are we," Lachlan said and with another bow and smile he sat in his chair. "We will not impose on your generosity. We will provide food and construct a temporary shelter for ourselves."

Sister Terese nodded, though Lachlan noticed the tight set of her lips. She appeared annoyed, but was wise enough to realize that any further debate was futile.

"This common shelter houses our sleeping quarters, which lie beyond that curtain," Sister Terese said with a nod toward it. "So, out of respect and courtesy, I ask that you not enter here unless invited."

"Of course," Lachlan said agreeably. "We do not wish to upset or interfere in your routine; only to help."

Sister Terese smiled and Lachlan felt a sting to his senses. Her prominent cheekbones took on a sculpted beauty and her blue eyes sparkled like a brilliant jewel. Once again warning signals went off in his head while his body was quick to heat.

Never-ending damnation, he silently reminded himself.

"I am sure you and your men will be busy hunting and erecting your shelter."

Erecting. Why did she have to use that word?

"That we will," he said quickly and wondered over the wisdom of his decision to remain there, especially since the only women he and his men would be around were five attractive nuns.

* * *

Lachlan and his men settled for the night not far from the common shelter. They had built a fire and afterward enjoyed the warm sweet cakes Megan and Hester had brought out to them. The men were quick to sleep after that, even Lachlan found himself more tired than usual.

He blamed it on the long, strenuous journey. He had intended to decide tonight on who would return to Caithness, but his exhausted body had other ideas. Morning would be soon enough. He pulled the blanket up over him to fully surrender to sleep. Just as his eyes were about to close, he thought he caught a glimpse of a moving shadow approaching their camp. He struggled to keep his eyes open, told himself to get up, wake the men and admonished himself for not posting a guard. Why hadn't he posted a guard?

His thoughts were foggy and he fought the heavy hand of sleep that seemed to squeeze at him. His eyes shot open wide, but only briefly. In that single moment he saw not one, but several moving shadows descending on him and his men. He thought to yell out, but instead his eyes shut and darkness swallowed him.

"Did he see us?" Terese asked Rowena.

"Not clear enough to identify anyone," she assured.

"How much time do we have?" Hester asked.

"Three hours to be safe, though the lot of them will probably sleep through until morning," Rowena said.

"We can't take any chances," Terese said. "Let's be done with it."

The five women hurried to the storage hut. They were quick and agile, though they had only the moonlight to guide their steps. Three went inside and shifted the baskets of food around, then brushed an area of dirt aside on the floor to expose a hatch. Hester swung it open and Piper dropped down inside.

Light suddenly spewed from the opening followed by bows and a cache of arrows. Rowena collected the weapons Piper handed up. In turn Terese, Hester, and Megan took them and one by one hurried them to their quarters.

When the women were finished and the storage hut returned to normal, the five nuns met in the common room. They sat around the long table looking from one to other.

Terese finally spoke. "We knew something like this could happen."

The other women nodded.

"If we keep our wits about us, we can get through this," Terese said. "I will insist that Lachlan make certain that the church knows that our work here has been successful. Once church superiors hear we are converting the pagans they will issue orders for us to continue. Lachlan and his men will leave and we will be left to ourselves once more."

Megan shook her head. "With the time they are going to spend here, they could easily discover the truth."

"She's right," Hester agreed. "They think to protect us so they will constantly be watching us."

"And we will be watching them," Piper reminded.

"And when the people need our help?" Megan asked. "How do we ride out of here with our weapons in full view?"

"That is why we are holding this meeting," Terese said. "We need to make plans, be prepared." She looked from Piper to Rowena. "I need you both to find a spot in the woods to hide our weapons."

"I know the perfect spot," Piper said. "We can have it done tonight."

Terese nodded and turned to Megan. "Make excuses to visit the farmers; while I know they will not betray us, they need to be aware of the situation."

Megan nodded and clenched her hands tightly.

Terese reached out, resting her hands over Megan's. "It will be all right. We will survive this."

Megan grabbed hold of Terese's hand. "The time I've spent here at Everagis is the only time in my life that I have ever felt safe."

Terese watched as in turn each woman nodded. "We have survived and grown strong together. We *will* remain so. I *promise* you that."

"But the church—"

Terese didn't let Megan finish. "I will do *whatever* is necessary for *all* of us to stay safe."

"You've already proved that," Hester said.

"Then trust me once more when I tell you we will be fine."

Piper jumped up, a flourish of dirt drifting off her. "There's time to get the first cache of weapons hidden."

As each woman stood Terese knew they proclaimed their trust in her. She was the last to stand.

"Together," Terese said and the women echoed her command.

A few hours later with perhaps four hours left until sunrise, Terese fell into bed exhausted. She hoped to drop right off to sleep, but past events came flooding back to torment her, as did worries for the future.

She wished she could have convinced Lachlan to leave, but it was obvious from the beginning that he would have it his way. He charmed, trying to make it seem that what he was doing was for the best of others, but it truly was to get his own way. She didn't doubt women easily submitted to that quirky charming smile of his, or that he was used to their surrender.

This time, however, he was dealing with nuns so he had to behave.

Though what if he discovered the truth?

It had seemed like an answer to her prayers five years ago, not that she had wished ill will on anyone. She knew her circumstances had been of her own doing. But when the nuns began to die of a sickness, she had realized she had a chance to be free, along with the other four women.

Mother Abbess had rescued each one along the way. Rowena had been beaten beyond belief and left to die along a lonely road. No one had expected her to live, but she had fought bravely for her life and thanks to the nuns' help she had survived. A near starved Hester had been saved from a selfish innkeeper. Mother Abbess thought she convinced the man to do the right thing and surrender the young woman, but Terese had paid several coins for Hester's freedom. As for Megan, she had been the worst of the lot. She had walked out of the woods dazed, bloodied and her garments nearly ripped off her. It took her months before she even spoke to anyone and to this day no one knew what had happened to her. Then there was Piper. One day she popped up out of nowhere, dirt streaking her clothes and skin and a dusting of earth trailing after her wherever she went. They soon learned that she loved the woods as she would a mother and knew it just as well.

Mother Abbess offered them a home at the convent, but only if they took vows. The women quickly agreed. With no place to go, no protection, what other choice did they have?

All plans fell apart shortly after their arrival. Mother Abbess was the first to fall ill, the nuns soon followed. Terese took command and soon had those healthy enough building shelters and preparing the land for planting. She also instructed the women in the use of weapons and horsemanship. And before they knew it they were defending the surrounding area from troubling bands of bandits. To keep their identity safe, they took on the persona of mercenaries and soon spread gossip about the fierce band in hopes of keeping trouble away.

When all was done, she and the four women were the only ones left. She wanted what those four women had—freedom.

She gathered the four women together and confessed her story. She told them of her father a powerful laird who felt his daughter a troublesome lot and wanted to be rid of her until she could serve a beneficial purpose. Then she explained that she wished to be as free as they were, and the only way she could do that was to die.

That day Alyce carved her own name in the cross that marked Sister Terese's grave and took her identity. She was finally free.

Chapter 3

Terese always rose just before sunrise. She loved to greet the dawn, watch as the first ray of light peeked on the horizon then slowly spread over the land. She felt as if the heavens touched her anew and it gladdened her heart each morning.

However, this morning her heart was a little heavy. Lachlan and his men were up at first light and asking permission to build a shelter much too close to the compound. They would hear everything the women were up to, and that wouldn't do.

Terese kept a pleasant smile as she walked Lachlan nearer to the entrance of the convent, away from the common shelter and the woods beyond. "I believe this area would better serve your purpose."

Lachlan glanced around.

Terese offered an explanation before he could protest. "It is the only entrance to the convent." She crossed her fingers behind her back for protection against her small lie, for she and the women had forged a significant entrance through the woods.

Lachlan nodded. "Then it will do."

•She pointed to woods opposite from where the weapons were hid. "You will find sturdy trees there to be build your shelter."

"Thank you and my men will hunt and provide fare for tonight's meal," he said.

Piper caused Lachlan to jump, startled by her sudden appearance. Not so Terese, she was used to Piper popping up when least expected. The wiry young lass was quick-footed and silent in her approach, though she made herself known when she wanted to.

"I'll show your hunters the best hunting ground," Piper offered.

Lachlan signaled to Evan and he hurried over. "Evan well knows the scent of the hunt in the woods."

Piper tapped her chest. "These are my woods."

Lachlan grinned. "Would you mind sharing them with Evan?"

Piper scrunched her nose and looked Evan up and down. "You can keep a good pace? I won't have to hold your hand?"

Terese kept herself from laughing and noticed that Lachlan did the same. She was glad to see that he wasn't insulted, but rather found Piper's remarks amusing.

Evan was quick to assure her. "No, Sister, you'll find me knowledgeable of the woods. There'll be no hand holding."

"There better not be," Lachlan said seriously, though his deep brown eyes twinkled with merriment.

Evan's pale cheeks turned scarlet while Piper shook her head and said to Evan, "Follow me."

"The lad is susceptible to your teasing," Terese remarked, watching the pair walk away and wishing that Piper could know how it felt for a young man to hold her hand. At nineteen, she was the youngest of the women and had confided in Terese that she knew nothing of men, but that sometimes she found herself curious.

"A teasing reminder," Lachlan said. "I want my men to remember that while you are all beautiful women, you are *nuns*."

"Are you saying that I'm beautiful, sir?"

For a moment he startled, presumably realizing he had just complimented a nun on her beauty. But he caught himself and delivered a charming smile.

"I meant no disrespect, Sister Terese, but when a woman is beautiful there is no denying it, whether a nun or not."

She felt her heart catch. While he was obviously a quick-witted charmer, she couldn't help think that it was the first time anyone had ever told her that she was beautiful. Usually, it was the opposite. An ugly shrew, that's what she had been called far too often.

Terese briefly savored the special moment then took control of the situation. "I will allow your compliment, but in the future, please refrain yourself."

Lachlan bowed his head respectfully. "As you wish, Sister."

"I did wish to discuss with you the contents of the message you intend to send to church officials," she said, reminding herself that there were more important matters to consider than being told she was beautiful.

"I thought you would, so my men stand ready to leave as soon as we finish discussing the matter."

"Your thoughtfulness is appreciated," she said. While she would have preferred to be more blunt, she had to remember she was supposedly a nun; a pious and patient woman. How far from the truth that was.

"I plan to inform the officials of your present status," Lachlan said.

"Which is?"

"That five of you are left out of the"— he paused a moment—"I believe I was told Mother Abbess, plus eight nuns and Alyce Bunnock had been sent here."

"That's correct," Terese said.

"That would mean that five succumbed to the sickness."

"Again correct."

"Then why ten graves?" he asked.

"We picked up a few women in need along the way," Terese answered, having prepared herself for his questions. She realized from the first that Lachlan Sinclare might appear a charmer, but he was far from a fool. Besides, she knew somewhat of the Sinclare brothers having heard her father speak with respect about them. They were well-honored and courageous warriors, which was probably why he requested help from the laird Sinclare in fetching his daughter.

"Perhaps one of them brought the sickness with them."

"It's possible," she agreed, though it had been one of the nuns who had fallen ill before the other women had joined them. "I don't think the church will be interested as to what caused the sickness."

"It isn't only the church I'll be answering to," he said. "As I told you last night, Angus Bunnock might have questions."

The image of her father rushed into her head. He was big and broad with a booming voice and snow white hair down to his chest and a bushy mustache that tickled her whenever he would pick her up and cuddle her when she was little.

She didn't know what happened to change things between herself and her father, or perhaps she did. She had developed a willful mind, though it had been he who encouraged it. She felt she merely was truly her father's daughter. She would do as she pleased, not as she was told and her mouth was sharp with retorts. Her father had warned her that no one would seek a union with her if she didn't watch her mouth. She was fine with that, for she wanted no master for a husband. Her father thought differently.

"As I told you, she is at peace. That should make him happy," Terese said.

"You spent time traveling here with Alyce Bunnock, what did you think of her?"

Terese wasn't sure what to say about herself. Did she tell him that Alyce was an intelligent woman, brave, adept with weapons, and could sit a horse with skill? Did she tell him that Alyce was good at tactics, having helped her father plan his battle strategies? Or did she confirm what he probably had heard; that Alyce Bunnock was not the easiest person to befriend?

"I spent limited time with her."

"Your choice?" Lachlan asked.

"Circumstances."

"Or is it that you wish not to speak ill of the dead?"

"Alyce Bunnock was not a bad woman," she said, no longer able to stand there and not defend herself. "And it is not appropriate to speak callously of the dead."

Her reprimand wiped the smile off his face. "I meant no disrespect. I only—"

"Wanted to satisfy your own curiosity," she finished for him and held up her hand to prevent further protest. "Alyce Bunnock is dead and buried. Let her rest in peace."

He nodded, though she could see he wasn't pleased by her command. He let a gentle smile surface and graced his tone with charm.

"I will inform the church officials of how dedicated you all are to the convent and how you all wish to continue your work."

"Please also add that we have worked diligently with the pagans in the area and they are prospering through our efforts."

"You have converted many?" he asked.

"Yes, we have converted many to our ways," she answered, not bothering to define *our ways* for him.

"The church, I am sure, will be happy to hear this."

She was counting on that and hoped the next couple of months would not prove as difficult as she feared. "Then let your men be off, so that this matter may be settled as soon as possible."

"I hope that our stay here will prove more of an asset than a hindrance."

She hoped the same herself, but a little help from the heavens wouldn't hurt. "God willing all will go well."

A raised voice caught both their attention. When Terese turned to see Megan marching toward her, her dark curly hair bouncing madly around her flushed face, and with one of Lachlan's men close on her heels, she feared the heavens might finally be upset with her never-ending string of lies.

"Tell this man . . ." Megan shook her finger at the warrior who now stood beside her.

Lachlan supplied his name. "Andrew. He is trustworthy and courageous."

"That may be the case, but I am in no need of him," Megan insisted.

Andrew offered an explanation. "She is, that is Sister Megan is, going to visit a few farms and I thought perhaps she could use help."

Megan looked to Terese. "And I told him I don't need his help, thank you very much."

Terese knew from the brilliance of Megan's green eyes that she was annoyed. It was a trait all the women were aware of and they treaded lightly around her at those times.

"It is very thoughtful of you, Andrew," Terese said and hoped her excuse would prove viable. "But Sister Megan always goes alone. She enjoys the solitary walks."

"But she's so-so-so—little," Andrew finally spit out.

Terese almost rolled her eyes, knowing his remark would only provoke Megan's annoyance more. And sure enough, Megan turned on Andrew with a flourish.

The six foot, lean-muscled man took a step back as Megan, all five feet three of her, vehemently shook her finger in his face, though she had to stretch her hand up to do it.

"You think size makes a difference? Why—why I could—"

Terese stepped in before Megan said something she would regret and would make matters worse for them. She grabbed hold of the waving finger. "*Sister* Megan, Andrew is merely trying to help, while here."

A reminder of who the man thought her to be had the desired affect and the color of Megan's eyes instantly softened. She was quick to offer a suitable apology. "Forgive me. I thought only of myself and the walks I so enjoy."

Andrew hastily offered a compromise. "I could keep a distance from you so that you feel as if you walk alone."

Megan smiled and all the women loved to see her smile, since it had taken almost two years after she had joined them for her smile to return. But her smile obviously had a different affect on men, for Andrew looked as if he had been punched in the gut, his soft blue eyes popping wide.

Terese looked to Lachlan and nodded.

He shook his head and with a sigh addressed the matter. "Perhaps another time, Andrew."

He didn't respond; he simply continued to stare at Megan.

"Andrew!" Lachlan said firmly.

"Huh?" Andrew said, turning his head so sharply that his black shoulder-length hair whipped him in the mouth and with a quick swipe he shoved the strands away.

"You can join Sister Megan another time," Lachlan repeated, then looked to Terese before turning his attention to Megan. "Of course, that is if Sister Megan doesn't mind."

Terese nodded at Megan to agree. Aware that Lachlan had gently ordered her to concur with him and being that it would give Megan time to inform the farmers of their situation, she happily complied with his silent command.

Megan understood and smiled once again. "I would enjoy Andrew's company another day."

"I assume we are finished here?" Terese asked of Lachlan. "I have duties to see to and I wish to speak with Sister Megan before she takes her leave."

Lachlan nodded. "You have been of great help. We will speak later."

"As you wish," Terese said and walked off with Megan at her side.

"What were you thinking?" Lachlan asked once the sisters were far enough away not to hear him. "Wait." He held up his hand and shook his head. "I know what you were thinking. Do you realize she is *Sister Megan?*"

Andrew shrugged and shook his head. "What can I say? She's beautiful, even more so when she smiles, and she's so damned petite. You know how I love petite women."

"She is a *nun!*"

"I know. I know. I'm going to burn in hell for my wicked thoughts."

Lachlan empathized with Andrew; since he'd probably be burning right along side him.

"Maybe it's better if you keep your distance from her," Lachlan suggested, thinking that he should take his own advice.

"I was afraid you would say that."

"And I'm afraid of what may happen if you don't," Lachlan said sternly.

"I understand, but you can't think I'm the only one looking at these women as women. Since not a one of them wear the traditional robes, it's hard to think of them as nuns."

He was right about that, not that Lachlan intended to agree, though neither could he appear blind to his men's plight. "Regardless, they are nuns and are due respect. Do I make myself clear?"

Andrew hung his head and sighed. "I will be ever vigilant." He raised his head. "But Sister Megan does need protecting, and I'd like to protect her." When Lachlan rolled his eyes, Andrew was quick to add, "You can trust me."

"For two maybe three months?"

Andrew looked stricken, but reassured him. "I give you my word."

That was good enough for Lachlan, since Andrew's word was his honor. "Then I shall take you at your word. Now go get five men, though not Kyle or Patrick, they will be the two who return home." He nodded to the cropping of woods. "Take the men and cut down what is needed for a shelter. The laborious chore will help clear your mind."

Andrew didn't argue; he did as he was told.

Lachlan remained where he was, glancing out over the convent. The time spent here would not be easy on his men, though he knew they would treat the nuns with respect, even if they silently lusted after them.

He cringed at the sinful thought, especially since he was no different. But that would stop this moment. There was work to do: men to send home, a shelter to build, hunting to see to. And then there were the mercenaries.

Alyce Bunnock wasn't his only reason for this mission. Cavan had gladly agreed to Angus Bunnock's request for help once he learned that mercenaries frequented the area.

Lachlan had come here to see if by any chance his brother Ronan was connected with them. He and his brothers Cavan and Artair had been searching two years now for their youngest brother, Ronan.

Cavan and Ronan had been captured in a battle with a northern barbarian tribe. Soon after, they had been separated. Cavan had found his way home after a year of captivity. Ronan was still missing.

Zia, Artair's wife and a healer, had tended their brother. The most shocking part of that news was that Ronan had left Zia's village, but where he had gone no one knew. They had been told by Zia's grandmother that if they found the barbarian's daughter Carissa, they would find their brother.

The brothers all agreed that there had to be something that kept Ronan from returning home. Though they didn't believe him chained or sequestered in a cell, somehow he remained a prisoner. But to whom?

Lachlan hoped the band of mercenaries might have some knowledge about his brother. Cavan had made certain that Lachlan had enough coins on him to buy such information, or if he was lucky and Ronan was among them, he could buy his freedom.

The warriors were aware of this and were prepared to battle if necessary to free Ronan. Lachlan's one concern was the nuns. If things didn't turn out well, they could suffer for his actions, which was another reason he was sending a message to church officials. Surely when they discover only five survived these past five years and were living more as peasants than nuns, the church would recall them home.

Besides, they should all be in the safety of a proper convent, clothed in proper garments. He couldn't understand how they had survived, actually thrived, this long on their own. With claims of mercenaries in the area, how had these women avoided being attacked by them?

He scratched his head, thinking there were many questions he needed answers to.

Chapter 4

L ate that night the women once again sat around the table to discuss and plan.

"Evan is attuned to the secrets of the woods. If we are not careful he will learn of our activities there," Piper said.

"He may be attuned to them, but you *know* the secrets. And you *know* how to cover our tracks," Terese encouraged. "And with vigilance we can succeed." She looked from one woman to another. "These men respect our status as nuns. We need to use that to our advantage."

"I agree," Megan said. "It is that very status that has kept us safe so far, and when I informed the farmers of our situation, they were deeply concerned. They do not want us to leave here, and they eagerly offered their help."

"It is good to know we can count on them," Hester said. "Good to know we have friends."

"That is all well and good, but what if the church recalls us home?" Rowena asked. "I, for one, have no plans of leaving this area. This is my home."

Each woman echoed the same sentiment.

"I feel the same as all of you," Terese said. "This is my home now and I don't want to leave it, but as Rowena has suggested there is always that possibility. In fact, it is inevitable. This land belongs to the church, not us."

"Just as these men are temporary residents here, so are we," Megan said.

Hester was the first to say what all the sisters felt. "What we need is a permanent home."

They all looked to Terese.

She smiled. "Then it is a permanent home we will find."

The women smiled and laughed with joy and soon were chatting about finding the perfect place and what would be needed and how it would take hard work.

The sharp rap at the door startled them all silent.

Terese felt for the dirk she kept in a sheath strapped to her leg before she stood. Satisfied that her weapon was handy if necessary, she signaled the women to remain quiet as she went to the door and asked, "Who's there?"

"Lachlan."

"Is something wrong?" Terese asked. "Is one of your men ill?"

"No, everyone is fine," he answered. "I am concerned about you."

She opened the door, "Why?"

"I heard raised voices," he answered, stretching his neck to peer past her into the room.

"We were praying."

He smiled, but it wasn't his smile that caught her attention. It was the dark shadows that cautiously moved around outside. He obviously had brought a few warriors with him.

"Isn't it a little late for prayers?" he asked.

"Are you accusing me of lying?" Too late, Terese let the biting tongue of Alyce Bunnock slip.

Lachlan took a step back and graciously bowed his head as if apologetic. "Not for a moment, Sister Terese. The sounds are what made me wonder if something was amiss, and I only wished to make certain of your safety."

She had warned the others to use their ruse to protect themselves and here her thoughtless action was placing them in jeopardy.

"Forgive my thoughtlessness," she said. "It is just that you interrupted a rousing vigil of prayer."

"I've never heard of a *rousing* vigil of prayer," he admitted.

"It works well for us. Now if you will excuse me, we must resume the vigil," she said, easing the door closed on him.

"Sister Terese."

She almost had the door closed and had to open it a bit to address him. She didn't like the glint in his dark eyes or his smile that suddenly looked ready to charm. "Yes?"

"Would more voices raised in prayer add to the strength of your vigil?"

He was a sly one; she would have to be more careful

around him. "It isn't the quantity; it's the belief that gives the prayer strength."

"Are you accusing me of not being a believer?" he asked.

He did not accuse with a testy tongue, as she had done to him, but rather winsomely.

"Nay, sir, I would never do that," she said gently and directly met his dark eyes with her blue ones. "When the moment is right, I shall request your assistance in prayer."

"And I will be at your service," he bowed gallantly and turned disappearing into the night before Terese could close the door on him.

The bright sun burnt off the mist that had accompanied the dawn, while an unusual warm breeze settled over the land. The pleasant weather had everyone smiling, happy to be busy with outdoors chores on this fine spring day.

Lachlan was pleased with his men's progress with the two shelters. A few more days and one would be habitable, the other would soon follow.

He had no time to lend a hand. He was more concerned with finding out what he could about the mercenaries. It was time he spoke to Sister Terese and see if she could tell him anything about them.

She had been planting in the field that ran the whole length of the convent, beyond the few structures and bordering the woods on two sides. It was a large field, providing more harvest than the sisters needed, but he imagined that they used the extra to feed the needy. There was also a garden on the side of the common shelter that appeared no one touched but Rowena, having found that out when Boyd entered the area thinking to snatch what looked to be berries. She chased him with a shovel.

The women worked well together, not a one of them complaining no matter what the task. They planted, tended the cows, sheep and horses, chopped wood, spun yarn, and cooked the most delicious meals he and his men had ever eaten. They visited the farms in the area on foot or horse and tended the ill that appeared at their doorstep.

They certainly were self-sufficient and comfortable with their surroundings and not at all fearful. How was it that the farms he and his men had stopped at along the way warned them of mercenaries, yet these nuns seemed unconcerned with their safety?

Mercenaries were known to spare no one—unless, could it be perhaps the nuns somehow had managed to strike a bargain with the band? The sisters were a resourceful lot and were not afraid to tackle any chore. And then, of course, there was their faith.

Lachlan approached Sister Terese with a wave. She stopped her planting and greeted him in similar fashion. She wore a welcoming smile and a large brimmed straw hat that shaded her face from the sun. She had rolled up the sleeves of her tired yellow blouse and had tucked her brown skirt between her legs, hooking the frayed end in her waistband to make it appear she wore pants. Her feet were bare and partially covered with the rich earth, and her slim ankles gave way to muscled calves. He forced his glance up to her face and silently warned his straying thoughts to behave.

"Such a lovely day, isn't it?" she remarked.

Lovely. That's what she was—lovely. He almost shook his head in an attempt to clear his musings, but corrected his action before it was too late and agreed with a firm nod.

"It surely is."

"Then why do you frown?" she asked.

Because I find myself attracted to you beyond measure?

The thought never made it past his lips. Instead, he got straight to his reason for disturbing her work. "I was wondering if you have had any encounters with the mercenaries I heard were in the area."

"We have been lucky, or rather blessed, since we have not been bothered by them."

"Why do you think that is?"

"Perhaps they respect the church," she said.

"Unlikely. They respect nothing but the coins their missions earn them."

"True enough," she agreed then shrugged. "But I have no other explanation to offer."

"Not a one of the mercenaries has darkened your doorstep? Not even an injured one?" Lachlan thought about how his brother Ronan had left Zia's village still recovering from his wounds and may have sought further care.

"The sisters and I do not question those who seek our help. If one of the ill had been a mercenary we would not have known it."

Lachlan had to know if his brother had been at Everagis so he asked, "Any man a few inches taller than me, with auburn hair—"

Terese interrupted with a question. "You look for someone in particular?"

Lachlan hadn't planned on confiding in her about his brother, but then, if he wanted her help, perhaps being truthful was his best choice.

"My brother Ronan," he admitted. "Last my brothers and I heard, he was recovering from injuries. Where he went afterward, we don't know, though we had been forewarned that if we found the daughter of the barbarian who captured my brother, we would find Ronan. We learned she might be connected with a band of mercenaries."

"You believe those mercenaries in this area?"

"More northeast of here, but you never can tell."

"Mercenaries are a band of misfits for hire. There are only poor farmers and pagans in this area. Nothing to attract the likes of mercenaries," she said.

"Perhaps it's simply a place of rest they seek."

She nodded. "Ronan looks like you?"

He laughed. "He's not as handsome as me."

Terese chuckled. "And is he a charmer like you?"

"You noticed my best quality."

"I don't know if I would call it a quality, and we waste time on you when it is your brother you should be describing," she chastised gently.

"You're right," he admitted. "As I said he is a couple of inches taller than me with auburn hair—"

She interrupted again. "If you know what wounds he suffered that might prove more helpful."

"If I recall what Zia told me . . ."

"Zia is your wife?" Terese asked.

"Good lord, no." Lachlan laughed and quickly apologized. "Sorry, Sister, but I have no plans of marrying any time soon."

"Why?" she asked before he could continue.

He spoke the truth. "I'm not ready to commit to a wife."

"Why?"

She asked why much too often, yet he felt compelled to answer her. "I enjoy the life I presently live."

"And what life is that?" she asked.

"A life of freedom," he answered with a generous smile.

"I understand," she said with a slow, continuous nod.

Oddly enough, he believed she did, though he couldn't say why.

"And Zia is?"

"She is my brother Artair's wife and a remarkable healer."

"Why did your brother leave her care?" Terese asked.

"We don't know. We can only assume that he has good reason for not returning home."

"His wounds," she reminded.

"Oh yes," he said and thought a moment. "I believe Zia said he suffered damaged ribs, a leg wound, a severe shoulder wound, and his face had been badly beaten."

"How awful," Terese empathized. "Someone recovering from such wounds I would have remembered. But I do not recall such a man seeking our help."

"But a band of mercenaries do frequent the area?"

"Yes, so we have been told," she said.

"And not once have they crossed any of the sisters' paths?"

Terese shook her head. "Such news surely would have been shared, but you are free to ask the others, if you wish."

"Perhaps Piper, with all the time she spends in the woods, would know something?" he suggested.

"As I said you are free to ask."

"You are generous and patient with us, Sister Terese," he said, suddenly feeling as if he and his men were imposing on her and the other sisters.

"Not at all," she argued with a bright smile. "We are here to help and be generous. It is what we do. And you have seen the fruit of our labor, which is why I am sure the church will want us to continue our work here."

He almost grabbed his gut, feeling such a sharp stab of guilt. Here he was sabotaging their plans, while she offered him help. Another reason for him to burn in hell . . . lying to a nun.

Sister Terese resumed planting, her foot easing the rich soil over the dropped seeds.

"You do not mind such a lonely existence?" he asked as he continued alongside her.

She laughed softly, never disturbing her rhythmic motion. "It is far from a lonely existence. The sisters and I have each other for company and we are constantly busy, as I'm sure you have noticed. Then there are the farmers we visit and those who come to see us. It is a good life."

"You don't find it confining?" he asked.

"How so?"

"You mostly work."

"And pray," she reminded him.

He nodded, though had to ask. "Work and prayer are enough for you?"

She stopped, looked at him and spoke bluntly. "You wonder why I chose this life over one with a husband and children."

"Forgive me, but I *am* curious why you chose to commit your life to the church rather than a husband."

Her blue eyes burst with brilliant color and she grinned. "For the very same reason you presently enjoy your life."

He stared at her confused at first then asked, "Freedom?"

"Precisely, I have more freedom here at Everagis than I would ever have with a husband." She laughed. "And don't try to debate the matter. You're well aware that a certain amount of obedience is expected from a wife, and no doubt you will expect it from your own. And as a husband you will have the last say in all matters."

"It is the way of things."

She shook her head. "How easy for a man to say that when life favors him."

"It is a good exchange between husband and wife. For her obedience I will take good care of her, provide for her and see her safe."

"So it is a bargain you will strike with your future wife," she said. "Love will not enter into the agreement?"

He rubbed his chin then turned a disarming smile on her. "I think I would rather wed a best friend then pledge an undying love."

"Why?"

"You do know you ask *why* much too often," he chuckled.

"It is the only way to get an answer"—she grinned—"which is what I'm waiting for."

"A best friend is always there for you, accepts you as you are, confides in you, laughs with you, cries with you, fights with you, but always—always forgives you, whether right or wrong. Love, on the other hand, can be unforgiving."

Her grin faded and she nodded slowly. "How right you are."

She continued her planting only this time he didn't follow alongside her. He stood watching her and couldn't help but wonder if perhaps she spoke from experience.

Chapter 5

~~∽∞∽~~

The next day the sisters had a couple of the men move tables from two other buildings outside. By early afternoon they had dressed the tables with fresh blue cloths and began adding platter after platter of scrumptiously scented food. To it they added pitchers of cider and mead.

The men stared from where they worked on the shelters, most wiping sweat from their brows. They were all hungry, since their first meal of the day hadn't been nearly sufficient enough, but they had yet to receive an invitation to join the sisters.

Terese corrected that as soon as she walked out of the common shelter. She approached Lachlan with a smile, noticing he already wore one. There were few times he didn't, though in those times, she caught a glimpse of the warrior within him.

For some reason, he fascinated her. She didn't know why, though it could be his affable nature. Most men she had dealt with were loud and demanding, not so Lachlan. He seemed ready to please whether with word or action and in turn others sought to please him. She had seen it with his men and the way he handled them, praising, though in command. Even the so-called nuns weren't impervious to his charm every now and again, and she had to remind them how intoxicating his charisma could be.

She wasn't adverse to it herself. Yesterday, she had actually enjoyed his company when they talked, though she remained on guard. The man could simply disarm with his clever tongue.

Gooseflesh prickled her skin when she suddenly thought of what it would be like to kiss him. Was she daft? It was a crazy thought and one that should never have entered her head.

She kept her smile bright and her musings on more important matters when she reached him. "We would be pleased to have you and your men join us for the meal."

A few men licked their lips, others mumbled beneath their breaths, and all of them looked with expectation to their leader.

"They'll wash up before joining you," he said and with his order given, the men rushed to obey. "Thank you for the invitation," he added as his men scurried around him.

"It's a beautiful day and we have plenty. Such a day should be shared with friends," she said.

"You think of me as a friend, Sister Terese?"

"All those who come here, we accept as friends," she said, though gave the notion thought. Was it even possible they could be friends?

"I'd make a good friend," he said as if wanting to persuade her.

"That is for me to judge."

He laughed. "True enough."

"But it is also for you to judge if you deem me worthy enough to call friend." Surprisingly, he appeared startled and to save the moment from turning awkward, she said, "The food will grow cold. Come and eat."

He nodded and they walked to the table in silence.

It wasn't long before a festive atmosphere filled the air and between mouthfuls tales were told, debates were argued, and friendships formed.

Terese knew Lachlan let the men linger instead of rushing them back to work. She was glad for it gave them all a reprieve to simply enjoy each other's company. And for the first time in five years, she realized that she did miss the company of a man. And she had a feeling the other women were reaching the same realization, all except Megan. There was still apprehension in her eyes, and Terese could only imagine the horrors of what had happened to leave such deep scars.

The men were about to return to work when Megan jumped up from the table and ran. Terese and the other women were right behind her when they saw what had caught her eye. She saw Lachlan signal his men who quickly grabbed their swords and spread out around the convent grounds. Andrew and Boyd joined him as he followed the women.

A man, gaunt and barely able to take another step, was assisted by a woman who looked too old to hold him. Two children, a lad and lassie around five and eight, their faces dirty and much too thin, held hands tightly and followed behind them.

Megan went to help the man, but Andrew gently eased her out of the way. "I'll do it," he said and relieved the old woman of her burden.

Megan instead helped the old woman and Terese went to the children, but they backed away from her with wide, frightened eyes. Even Piper, who children were always drawn two, couldn't coax them near.

"They joined us along the road, though it took time for them to be able to walk near us," the old woman explained with a tired breath. "They haven't spoken a word."

Lachlan hunched down in front of them and with a broad smile introduced himself. "I am Lachlan of the clan Sinclare."

There was hesitation, but it seemed that determination took over and the little girl attempted to step forward, though the lad fought to hold her back with a firm hand. She would have none of it and took an exaggerated step. Her red hair was heavy with grime, her face streaked with dirt, and her clothes so worn and tattered there was barely anything left, and her little feet were bare and filthy.

"The Sinclares are brave warriors?" she whispered to Lachlan.

"Aye, that we are, and I can offer you my protection if you will have it."

Tears stained her soft blue eyes, and she fought bravely not to let them spill. "Truly, you can?"

"I give you my word as a Sinclare warrior," Lachlan said strongly.

"Will you offer the same to my brother?" she asked, her bottom lip quivering.

"I will protect both of you with my life," Lachlan said.

The little girl threw herself into his arms and wept.

Lachlan wrapped a firm arm around her, stood and held out his hand to the lad.

"We are grateful, sir," the lad said then took his hand.

Piper sniffed back tears, Rowena let hers fall, and Hester smiled through tear-stained eyes. Megan remained her stoic self and they all walked to the common shelter.

"Food," the lad said with desperation when he spied the table with nearly empty platters.

"I think it would do well if we feed them all before seeing to their care," Terese said and nodded to Hester and Rowena to bring more food.

As they settled the four at the table, Terese heard Lachlan whisper orders to Boyd.

"Take some men and check the area for others or for trouble," he ordered, sending Evan as well.

Terese looked to Piper and she took off, though not in the same direction as Evan.

The little girl sat on Lachlan's lap while she ate; grabbing hold of his hand every now and again as if to make certain he was still there.

While the children and two adults ate their fill, Terese and Lachlan talked with them. The other women prepared to tend them and provide them with fresh clothes.

"I am Beatrice and my brother is Harry," the little girl informed them.

The older woman was Frances and the man Henry.

Beatrice glowed when Megan handed her a sweet cake. She was about to tear it in two to share with her brother when Megan handed him one.

"All for me?" Beatrice asked with wide eyes.

"All for you," Megan assured her.

Beatrice said no more, too busy enjoying her treat.

It wasn't until the children went inside the common shelter, Lachlan having had to walk Beatrice in and promise her she would be safe, and that he would be right outside, that Terese and he spoke freely with Frances and Henry.

"Once the sisters are done with the children, they will tend you both," Terese said. "At the moment, however, we'd like to know what happened to all of you?"

Henry explained. "Frances and I found each other along the road in the wake of two warring clans. They're taking food and whatever else they need from the farmers while they wage their war." He wiped tears from his eyes. "I lost my wife."

"I, my husband of thirty years," Frances said sorrowfully.

"I'm so sorry for your losses, but I must ask, does the fighting spill past the boundaries?" Lachlan asked.

Henry shrugged. "They'd have to make it past the mercenaries."

Lachlan leaned forward. "What do you mean?"

"There's a band of mercenaries who are making their presence known in the area," Henry said. "From what's been heard they're fierce warriors and claim what they will. It's really what started the clans to warring."

"How so?" Lachlan asked.

"One thought the other hired the violent band to help conquer." Henry shook his head. "But it was the clan leaders' fears and hatred for each other that provoked the start of it all and then . . ." He shrugged again.

"It escalated out of control," Lachlan said knowingly.

"Now the mercenaries sit by and wait," Henry said.

Frances nodded in agreement. "And then they will finish it all and our lands will be forever lost to us."

Night settled over the land. The children had long fallen asleep, exhausted from their ordeal. Frances and Henry had also dropped into a dead sleep after the sisters had seen to their care, offering baths and clean garments. Lachlan's warriors had found nothing, and Evan confirmed the same when he returned. Not a trace of anyone in sight.

Still Lachlan could not sleep. He felt unsettled, as if there was something he should know, but could not grasp. He sat by the campfire warmed by its flames, the night having chilled considerably. His men slept around him, with a few standing sentry around the convent.

He caught the moving shadow out of the corner of his eye, and it took him a moment to realize that it was Sister Terese. She blended with the night shadows to slip silently along the edge of the woods.

Lachlan didn't give it a thought; he followed her. It was much too late for her to be up and about, especially going off alone. He worried over her safety, but more he wondered where she was going and why.

He came upon her sitting on a boulder looking over the entrance of the woods and what he imagined would be a perfect spot to be at sunrise. But it was far from sunrise, so why was she here?

She sat with arms wrapped around raised knees, a dark green wool shawl draped around her and her hair was free of the usual braid she wore. It fell to her waist and glistened like strands of shimmering silk in the full moon's light.

His tightening loins suddenly warned him to leave, get away, do anything but approach her.

"You're welcome to join me if you'd like," Terese said.

Oh lord, that was all he needed . . . an invitation.

Of course, he accepted and was soon sitting next to her. "Is this a favorite spot of yours?"

"I come here when I can't sleep or at sunrise," she answered, on a yawn.

"I know the feeling," he admitted and found himself wanting to draw closer to the heat of her body, but respectfully kept his distance.

"There's a distinct chill in the air tonight," she said and stretched out her legs to wrap her shawl more tightly around her.

How he wished he could wrap his arm around her, draw her near and keep her warm against him, wrapped solidly in his arms.

You will definitely burn in hell, Lachlan Sinclare.

He continued to heed the warning and asked, "Why can't you sleep?"

She shrugged.

He sensed she knew, but didn't wish to discuss it.

"And you?" she asked. "Why can't you sleep?"

Because you haunt my thoughts. He couldn't speak the answer aloud so he also shrugged.

"Too many thoughts that need vanquishing?" she asked.

"Precisely," he agreed and wondered if her musings were as improper as his. He became curious and asked, "Why did you join the convent?"

She took a moment to answer him. "I truly had no choice."

"Why?" he asked, now even more curious.

"I had no place to go, no place to feel safe."

"Why?"

She turned and smiled softly. "Now it is you who ask why too much."

"Guilty," he admitted. "But also curious."

She hesitated.

"I don't mean to pry."

"No, it's all right. It's just a bit difficult for me to

talk about," she said and continued. "My family didn't want me. I was a burden to them."

Damn if he didn't feel a stab to his heart. How could someone so beautiful and selfless be a burden? He didn't think when he blurted out, "That's utter nonsense."

Her smile brightened. "You say what a friend would say."

Since there could be nothing more than friendship between them, he was grateful for the acknowledgment and wanted her to know the same. "I am your friend."

"That is good to know."

"You can count on me if ever you are in need," he assured her.

"That is generous of you, I shall remember that."

"You have not heard at all from your family?" he asked.

Again she hesitated, wrapping her arms tightly around her chest as if protecting herself. He could only imagine the painful memories that must haunt her.

She shook her head. "You are lucky to have such a loving family."

"They have their moments," he admitted with a laugh.

"Your mother and father must be proud."

His smile faded along with his laughter. "My father has passed."

"I'm so sorry," she said, her hand gently resting on his arm, offering comfort.

Her warm flesh and tender touch tempted, but it

was her sincere empathy that caused his desire to soar
. . . much too high. That she truly had a caring heart
fired his passion beyond belief, and he wanted nothing
more than to bury her in his embrace.

Instead he maintained control, though with great
difficulty.

"You must miss your father," she said.

"I do," he admitted, realizing it had been the first
time he had voiced it. "I truly do. He was a loving
father, a great man and a wise laird."

She patted his arm. "He must have been a loving
father, for you spoke it before anything else."

"You're right." He nodded slowly realizing how
true it was. "My father always had time for me and
my brothers, and especially my mother. They were
inseparable."

"Raised with such love, I'm surprised you don't look
for it yourself. Or perhaps you do and don't know it."

Her hand drifted away from him and he suddenly
felt chilled, as if all warmth had gone with her. And
oddly enough, he wondered if she could be right. In
his endless quest of women, could he truly be searching for love?

She yawned and rubbed the back of her neck.
"I should be able to sleep now." She turned to him.
"Thank you for the company and the conversation."

"You are most welcome," he said standing and
reaching out his hand to help her up.

She hesitated briefly before accepting, and once
she stood she walked away without saying another
word.

It was just as well for in that brief moment when her hand rested in his, he was overwhelmed with the desire to kiss her.

The flames of hell are waiting for you, Lachlan Sinclare. You're going to burn, burn, burn!

"Shut up!" he yelled at himself and stomped off, knowing that sleep would not come easily tonight.

Chapter 6

Piper woke Terese about an hour before sunrise. She knelt next to Terese's bed and whispered, "There is something you must see."

Rowena was already up busy making honey bread.

"Keep our absence secret from our guests as long as possible," Terese instructed Rowena and with quick, silent steps followed Piper over the convent grounds and into the woods.

The sun was a bright, half orange ball on the horizon when they reached their destination, Terese knowing she had slowed Piper down. It amazed her how familiar the young woman was with every inch of the woods, and it was that way with any forest. Once in it, Piper was as comfortable with it as with an old, dear friend.

Piper dropped to the ground and carefully brushed leaves out of the way to reveal tracks. "There were two of them, one heavy-footed and one nimble. They're scouting."

A chill ran through Terese as she bent down alongside Piper to take a look. "Do you know who?"

"Look here," Piper said, pointing to one hardy imprint in the ground. "This was made by a sandal. Mercenaries mostly wear boots."

Terese frowned, leaning back on her haunches. "This confirms a fear I had. At first when Henry mentioned the mercenaries, I wondered if perhaps the gossip we perpetuated about our little group had grown out of hand. Then I wondered what if . . . What if it had nothing to do with us at all?"

"It doesn't bode well," Piper agreed, then added proudly, "but we are warriors. You have seen to that."

Perhaps so, but Terese worried regardless.

"I would guess that the warring clans sent scouts to see if a surprise attack against the mercenaries was feasible," Piper continued.

"And if they're successful, they may just keep going, claiming everything in their path."

"A very good chance that's exactly what they'll do," Piper said.

"Is this as far as the scouts have gone?"

"They circle for the moment, concerned with their plan of attack," Piper explained. "They will probably continue to scout the remaining area afterward."

"And come upon the thriving farms," Terese said shaking her head. "Once they discover the farmers don't belong to any liege lord, their lands will be confiscated and they'll be free no more."

"And the convent?"

"They will not hurt us, but we will find our activities restricted."

"What can we do?" Piper asked anxiously.

Terese paced, the dried leaves swirling around her scuffling feet. She stopped suddenly and one or two leaves attached themselves to the hem of her brown skirt. "There's only one solution to this problem."

Piper waited expectantly.

"I go see the mercenaries."

Lachlan woke just after sunrise and following a hurried stretch he made his way to where he was certain he'd find Sister Terese enjoying the morning sunrise. He stopped when he saw that she wasn't there. He grew concerned that perhaps something happened to one of the children, or possibly Henry or Frances.

With quick steps he made his way to the common shelter. He almost collided with Sister Hester when she hurried out the door, a basket on her arm.

"Good morning, sir," she said with a nod.

He had given up on trying to convince the nuns to call him Lachlan.

"I'm taking fresh honey bread to the men." Hester pulled back the cloth for him to see.

The delicious aroma had his stomach crying out.

Hester smiled and handed him a slice, which he gratefully accepted.

"I'm looking for Sister Terese," Lachlan said before popping a piece into his mouth and relishing the sweet taste.

"I'm not sure where she is, though I believe Sister Megan knows."

"Where can I find her?" he asked.

"She's left for one of the farms. A babe needs delivering."

"What farm? Where?" Lachlan asked.

"Sister Piper would know that," Hester said, slipping him another slice before walking away.

"Where's Piper?" he called out.

Hester turned and shrugged. "I'm not sure."

He stood eating the bread and wondering over his next move. "Evan!" he said aloud.

"He's off in the woods," Andrew said, causing Lachlan to swerve around at his unexpected arrival. "He's holding the work up again."

Lachlan cringed. "What this time?"

"Fresh nests. Evan says the trees with the nests we can't disturb. He's marking the trees we can use. So, what are you going to do about it?" Andrew challenged.

"*You're* going to do as he says," Lachlan ordered.

Andrew shook his head. "Why do you allow him such fancies?"

Lachlan raised a brow. "You question my command?"

"Never," Andrew assured him. "I will get the men to work as soon as Evan finishes."

Lachlan placed a sturdy hand on Andrew's shoulder. "Evan tracks like none I have ever seen."

"True," Andrew nodded. "Very true. The men even talk about his exceptional skills."

"Now tell me, have you seen Sister Megan this morning?"

Andrew shook his head vehemently. "I keep my distance when at all possible."

Lachlan grinned. "I am not accusing you of anything. I need to know if you've seen her today."

Andrew answered reluctantly. "I saw her for only a moment. She was in a hurry, clutching her basket, telling me she had to be on her way. She smelled like freshly blossomed flowers and her cheeks were flushed pink and—"

"Enough!" Lachlan ordered. "How many times am I going to have to remind you that she is a nun?"

"She does not look nor does she act as a woman who has avowed herself to God, and you can't tell me you haven't thought the same watching the women."

"I can understand your apprehension. The women do not dress in the proscribed robes or act as piously as we would expect, but their reasoning makes sense. How could they possibly do the required work in such cumbersome garments or be lax in their chores?"

"Now you sound like your brother Artair," Andrew argued with a grin.

Lachlan shook his head and laughed. "Never will I be that practical."

"Thank the heavens," Andrew said with a smirk and playfully folded his hands in gratitude to the heavens.

"Back to more important matters," Lachlan instructed, anxious over Sister Terese's absence. "You've seen nothing of Sister Terese this morning?"

Andrew rubbed at the back of his neck. "Come to think of it, I don't recall seeing her at all."

A shout from one of the men had Andrew running off to get the shelter work started, leaving Lachlan to stew in worry. If sisters Megan and Hester were accounted for, all that was left was for him to see if Rowena or Piper knew anything.

He assumed Rowena to be in the common house tending the recent arrivals, but a quick peek inside found the room empty. A squeal of laughter had him smiling. Beatrice evidently was feeling safe enough to laugh.

He walked around the side and saw Beatrice running in circles, her brother Harry chasing her with a worm that looked to have been plucked fresh from the garden. He was glad to see their pale cheeks colored pink and while sadness remained in their young eyes, they had found the resiliency to play as carefree children once again.

When Beatrice spotted him, she reached her arms out to him and called out with a smile, "Save me, brave warrior, save me."

Lachlan understood her actions were more than simple play. She was testing him to see if she truly could depend on him. He immediately went to her rescue; scooping her up then playfully grabbing hold of Harry and ordering him drop his weapon. Harry giggled and dropped the worm to the ground.

"You are my hero, brave warrior," she sighed and wrapped her small arms tightly around his neck.

She stole his heart right there and then, and he hugged her, wanting her to know that she was safe. She looked so much better than yesterday, all cleaned up and with fresh clothes, a little too large, but tucked and tied in places that made them fit reasonably well.

She was actually very pretty with a spattering of freckles across her small nose and bright red hair that curled nicely with all the grime gone.

Lachlan noticed how good the rest of the recent arrivals looked. Frances even appeared to have less wrinkles than yesterday. But then, he knew from experience, being half starved and fearful undeniably marred not only the soul, but the body as well. He had become all too familiar with the ravage and results of battle.

The sisters should be proud. They had taken hungry and battered souls and tirelessly tended them, nourishing their every need. Guilt stabbed at him again for having alluded in his message to the church that the sisters should be returned home. They did good work here and were truly needed.

"Sister Terese, my hero saved me!"

Beatrice screeched near his ear and made him cringe, though he did it without disturbing his smile and quickly looked around for the woman who had eluded him since morning. He saw the strain of worry on her face as soon as their eyes met. It pinched at the bridge of her slender nose and forced a wrinkle or two at the corners of her blue eyes.

"How wonderful for you, Beatrice," Sister Terese said, her smile genuine, though worry remained evident as she stopped beside him.

"He can be your hero too," Beatrice said and leaned close to whisper to Terese. "We'll share him."

Lachlan heard and his heart melted even more for the little girl.

"You are most kind," Terese said and kissed Beatrice on the forehead.

"Beatrice, Harry, would you like to help me with the garden?" Rowena called out.

Beatrice kissed his cheek before she wiggled out of his arms and ran after her brother eager to help.

"I have been looking for you," Lachlan said.

"A nearby farmer has been ill for near a week now, and he feared his time had come and wished spiritual comforting," she said, walking over to sit beneath a tall pine, its fallen needles cushioning the ground.

He joined her. "His death leaves you troubled?"

She casually placed her hand over his. "What doesn't trouble me? I worry over the fate of those who arrived here in need and wonder if more will seek refuge. I worry that this senseless battle will spread and consume the farm families. So, yes, much troubles me. But that is the very reason I am here . . . to offer help and comfort."

Suddenly his guilt over wanting the sisters returned home vanished. Now he simply wanted Sister Terese safe and free from worry.

"You cannot possibly care for everyone," he assured her.

"I can try," she said emphatically.

"You are but one person."

"If not one than how many," she snapped. "How many will it take to help those in need, those suffering, those children that wander alone, hungry and frightened."

She certainly made him feel the selfish fool.

"You are good with children," she said more calmly. "You will make a good father."

"When the time is right," Lachlan said.

"There is a right time for children?" she asked curiously and answered her own question. "I always thought a babe chose his time."

"I will wed and have children in my time," Lachlan confirmed with a nod.

"You are so sure."

"I know what I want, and I will have it all in good time."

"How nice for you," she said with a gentle smile. "To be so sure of what your life will bring."

"I am confident I will find the perfect woman to wed," he said with a teasing glint and was surprised when she scrambled to her feet, a sudden scowl on her face, and he worried that he somehow upset her.

"I must go. I will be gone for a few days."

He jumped to his feet, intending to stop her from running from him, while wondering why she felt the need. "I will go with you."

"No, I will go myself."

"No, you will not," he argued.

"You have no right to dictate to me. I obey the church, not a Sinclare. Where I go you will not be welcome."

"Then you will not go," he ordered, thinking her too stubborn for her own good.

Her hands went to her round hips and the smirk on her face dared him to challenge her again. "I go where I please."

"I am here to protect—"

"We protect ourselves! You remain here out of *our* generosity! *Do not* for once think you can command me!"

Lachlan stood staring at Sister Terese, the force of her voice and her commanding stance made him look twice to be sure he spoke with the same woman.

"Sister Terese," Piper said appearing out of nowhere. "I need to speak with you."

The two were gone in a flash, Sister Terese acknowledging her departure with nothing more than a bare nod.

He wasn't sure of what had just happened, but he knew one thing. Sister Terese wouldn't be going anywhere without him.

Chapter 7

Terese took a deep breath and walked around the back of the common shelter with Piper. Once out of Lachlan's sight she took another deep breath, squeezed her eyes shut, and dropped back against the rough-hewn wall.

"You nearly lost your temper," Piper said, though not accusingly.

Terese's eyes popped open and she sighed with a nod. "He got me so mad, dictating to me."

Megan approached having seen the whole exchange and followed the two sisters. "We have gotten too used to being on our own, with no one to give us orders, no one to command our lives. We live as we please."

"I like it," Piper said.

"As do we all," Megan agreed, "which is another good reason we should find a new home."

"Unfortunately, the search must wait," Terese said. "We have more important matters."

She shared the news about the mercenaries with Megan and the woman paled.

"What are we to do?" Megan asked anxiously.

Terese motioned for the two to follow her. They made their way a few feet into the woods where the dense trees and thick foliage concealed them from prying eyes and ears.

"I am going to speak with the mercenaries," Terese said.

Megan objected with a firm shake of her head. "That's much too dangerous. You take a serious chance of being harmed."

"Not if I arrive wearing my nun garments and with news that would benefit them," Terese suggested. "This would surely put me in their good graces and in turn benefit us. Besides, I must learn their intentions here."

Megan stopped shaking her head. "It is an idea that could work, but it still remains dangerous."

"I thought the same," Piper added. "Though what other way is there?"

Megan nodded and asked, "Piper will go with you?"

"Yes, I need her. And it is wise that we take our leave as soon as possible and have done with this matter," Terese said, "though I will need your help in distracting Lachlan. He thinks to come with me."

A scream interrupted any response and excited, though unintelligible shouts followed. All three women hurried to see what the commotion was about. In the end it was the unexpected fuss that gave Terese and Piper the cover they needed to sneak away.

The three women were startled to see Beatrice and Harry fling themselves into the arms of a tired and ragtag couple who would have dropped if it had not been for the children's hardy embrace.

That Beatrice and Harry should be reunited with their mother and father, everyone agreed, was nothing short of a miracle. Some chaos pursued since everyone seemed to be talking at once, while the children, teary-eyed, clung to their parents. Neither children nor parents expected ever to see each other again. They had been separated in the mayhem of a battle that had spilled onto their farm. The children witnessed the carnage and believed their parents dead. The frightened brother and sister left thinking they had no one but each other. Ever since that day the parents, George and Gelda, had searched tirelessly for them.

All were caught up in the joyous reunion; it was Megan who saw opportunity in the moment and urged Terese and Piper to take their leave before anyone noticed.

They did. The last thing Terese saw of Lachlan was his charming smile as he spoke to the happy parents about their daughter and son's bravery. She bid him a silent good-bye, and oddly enough, realized that she would miss him.

A crazy thought, that should never have entered her head. And she suddenly felt guilty for having snapped at him. It was nonsense to be angry with him simply because he knew what he wanted and more than likely would get it.

She had been foolish to ever think her father would actually let her live her life the way she chose. He had reminded her often enough of her duty to him and the clan. And while he had encouraged her boldness, her need to be herself, when the time came, she was expected to reign in her independent nature and be a dutiful daughter.

Unfortunately, she could never accept that, so she had no other choice but to die. And she had better remain dead if she wanted to live free, which was why she had to remember she was the understanding, patient Sister Terese, not the snappish, shrewish Alyce Bunnock.

Terese and Piper made their way through the forest, their nun attire tucked in the cloth sacks that hung on their arms, along with other essentials. Terese would do what was necessary and then return to the convent, hopefully with this ordeal laid to rest.

Lachlan couldn't believe that Sister Terese had left when he had ordered her not to go alone. He hadn't learned of her absence until hours after she had been gone. He had been so caught up in the children's happiness and too intent on finding out more, if possible, about the warring clans from the parents, that he had forgotten about Sister Terese.

No, that wasn't completely true. He had assumed she would listen to him, follow his orders and wait for him to accompany her to wherever it was she wanted to go. When he discovered from a reluctant Sister Rowena that Sister Terese had gone deep into pagan territory, he grew even more annoyed.

She was placing herself in danger, though no one else seemed to agree with his assessment of the situation. The other sisters assured him that Sister Terese would be fine; she had been there many times before without incident. His men even seemed unconcerned, Boyd suggesting that Sister Terese could look after herself.

Nothing anyone said mattered and he planned on following her with Evan's help. Evan had gone into the forest just a few moments ago to see if he could pick up their tracks. Lachlan waited impatiently, Andrew joining him.

"Sister Megan assured you that Sister Terese would be gone two, maybe three days at the most," Andrew reminded.

"And much can happen to her in that time," Lachlan said.

"She's a resourceful and determined woman."

"And a beautiful one," Lachlan snapped and cringed at his words.

Andrew pursed his lips to prevent a grin.

"Don't say a word," Lachlan warned.

Andrew obeyed, though he couldn't keep a grin from bursting clear across his face.

He was doomed to damnation for even allowing himself the thought that he would miss her. He found he enjoyed conversing with her, or simply spending time with her. Her smile was always pleasant and her tongue thoughtful, though he could see that a spark of temper lay beneath her agreeable nature.

Lachlan saw Evan before he heard him, his steps too light to make a sound.

"I've never known anyone with Piper's skills," Evan said as if in awe.

"Which means you can't pick up their tracks," Lachlan said annoyed.

"Not a sign." Evan smiled broadly.

"And why does this make you happy?" Lachlan asked, growing more annoyed.

Evan wiped the smile from his face. "I'm not happy, not happy at all. It's just that . . ." He ran his hand through his tousled brown hair. "She's amazing. I've never seen anyone cover tracks with such skill. Not a footprint or scent. Nothing."

"Are you telling me that she covered her tracks on purpose?" Lachlan asked, now angry.

"That she did," Evan confirmed.

Lachlan began to pace. "She made certain no one could follow. She paid no heed to my order at all."

Andrew and Evan nodded, both knowing it was their safest response.

Lachlan stopped and glanced at the woods as though it waited to swallow him up if he should enter. He tempered his anger and instead asked himself why. Why did she feel the need to purposely leave him behind?

Lachlan turned suddenly and asked Evan, "Have you noticed how much time Sister Piper spends in the woods?"

Evan smiled and nodded. "Much more than I do."

"Which means she practically lives there," Andrew said.

"And what of Megan?" Lachlan asked turning to Andrew. "How often is she gone from here?"

Andrew rubbed his square chin. "Come to think of it she's always taking off with that basket of hers on her arm."

"Sisters Rowena and Hester are always about," Evan remarked.

"Are they?" Lachlan asked. "We assume Sister Rowena is always in the common room cooking, but we don't know for sure. And as for Sister Hester, she's here and about, but if we think on it, how much do we really see her?"

The three men grew silent.

Lachlan spoke first. "I think it would be wise to keep an extra watch on the sisters."

"What are you thinking?" Andrew asked.

"I'm not sure," Lachlan admitted. "But something doesn't seem right. Why wouldn't Sister Terese want me to go with her? With news of clans battling and confirmation that a band of mercenaries have claimed land here, wouldn't she be eager for protection?"

Evan offered another explanation. "But Piper knows these woods and could probably get Sister Terese more safely to her destination than you could."

"That's true too," Andrew agreed.

"It's questionable," Lachlan said, "therefore we keep an eye on the sisters' activities. I'll instruct Boyd to help, no others need to know."

The other two men nodded and then the three walked off, Lachlan certain he'd find answers soon enough.

Terese wore the nun garb proudly. After all, it had allowed her freedom. She and Piper arrived as night cast deep shadows over the landscape. They were escorted into the mercenary camp by a giant of a man, in height and width, though his girth was all muscle. His steps were confident as was his manner and she noticed that men quickly cleared a path for him if they should happen to be in his way.

His name was Hagen. He had made it clear that they were to follow him after Piper had surprised him at his sentry position in the woods. He had been so startled that he stood staring down at Piper as if he hadn't been certain she was really there. He had scratched his bald head and rubbed his chin taking time to determine how the wisp of a woman suddenly materialized.

Terese at first thought to explain to the large man that they needed to speak with his leader, but it didn't seem necessary since Hagen seemed to know what they wanted.

The camp grew eerily silent the further they ventured into it. Piper took hold of her hand and Terese squeezed it to let her know all would be fine, though she wondered over the wisdom of her actions. There were many more men than she had imagined and with each campfire they passed, the faces became less and less friendly. You could see from the heavily scarred faces and broken noses that never properly mended that these men were battle worn. They probably had stared down death on so many occasions that they didn't fear it anymore. And that made for a dangerous man.

At that moment, she couldn't help but wonder if her decision had truly been a wise one.

Hagen stopped at a campfire where two men sat and neither got up or acknowledged them once Hagen sat beside the smaller and stouter of the two.

Piper moved closer to her, and Terese felt a tremble ripple through her thin body that left the young woman shivering.

"I would like to speak with the leader," Terese said softly.

No one looked her way.

"I have important information," she tried again and the stout one snorted. She kept calm, though her heart beat madly. "It would serve you well to listen."

After one said something in a foreign tongue, the three men laughed.

That they simply ignored her out of arrogance sparked her temper. She had experienced the same in her own family and could never stomach it, which was why her mouth had turned bold. It was a weapon that always worked well for her and she thought gave her courage.

"Since the three of you are so stupid, I guess you all deserve what awaits you!"

Piper stiffened beside her, not a ripple of a shiver remained.

The three men's heads shot up and their eyes glared like the fires of hell at her.

"Your attention at last," she said sarcastically. "Do you now want to hear what goes on in the woods around you while all of you sit here chatting like empty-headed women?"

Terese didn't need to look at Piper to see that she had paled as if death's cold hand had touched her; she felt it in the defeated slump of her body. But Terese had no time to deal with Piper's fear. She was too enraged by the situation and determined enough to see it through.

The man in the middle stood slowly and Terese had to stretch her head up to look at him once he reached his full height. Dirt marred his face, but not his handsome features, add to that long dark hair and black eyes that impaled with a shiver.

"Speak," he ordered.

"I am not an animal," Terese said.

His head reared back as if feeling the sting of her sharp tongue. "Then why do you bark and bite?"

The other two laughed.

"How else do I communicate with you, but to speak your language," she retaliated and was surprised to hear a tiny chuckle from Piper.

"Watch your tongue, woman," the tall man warned.

"I am Sister Terese," she said with a proud toss of her head. "And this is Sister Piper. We have come to offer help and to ask for it."

He laughed. "Do we look like we need help?"

"In more ways than one," Terese snapped.

He growled like an angry animal. "It is a good thing you wear those robes, or I would teach you your place."

"Just like a man, needing to suppress a woman so that he can feel courageous."

"I should cut your tongue from your mouth," he sneered at her.

Terese lifted her chin. "I've been threatened with worse. Now do we talk, or do Piper and I leave you to await your deaths?"

"Tell me," he ordered sharply.

"Are you the leader?" she asked, wanting to know as much about these men as she could. She supposed it had always been in the back of her mind that perhaps she could find out if Lachlan's brother or the woman he searched for was in anyway connected to this group.

"That's none of your concern."

"I will speak to the leader," she demanded.

"Tell me!" he repeated with a shout.

"You are not the leader," she accused.

"How do you know?"

"You would have confirmed it immediately," she said.

This time he smiled, and Terese was struck by just how handsome this man was, even covered with dirt and dust.

"Perhaps we should keep you. You might prove an advantage to us."

"You would tire of my blatant tongue soon enough," she advised.

"True," he agreed and answered her query without her having to repeat it. "Our leader is not here."

"I am from Everagis Abbey, a short trek through the woods and over a hill or two. And you are?"

"I am Septimus."

"A seventh son," she said knowingly.

He confirmed with his own nod. "I suppose this help you can offer us comes with a price?"

"No, it comes with no attachments, though your help I would appreciate."

"Let me hear what you have to offer."

"Two clans north of here fight," she said.

"The MacMurdos and the Longhills," Septimus confirmed. "They know better than to bother us."

"I don't believe so," Terese disagreed, shaking her head. "Two men now scout your land, I believe in preparation of an attack."

"How do you know this?" he asked skeptically.

"Sister Piper is intimate with the woods, knowing its every sound, sensing its every presence. She came to me with the news and then showed me the footprints these men have left on your land and ours."

He remained silent for a moment and then once again spoke in a foreign tongue and the two men who had remained seated stood and rushed off.

"Sit," he said.

Terese, with Piper still clinging to her hand, sat near the fire.

He sat across from them. "Now tell me what I can do for you."

"Presently, the church has sent a small group of

warriors to protect us, but they will leave in two or three months."

"Leaving you vulnerable," he said.

"Not only the convent, but the farms around us," Terese confirmed. "In exchange for your protection of the convent and the farms, we will share our harvest with you and tend your ill or injured."

"How do you know you can trust us?"

"You are men for hire," Terese said confidently. "I offer you a good exchange, one that will benefit you. You would be a fool not to accept."

"Your tongue is too sharp."

"My tongue is honest," she snapped. "I present a decent, honest trade."

"Take the offer and share our bargain with no one, or it will be no more."

The bone-chilling voice commanded with a strength that sent a shiver through both women. Terese knew the voice came from somewhere in the dark that surrounded them. She also instinctively knew by the power of his voice this was not a man to cross.

It wasn't only the coldness of his voice, but the emptiness of it that frightened her. To her, this man had no heart.

"I give my word," Terese said and shivered once again, for she feared she had just signed a pact with the devil.

Chapter 8

L achlan stood and stared for a moment before he walked up to Sister Terese, wondering if she was truly there, when on the third morning he woke just before sunrise and found her in her usual spot waiting for dawn. He had gone there the past two days since her absence, hoping she had returned and now that she had, he wanted simply to hug her.

Damnation!

He didn't need to be reminded he was once again tempting the fires of hell.

"Did you miss me?"

Her query stunned him, though he regained his composure fast enough and with a smile sat beside her and admitted, "I missed our morning chats."

"I've grown accustomed to sharing the sunrise with you, Lachlan," she said, keeping her glance steady on the brightening horizon.

At the sound of his name spilling from her lips, he felt his heart catch as if for a brief moment a hand had squeezed it.

"You are an interesting man to talk with."

Interesting?

Most women found him charming, but none had ever found him interesting.

Woman? She's a nun! The warning resonated like a church bell clear and loud in his head.

"Where have you been?" he asked, wanting to distance himself from such wicked thoughts and wanting answers to several pending questions.

"To assist pagans who needed our help."

"Why didn't you let me go with you?"

"The pagans are a strange lot. It took much work to have them accept us," she said.

Her explanation seemed reasonable enough, yet it didn't satisfy him. "You could have given it a chance."

She turned then and smiled at him, and he thought his heart would stop beating. The sun was just rising and its brilliant glow illuminated her face. He was struck with awe by her beauty.

"Your tongue charms easily enough, but the pagans look for more in a man."

"And you don't think there is more to me?"

"I think there is much more to you," she said, "though you let no one see it." She scrunched her brow. "Why do you hide?"

"I don't hide," he objected.

"You do," she nodded. "You hide behind your calculating charm, afraid to let people know you are a truly selfless and caring man." Her smile returned. "Is it a way for you to be different from your brothers, in a sense your own man?"

He laughed. She was too astute for her own good.

She laughed along with him. "I knew it. I'm right."

"Two older brothers and a favored younger one, what was I to do?" he asked with a shrug and a smile. "I had no choice. I had to find something that would make me stand out, while allowing me to be me."

Her smile broadened, and she nodded slowly as if she truly understood him and her reaction encouraged him to continue.

"I discovered that I could coerce with words. Even my brothers were susceptible to my charm, and once I learned that . . . there was no stopping me."

"Did you ever think it wasn't your charm but perhaps your honorable nature that did the coercing?"

He paused to give her suggestion thought. He recalled how often his father discussed pending clan matters with him and asked for his opinion. Afterward, he would tell Lachlan that he admired his perceptive nature and that he should use it more often instead of relying on his charming tongue. His mother, in her own way, had advised him to be who he was.

"You're thinking on how right I am," Sister Terese said confidently.

"You are an insightful woman."

"It is needed in my position," she said.

How I wish you weren't in that position. He almost cringed at his thought, but managed to remain composed.

"You have much responsibility," he said, reminding himself of his own responsibility.

"I enjoy it," she said, scooting her knees up to wrap her arms around. She breathed deeply and raised her face to the morning sun. "Sunrise is so very beautiful."

"Beautiful," he whispered, looking at her, for her beauty truly astounded him. He felt a punch to his gut as if someone attempted to remind him of his manners.

She turned to him again. "I was wondering if perhaps you could offer George, Gelda, and their children a home with your clan? I know if they are with you, they will remain safe."

That she had such confidence in his ability to protect made him all the more intent on protecting *her*. Actually, it was a necessary need in him to make certain she remained safe, though it didn't lessen his guilt about seeing that he would be the reason she and the other sisters were returned home.

But wasn't Everagis their home now? They certainly had worked hard to make it so. And if they could not remain here, where would church officials send them? Would they separate the women who seemed as close as blood sisters? And more so, after his time here was done, would he ever see Terese again?

He chased such questionable thoughts away and answered her. "They are welcome at Caithness, home of the Sinclares. I believe there is even a vacant farm that needs a tenant."

Terese laid a gentle hand on his. "Beatrice is right. You truly are a hero."

Her warm palm tingled his flesh, but then her innocent touches always did. He knew they were meant to comfort, nothing more, but that didn't matter; his body responded anyway. Whether she laid a hand on his hand or on his shoulder, her touch sparked something inside him that he could not deny. He had known many a woman's caress, but none, not one, had the power to stir his passion so easily.

While he loved the pleasure of her touch, he knew it was wrong. And he wished that he could shove her hand away, but that would be rude. Instead he kept his eyes on the bright ball of sun.

"I am no hero," he told her.

She chuckled and gratefully her hand drifted off him. "I would say you are modest, but I know better."

He laughed. "You have gotten to know me well in the short time I have been here."

"You have made it easy for me to get to know you."

"How so?" he asked curious.

"Our talks," she said brightening. "When two people spend time talking they are bound to get to know each other."

"And become friends," he said, wanting her to know without a doubt he was her friend.

"And become friends," she repeated.

They both turned to stare at the sun high in the sky. He was glad she thought of him as a friend, but if he were honest he wished there could be more between them. He berated himself for such sinful thoughts. He had to forget how her lips were perfect for kissing, how he itched to take hold of her slim waist and then roam his hands over her generous hips. And finally cup her firm backside with eager hands.

He stood quickly, needing desperately to put distance between them. "I will see you later."

He hurried off and because he never looked back, he never saw the look of regret his hasty departure had left in her eyes.

Later that day, Terese wasn't surprised to learn that Frances and Henry would also find a home with the clan Sinclare. She had expected as much from Lachlan. While she could spy the warrior within him, she was more interested in the man who seemed to truly care about people. Unlike many warriors in her clan, he wasn't always commanding, demanding, or loud. What surprised her most about her talks with him is that he listened. He truly seemed interested in what she had to say.

He was the type of man she could have feelings for, but knowing that was impossible she chose to have him as a friend.

Terese stood in the field continuing to daydream instead of finishing the planting.

It was Megan who startled her out of her musings. She wore a smile, but her words expressed the opposite. "I believe Andrew keeps a watch on me."

Terese covered her own concern with a pleasant grin, wanting no one to suspect their conversation was anything but ordinary. "How so?"

"He's been lingering around me. He thinks I don't notice him, that I'm too absorbed in my chores, but I see him. And he followed me to one of the farms the other day."

"You let him?"

Megan nodded, her forced smile spreading. "It was a visit to the Timmins farm."

Terese nodded knowingly. Rachel Timmins would birth her third babe in a month's time, so there was a good reason for Megan to be there. Of course, Rachel and her husband Robert knew the truth about the sisters and were staunch supporters.

"I have noticed that I'm not the only one being watched," Megan said. "I see that Boyd and Evan have kept keen eyes on all of us with Lachlan keeping the keenest eye on you."

"What do you mean?" Terese snapped and realizing she had shown her temper quickly renewed her smile.

Megan covered her chuckle. "Lachlan is smitten with you."

"Don't be silly," Terese said but wondered if it dare be true.

"If he didn't believe you a nun, he would have made his feelings known by now."

"He charms, that's all," Terese said trying to dismiss it as nothing, while secretly thinking . . . was it possible?

Megan shook her head. "No, this is more than charm. He worried incessantly about you while you were gone. That's not merely charm, that's caring."

Terese tried to dismiss it once again. "He's just a friend."

"He'd be more if he could."

"How would you know?" Terese challenged, wishing Megan could confirm it, since no man had ever cared in such a way for her. And it touched her heart and tempted her dreams.

"Let us continue planting as we talk," Megan suggested, "so no one will suspect anything of us."

Terese quickly followed her lead, eager to hear more.

Megan continued as they dropped seeds on the prepared ground. "I have seen more lust in men's eyes than I have seen love. But when I did, it was so genuine that it moved me to tears. I see that memorable look in Lachlan's eyes when he looks at you."

Terese felt a catch to her heart. Why did it have to be now, like this . . . when she wasn't free to love this man?

"You loved once?" Terese asked, needing time to digest the thought.

"More importantly," Megan said softly, "*I was once loved.*"

Conversation ceased and Terese's only thought was that after all she had been through, all she had fought for, that there was finally a possibility that love was knocking at her door. And the sad part was . . . she couldn't answer it.

Chapter 9

The summons for help came just before dawn, while the whole abbey slept. Piper was the first to hear the familiar, continuous screech of a bird that was no bird, and alerted the other women. They donned men's clothing and with silent steps snuck away from the abbey so as not to be heard. They fetched their weapons in the woods and proceeded to the Timminses farm, where their horses were kept. Then without hesitation they rode to Gillian's, the farm that was under attack.

Terese knew that once Lachlan departed the abbey Septimus, by order of his leader, would have his men guarding the area, and there would be no more need to continue the ruse of mercenaries. Until then, when a summons for help came, the women would have to answer.

The women arrived before any severe damage could be done to the family or the farm. It took more than a skirmish to conquer the small group of clan warriors who had made it past the mercenary camp without detection. It took all of the women's skills and strengths, the use of wit rather than brawn, and Terese's strategizing skills to combat them.

The women made the warriors believe there were more fierce mercenaries than the five of them. Piper set traps in a particular area and the other women made certain they drove the warriors right into them.

Unfortunately, as the conquered warriors beat a hasty retreat, one released an arrow that found its way into Terese's upper arm. Before the other women could retaliate, Septimus and a few of his men appeared and finished off the retreating warriors.

Septimus's black stallion pranced majestically around her chestnut mare. "What foolishness is this?" He reached out and pulled off the stocking cap that kept Terese's long blond hair hidden, the silky strands falling in a mess around her face. "If I hadn't recognized you, you would all be dead right now."

"You're the one that let this group get past your camp," Terese shot back as she fought the burning pain in her arm.

"Let her be," Hester warned, riding up beside him brandishing her sword.

"You are a fool," Septimus spat. "Are you blind to the many men that surround you?"

Hester laughed. "It takes only one sword to kill one man."

Septimus grinned and looked to Terese with a shake of his head. "You taught these women courage, didn't you?"

"What difference does it make?" Hester demanded.

"Few truly brave leaders exist," Septimus said. "I and my men respect those who do. Sister Terese has earned our respect."

"And that means . . . ?" Hester challenged.

"More than you know," Septimus said with a cold stare that turned Hester silent.

"How did you know we were here?" Terese asked, turning paler by the minute.

Rowena rode up just then and shooed everyone out of her way. "You need to be off your horse so that I can tend that."

"I wouldn't do that," Septimus said. "There's a contingent of warriors from your abbey headed this way and something tells me that they don't know about your warrior skills."

Terese shook her head, trying to keep her mind focused, but the pain was taking its toll.

"Go," she ordered Septimus. "They must not know about you and your men."

"What of you?"

Terese sent him a hard glare. "You doubt my ability to handle this?"

"No, I would never be as foolish as the man who comes for you."

Her eyes widened and Septimus eased his horse closer to hers.

"Neither I nor my leader are fools. He advises caution with this game you play, for he has no doubt it will bring retribution."

Terese groaned as he rode away, his men following. Septimus intimated that he knew that she and the other women weren't nuns, but did he? She had no time to think on this new worry. Gratefully, all four of the Gillians were fine and William, the oldest son, offered to help return the horses to the Timmins farm. And the women needed to return to the abbey with all haste, while hopefully avoiding Lachlan and his men in the process.

"Piper," she called and the wiry young girl appeared in a flash. "Can you misdirect them?"

"Yes," she answered without hesitation. "I know how they picked up our trail."

"How?" Terese asked, the other women, just as curious, having joined in.

Hester answered. "It was me. I had forgotten the extra cache of arrows and backtracked to retrieve them, not covering my tracks good enough."

"What's done is done," Terese said. "What matters is what we do now." She ordered with the confidence of a true leader and in minutes the women set to work.

When it was only she and Rowena, Terese asked, "How bad is the wound?"

"The arrow went clean through the fleshy part of your arm," Rowena explained. "It's going to hurt like hell removing it, and it may require a few stitches if the flesh tears. Then we have to be careful of poison setting in and of course fever—"

"No more," Terese protested, her head spinning and

her arm already unbearably painful. "Let's be done with it.

"I'd prefer if we waited until we return to Everagis," Rowena said. "Piper will have Lachlan and his men running in circles, which will delay their return, giving us time to properly mend you."

"It's quite a chance we take sneaking back to Everagis with an arrow through my arm."

"A necessary chance," Rowena said firmly. "I have all I need there."

Terese nodded and while Piper saw to her chore, Megan and Hester, with William's help, saw to the care of the horses and stowing the weapons.

Just after sunrise, she and Rowena managed to sneak in through the secret entrance the women had installed in the back end of the common house. It was a good thing too since Terese collapsed in a chair unable to bear much more pain.

Rowena opened the wood shutters just enough to peek outside to see a few warriors prowling about. "You were right," she said, returning to Terese's side. "Lachlan did leave some men behind."

"A seasoned warrior would," Terese said. "That's why I worry he will return sooner than expected, so we must hurry and remove this arrow and mend me."

Rowena nodded and hurried to gather everything she needed, and just before she was ready to begin . . .

The door crashed open, slamming against the wall, and in strode an enraged Lachlan. Megan, Hester, and Piper were forced in behind him by Andrew, Boyd, and Evan.

"I want the tru—" Lachlan's shout ended abruptly. "What happened?" He was quick to go to Terese's side.

"What does it look like?" Terese said snappishly and Rowena nudged Terese's foot with her own.

The warning came too late. Lachlan slammed his fist on the table, causing not only the items there to jump, but everyone in the room. "You will tell me the truth . . . all of it."

Terese was in no mood to play nice, especially since he was being so forceful and besides her arm hurt like hell. "And I shall do that now while my arm is turning poisonous?"

After a deep breath he calmed and asked, "How can I help?"

Before Terese could tell him his help wasn't necessary, Rowena spoke.

"Your strength could be an advantage in removing the arrow. The men must leave and the sisters need to see to their chores." The three women nodded and hurried to their rooms to change into their own garments.

Terese was about to protest Lachlan's help when he leaned down and pressed his nose to hers. "Not a word."

His command hadn't stifled her objection; it was the suffering in his dark eyes. It was as if he shared her pain and the realization stole her breath, making her gasp.

"What's wrong?" he asked with an anxious yet gentle hand to her shoulder.

"Nothing," she said, still feeling breathless.

Lachlan hunched down in front of her. "I am so very sorry that you suffer this pain and that I will cause you more pain removing it."

Terese didn't think; perhaps it was the pain, or maybe she just needed to touch him, for that's what she did. She placed her hand upon his cheek and his warm flesh was the tonic she needed to soothe her soul. And with caution gone, she rested her forehead to his and said, "I need you."

She felt him ease away from her and say, "She's delirious from the pain."

Terese raised her head, shaking it. "No, I'm not." She then looked to Rowena. "We can't hide the truth any longer. They are bound to discover it sooner or later and we've burdened ourselves long enough with it."

"What are you talking about?" Lachlan asked.

"First, the arrow," Rowena advised. "And the others should be here when . . ."

Terese nodded her agreement. "You are right." She looked to Lachlan. "Take the arrow out and then I will tell you the truth." Though she would not reveal her true identity. Never would she tell him her true identity.

Rowena twisted Terese's long hair up and secured it with two combs. She then ripped the sleeve off and away from around the wound and handed her a piece of wood. "To bite down on for the pain."

Terese took it with a smile, though she felt anything but brave.

Lachlan spoke quietly with Rowena for a few moments and then it was time. Terese closed her eyes and clamped down on the thick stick with her teeth. She didn't have to worry, with the first onslaught of intensely burning pain she passed out.

She was stretched out on something hard and her eyes fluttered open; through hazy vision she could make out Rowena standing over her.

"Good timing, I'm all done," Rowena said.

Lachlan popped into view. "It was better you fainted. The arrow was stubborn and didn't want to let go of you."

Terese went to move and a searing pain shot through her arm. She groaned and grimaced.

"It will be painful for a while, then merely sore and finally heal as long as—"

Terese shook her head. "I don't want to hear all that could go wrong. Just tell me what I need to do to keep it right."

Rowena went into a list of things, finishing with, "But I don't expect you to listen."

"I'll see that she does," Lachlan said.

"That might work," Rowena said with a chuckle.

"Help me up," Terese ordered.

"See, already she doesn't listen," Rowena said but did as Terese asked, though Lachlan took over and assisted Terese, his arm going around her.

Terese kept her arm wrapped around Lachlan's after he had helped her to sit up. It was a good thing too, since she felt dizzy. She rested her head to his shoulder. "The room spins."

"Take your time," Lachlan said, holding her firm.

She wished she could stay there resting against him. That he was muscled, his body taut, was obvious, but it was the warm comforting feel of him she liked the best.

Her vision cleared completely, the dizziness passed and she was able to sit without help, so she had no choice but to let him go. But she didn't. She held on to him for a few more moments until common sense warned her to release him.

When she finally did, he seemed reluctant to let her go. "Are you sure you feel well enough?"

"I'm fine, though you could help me to a chair," she said and was surprised when he carefully scooped her up into his arms and placed her gently on a chair. It felt even better resting against his chest, the woodsy scent of him teasing her nostrils and her senses.

It was over too soon and too soon she would have to tell him the truth.

"The others wait outside," Rowena said.

Terese had forgotten Rowena was there. For a moment she only had thoughts of herself and Lachlan. Could that be why she wanted the truth revealed? Did she want Lachlan to know her a woman free to do as she chose?

"Bring them in," Terese said before her thoughts turned too crazy.

Megan, Hester, and Piper entered and joined Rowena and her at the table. Lachlan chose to stand, arms folded across his chest.

"Before you start I'd like to have a say," he said.

Terese nodded.

"I thought more was going on here than met the eye. I must admit I never expected that the five of you had taken on the persona of mercenaries. I'm sure you had a reasonable explanation, and I can assure you that neither I nor my men will reveal your secret to the church. Of course," Lachlan said with the hint of a smile, "there is the stipulation that you never again do such a foolish thing."

Terese knew the other women felt as she did, that they would allow no one to dictate to them. They had survived on their own this long and they would continue to do so.

"What you tell to the church doesn't matter to us," Terese said.

The other women nodded in agreement.

Suspicion dawned in Lachlan's eyes. "And why is that?"

"It's simple," Terese said. "Not one of us is a nun."

Chapter 10

Lachlan shook his head.

"You heard me right," Terese confirmed.

He thought he had, but it was too crazy too think it was the truth. "None of you are nuns?" he asked, looking yet again for validation.

Terese glared at him. "Not a blessed one of us."

"Explain," he said tersely, not certain if he was feeling angry or foolish over the revelation.

"We are women—"

"Misfits to most," Megan threw in and all the women nodded.

Terese continued. "The sisters picked us up one by one along the way and offered us shelter and a home if we wished to take vows. But before anything could be decided the nuns took ill. We looked after them, tended them and then buried them. Everagis was our only home, and so we took on the identity of nuns."

"That's two guises so far, nuns and mercenaries," Lachlan said. "Are there any more I should know of?"

"Not a one," Terese said, knowing she lied again, yet knowing it was necessary.

"What of your names?" Lachlan asked. "Are they your own?"

"They belong to us," Terese said.

"Is there any more you need to tell me?" he asked.

"There is nothing more," Terese said.

Lachlan looked at the lot of them then settled his eyes on Terese. "You lead them?"

"I do, and proudly."

He nodded slowly and after a moment of silence he said, "Rest your wound, I will speak with you later about this." And with that he marched out of the room, shutting the door none too gently behind him.

His men moved out of his way, his intent steps and the rare look of anger in his eyes warning them to stay clear. He grew more angry when he found himself at the spot where he and Sis— He stopped himself; Terese was no Sister. She was a woman like any other woman and . . . again he stopped and realized what this revelation meant.

She was a free woman and he had had an itch for her since he had first seen her. How he had suffered over what he had thought sinful musings. With this news, he would no longer have to worry about eternal damnation.

He could kiss Terese, and that prospect set his loins to aching.

I need you.

That's what she had said to him and at the time, he wished he could have told her he felt the same. He needed her. He needed to ease her pain, keep her safe, kiss her, touch her and damn . . . he wanted to make love to her.

He had believed that all out of his reach, but now . . . now things were different.

Very different. He rubbed his head and near groaned. Once his men discovered the truth they'd be sniffing after the women like animals in heat, especially Andrew. He was already smitten with Megan and once he learned that she was not a nun . . .

Lachlan groaned again and shook his head. He would have to gather his men together and set down some rules. They might not like it, but they'd obey. Or else they would face dire consequences from Cavan, their laird, and not a one of them would want that.

He needed to address this matter immediately and later he would have a talk with Sis— He shook his head. *Terese.* She was now plain and simply *Terese.* Not that, by any means, Terese was plain and simple. No, she was a beautiful woman he planned on getting to know more personally and he was confident that she wanted to get to know him just as much.

Feeling lighter in his step, he walked away to deliver the news to his men.

Andrew got Lachlan alone, as Lachlan had suspected he would, after the men dispersed smiling and mumbling among themselves. Lachlan had made it clear that they were to behave. He didn't ban them from talking with the women, but he did warn that if the women showed no interest, not even in a conversation, then the men were to leave them alone.

"I think Megan's just skittish around men," Andrew said as he and Lachlan walked away to talk on their own. "If I could just get her to know me better, I think she'd like me."

"I can't make an exception," Lachlan said. "I'll have a revolt on my hands if I grant you special privileges."

Andrew moaned with frustration.

"Use your wits and find a way for her to talk with you," Lachlan suggested.

"How?" Andrew bemoaned. "I've tried and she just gives me a cold stare and walks away. Even when I offer help, she turns me down. What else can I do?"

"What do you like about her?"

Andrew grinned. "Her tenacity."

"Then show her your own," Lachlan said and gave him an encouraging slap on the back before walking away.

Lachlan made a point of talking with each of the women and informing them that his men knew the truth, and also the strict orders his men had been given regarding the women. Each of them was appreciative and thanked him profusely. He saw no worry in any of their eyes, except for Megan. She actually paled.

"None will bother you," he assured her.

"They better not," she said and stormed off.

The news changed nothing for the others at the convent, Frances summoning it up the best. "Nuns or not, they are good, kind, generous women."

* * *

It was four days before Lachlan got to talk with Terese, not that he hadn't tried before that. Rowena had told him that she slept and was in too much pain to be disturbed. He wasn't sure if he believed her, but when she walked him down the hall and eased the door open to Terese's room, he saw for himself.

She lay pale and sleeping, and tucked under a mound of blankets.

"The chills," Rowena had whispered, but had assured him not to worry.

He continued to inquire about her progress and on the morning of the fourth day he woke before sunrise and saw her. Her long blond hair was free and fell slightly unkempt around her face, and she hugged, with a degree of difficulty, a green wool shawl around her as she walked to her favorite spot on the hill.

He caught up with her and slipped an arm around her to help her sit.

"You are a gentlemen," she said.

He turned his charming smile on her. "At times."

"And other times?"

"That would depend on the women you asked."

Terese smiled and shook her head.

"I am glad to see that you're feeling better."

"Rowena told me that you frequently inquired as to how I was doing."

"I was concerned," he said. "Not all wounds heal as they should."

"No . . . No, they don't," she agreed slowly, making him wonder what wound she was recalling that hadn't healed.

"I'd like to know who you really are."

"Nobody," she said softly.

He felt the pain of her response. It was like a stab to his heart and he wanted to beat the person who had hurt her.

"That's not true," he said adamantly. "You are a courageous and beautiful woman."

"You stand alone in that opinion."

"Mine is the only opinion that matters." He smiled, but in his eyes there was a fire.

"A champion," Terese said as if giving it thought. "I've never had one."

"You do now," Lachlan assured her.

"Why?" she asked on a soft breath.

He leaned closer. "You deserve one."

"I do no—"

He pressed his finger to her lips. "You deserve much more, like the kiss I've wanted to steal from you ever since I met you."

"You don't have to steal it," she encouraged.

"I'm glad to hear that," he said and leaned in close to brush his lips across hers as if first familiarizing himself with her and letting her do the same with him. She eagerly returned the favor and soon their lips were seeking more. She was confident in her kiss, with a firm certainty that sparked his passion. She wanted him and she wasn't afraid to show it.

Their kiss deepened and his arm slipped around her, carefully so as not to cause her injured arm pain. Her little moans and groans excited him and damn if he didn't want to make love to her here and now. But it wasn't the time or place, and there was her wound to consider.

"You taste good," she said with candor when he eased their kiss to an end.

"And you are intoxicating." He pressed his cheek to hers and lingered in the cool softness.

"We have a situation here, Lachlan."

His name rolled so comfortably from her lips, as if she were familiar with it and liked the taste.

"We certainly do," he agreed.

"What do we do?" she asked, though he thought she already knew the answer just as he did.

"We let it happen," he whispered and kissed her cheek.

"You are not angry with me?"

He understood her query. "I must admit that at first I was, but my anger was more over my own foolishness than anything else. Giving the matter more consideration, I realized the situation you all were in and the wisdom of your choice."

She scrunched her brow. "You are so very different from the men I have known."

"And how many men is that?" he asked, unable to hide his annoyance.

She quickly explained. "I've bedded no man. I compare you to family and clan members."

His annoyance instantly evaporated. "I'm one of a kind."

She laughed lightly. "I'm beginning to realize that."

"But so are you, which make us the perfect pair."

"I agree."

Lachlan took her hand and raised it to his mouth for a kiss, but her grimace stopped him short. "I'm sorry," he said, easing her arm down to rest their clasped hands on his lap.

"My wound is truly much better then it was," she assured him.

They stared at each other and the sun came up around them, a brilliant ball of orange that kissed the land and their faces as they came together in their own kiss. It stole their breaths and sparked their passion. When it finished they rested their foreheads against each other, allowing their breathing to return to normal, though it would take more time for their desire to abate.

He chuckled, his forehead continuing to rest against hers. "I'm relieved you never took vows."

"They are not meant for me," she said, turning her head from his to tilt it back so that the morning rays could toast her face.

"What is meant for you?"

"Freedom to live my life as I wish."

"Few people have freedom to do that," he said.

She shrugged. "Then I will be one of the few."

"You are obstinate."

She smiled. "Will that hurt our friendship?"

"Nothing can hurt our friendship."

"You never know," she said, shaking her head.

"Then you never had a true friend."

She stared at him, her blue eyes matching the color of the morning sky and making him think he had never known the color to be lovelier.

"Good friends," he continued, "are there for each other through the good and bad of things. They don't judge or condemn."

"Promise me that?" she asked. "Promise you won't judge or condemn me."

"I promise," he said without hesitation.

But she looked skeptical and again he wondered who had hurt her. He'd find out in time, for as their friendship grew so would trust.

"Will this information change your departure time?" she asked.

"It changes nothing. You are women in need of protection—" He stopped abruptly and grinned. "Maybe not as much protection as I first thought."

She took his remark as he had intended it, as a compliment. "Thank you," she said.

"However, there still remains a problem."

Terese nodded. "We occupy church land and will not be allowed to remain here."

"No wonder you lead; you have a sharp mind."

"All the women do. I just happened to fall into the role."

"It may seem so, but leadership was truly yours from the start as with all great leaders. They never seek it; instead it finds them," he said.

She seemed uncomfortable with yet another compliment, and he wasn't surprised that she chose to ignore it.

Instead she inquired, "Do you think the church will send others to replace us?"

"I would say that's a good possibility, especially since you and the others have proved so fruitful here."

"Our good deeds will see us homeless," she said rather sadly.

He squeezed her hand lightly. "I will not let that happen." It produced the smile he was hoping for. "Your smile is like the sunshine, warm and pleasant."

"*Pleasant?*" she queried with a chuckle.

"*Very* pleasant," he confirmed. "It defines your lovely nature."

She stared at him as if befuddled.

He simply smiled. "I speak the truth, so accept it. You are *pleasant* and *lovely*."

Her expression softened. "You may reclaim those words one day."

"Never," he insisted adamantly. "They are words spoken from my heart and will forever remain so."

She slipped her hand out of his and gently laid it against his cheek. "Then know they are gratefully accepted and forever tucked in *my heart* for safekeeping."

He placed his hand over hers that rested against his cheek. "That would mean that each of us is in the other's heart forever."

"A safe place to be?" she asked on a whisper.

"Very safe," he assured her.

Their hands dropped away and their lips drifted together until they lightly touched and a heated spark jolted them. Their wide eyes acknowledged the passion that had struck them like a bolt of lightning, and they both knew without a sliver of doubt, that soon, very soon, they would surrender to it.

Chapter 11

Terese sat under a tree, her back braced against the thick trunk and its fallen leaves beneath providing a comfortable cushion. It had been hours since she and Lachlan had talked, with him leaving her at the bottom of the small hill to see to his men and her to rest as he had gently, but firmly suggested.

She had offered what help she could reasonably give to each woman and one after the other they had turned her away, insisting she rest, and so she did what everyone had advised.

She had chosen a place beneath a large oak tree, for it gave her a generous view of the convent, though it actually didn't— it never resembled a convent and now it looked even less like one. Everagis appeared more like a pregnant land laboring to give birth to a village and the thought made her smile.

There was camaraderie among the inhabitants that filled the air, and smiles that couldn't be denied. Everyone seemed genuinely content. And the men had wasted no time in pursuing the women.

Terese noticed immediately how Piper and Evan talked more freely and huddled hunched down on the ground, Piper drawing in the dirt with a stick and Evan eagerly nodding. Hester was pleasant to the men who approached her, but appeared not interested in a one of them and made that clear.

And Megan? Terese knew she would let no man near her and felt sorry for Andrew, who seemed truly interested in her. He didn't push or demand; he simply would approach with a question. Unfortunately, it appeared it was one that she could easily answer with either a nod or a shake and with nothing more left to be said he'd walk away. But he would return, do the same and walk away again, but not once did he give up. He kept going back.

Terese wondered if perhaps he would wear Megan down, and she would eventually see Andrew for who he was . . . a man willing to patiently wait for her.

She felt a stab of guilt. Here she was hoping Megan would see Andrew for who he truly was while she hid who *she* was from Lachlan. Her guilt quickly turned to sorrow for she realized that Lachlan was attracted to Terese, not Alyce.

And how would he feel when he discovered she played at yet another ruse, one that could damage more deeply than the other two?

He had promised her he would never judge or condemn her, but then that promise had been made to Terese, not Alyce. She shook her head. She didn't even know who she was anymore. She had been living so long as Terese she almost believed Alyce dead. But then it was as if Alyce would awaken and break free. Sometimes she would be happy to be reunited with her, for she knew that her sharp-tongued nature was needed, especially in difficult situations. And then she would slumber once more.

Terese had to keep things in perspective. This friendship and attraction to Lachlan could go no further than that. She had to keep reminding herself that he would be leaving, and that he *must* leave when the time came, and she must go on as Terese.

The thought of his eventual departure left a solid ache in her stomach, but that couldn't be helped. She already knew that her friendship with Lachlan had been growing deeper by the day, and she didn't want to jeopardize what was or would be between them.

Hester's wave and approach drew Terese out of her musings and she soon joined Terese, the basket on her arm revealing a bounty of food for them both.

"Rowena says eat then rest," Hester said, spreading out a white linen cloth to place the food upon.

"All goes well?" Terese asked, realizing just how hungry she was upon smelling the delicious fare.

"Lachlan is true to his word. His men behave," Hester said, pouring them each a tankard of freshly brewed cider.

"You fancy not a one of them?" Terese asked with a smile.

Hester didn't smile, she was blunt. "I want no man. I'm happy as I am."

"Piper seems busy with Evan," Terese said.

That brought a smile to Hester. "Those two are alike, both loving the woods. She even confided to him that the woods had birthed her and was her mother."

"What did Evan say to that?"

"I was impressed with his response," Hester said. "He told Piper that her mother had taught her wisely, and he would like to learn what she knew."

"Evan's a good man, don't you think?" Terese asked.

"Is he a good man for Piper is what you're asking?"

"Piper deserves someone good, if that's what she chooses," Terese said. "And he does share her love of the woods."

"It wouldn't work," Hester said. "Evan wouldn't leave the Sinclare clan and make his home here and Piper will not leave."

"I suppose that would be a true test of things," Terese said.

"And what of you?" Hester asked and shook her head when Terese appeared to protest. "Don't deny it. I and the others have seen the way you and Lachlan have been meeting on the hill in the morning, how he keeps you company while planting, and most of all how you look at each other."

"And how is that?"

"With a desperate longing," Hester said with a merry glint.

"It's that obvious?"

"Only to those who know you," Hester assured her.

Terese sighed. "I had resigned myself to never knowing a man . . . then Lachlan came along and I began to wonder."

"I wonder if it would not be better for the warriors to leave," Hester suggested with reluctance. "It seems the longer they remain here, the more they learn. And that could prove dangerous for you."

"Lachlan has informed me that he has no intentions of leaving."

"Then be careful," Hester warned. "You don't want to lose more than you're willing to give."

"I will give sparingly."

"But will your heart?" Hester asked.

The men kept busy building extra shelters, having generously given the first one finished to the Moore family. Beatrice and Harry were thrilled and their parents grateful. Soon George and Gelda had prepared a patch of land for a garden and were planting seeds the women had given them.

Lachlan had set the men to erecting a small cottage a good distance away from the others and from the common house. It would be for him and he hoped Terese. He had never failed to charm a woman into his bed, but this was different. He couldn't even say for sure how it was different; he only knew how it felt.

With other women, they didn't matter to him beyond the bed. With Terese, she seemed to matter to him all the time. He had never felt so relieved when she had confessed that she was not a nun. He had been having nightmares about burning in the fires of hell, the flames scorching then devouring his flesh, yet his wicked thoughts refused to leave him alone.

With no further worry over that prospect he was free to pursue Terese, but it wasn't only his bed he wished to get her in. No, he wanted more from her, but again just what that more was he wasn't sure.

He did want to learn more about her, where she was from, about her family and who in the past had hurt her so badly. He liked that conversation never failed between them. They always found something to discuss or debate.

Most of all, he liked the way she kissed. She hadn't shied away from him; she was as eager as he. And she freely admitted that he tasted good. He thought about that moment often since it had happened two days ago. Unfortunately, he had little chance to spend with Terese since. When he was free she was resting, when she was free he was busy with his men.

It seemed everyone was busy. Everagis was growing with the help of him and his men, and he was beginning to wonder if there was some way he could make certain the women remained in the home they had forged with their own hands. He would give it thought and see what he could do.

"Can I interest you in a walk?"

Lachlan spun around with a smile and as soon as he saw Terese with a glow to her cheeks and her honey blond hair secured in a braid, he knew she was well.

He crooked his arm for her to take and she did with a smile and without difficulty.

"You're feeling much better?" he asked as they began their stroll around the convent.

"It still pains me at times," Terese said, "but Rowena was quick to show me how well the wound was healing between bandage changes, though cautioned against too strenuous work."

"Then what are your plans for today?" he asked, ready to suggest something that would involve just the two of them.

"I thought to take a walk in the woods and gather branches to make baskets. We have need for more and"—she said with a teasing grin—"I need help."

"I'm at your service." He gave a quick bow of his head.

She hugged his arm. "I was hoping you'd say that."

He leaned close. "And I was hoping you'd ask."

They walked away arm in arm smiling, oblivious to the curious stares and smiles that followed them off the convent grounds. They didn't go deep into the woods and were quick to hold hands rather than remain locked arm in arm. It made it easier to walk the uneven terrain and make their way around large rocks and fallen trees.

"Your hand feels good in mine," she said. "I like the feel of you."

Lachlan enjoyed her candid proclamations; they stirred his blood. But then he didn't need much stirring when he was near her. Her closeness alone could spark his passion for her.

"I like your bluntness," he said emphatically.

She stopped, though her hand remained firm in his. "Bluntness is not an attribute."

He rested his other hand lightly on the curve of her waist and eased closer so that their garments brushed. "It is with you."

She laughed. "Again you would be alone in your assumption."

He gently squeezed her waist, lingering in the feel of her tender curve. "Whose tongue has wounded you so badly?"

"It matters not," she said.

When she attempted to walk away, he stayed her with a slight pressure of his hand. "He matters to me."

Her eyes turned sad for a moment and then brightened. "I forget you are my champion."

"I didn't forget, and I never will," he said firmly and released her hand to hug her waist and draw her close. "I've been aching to kiss you."

"Then what are you waiting for?" she asked and melted against him.

He claimed her mouth like a starving lover, while their bodies entwined in a hungry embrace. It was as if they had waited years to come together and now they could not get enough.

Their kiss exploded with passion and their hands roamed tentatively, eager but unsure. It was Terese who took the first step and slipped her hand inside his shirt to splay her hand over his chest. At that moment

Lachlan felt branded, forever marked by her and oddly enough he relished the thought.

She spread his shirt open and her hand roamed his naked chest at will, he hoping she would travel down further and further. His lips drifted off her mouth to impatiently explore along her neck, sweet and soft and ever so intoxicating.

She took hold of his face and forced his mouth to hers once again, hungrier than she was before, but then his appetite was just as ravenous.

When breath was needed she rested her cheek to his and whispered, "I need you. I have never known such a need."

Lachlan near growled with desire and the thought that she had never known a man, that he would be the first to touch her, to teach her, only made his passion more potent.

But the woods and hard ground was no place for her first time. He wanted it special for her, for them to always remember.

He eased away, taking hold of her hands and the ravenous desire that had turned her sky blue eyes stormy almost made him change his mind.

"Not here, not now," he said softly.

"Why not?" she asked anxiously.

"You deserve more."

"I have more." She gripped his shirt. "I have you."

"And so you shall," he promised with a kiss. "You shall have me all night and wake in my arms in the morning."

"Why must we wait?" she asked annoyed.

"Why must we hurry?"

"Your time here is short," she said on a sigh. "I wish to make the most of it."

He pressed a gentle finger to her lips. "There is no time when it comes to us. There is only now."

He kissed her again and they lingered in it, nibbling and nipping, but this time not touching for he had taken hold of her hands and held them tight, knowing if he let her touch him, he would surrender.

Chapter 12

~~~⌒⌒~~~

Terese spent the afternoon trying to make baskets with Megan, but she snapped more branches than she bent into shape. Finally, Megan shoved her aside and ordered her not to touch another branch.

"We'll soon have no branches left and only one basket has been made."

Terese apologized. "I'm sorry." She plopped down in the chair at the table where Megan worked. Sun filtered through the open door and the wooden shutters had been thrown open to allow for even more light. The small cottage was used mostly by Megan who cherished her solitude more than the others. She made baskets, wreaths, worked on the loom, and spun fine wool for their clothing.

A spring breeze drifted in and around them as Megan continued to work and Terese sat and watched.

"You seem dazed, not yourself," Megan said, her fingers bending and rounding the branch to skillfully form a large basket.

"It's Lachlan," Terese said honestly.

Megan shook her head. "No good can come of that."

"He is not like other men."

"I thought that once." Megan again shook her head. "It wasn't so."

"I'm attracted to him."

"He will hurt you; all men do," Megan said coldly.

"I'd like to believe differently."

"Wouldn't we all?"

"He will leave and it will be done," Terese said as if it didn't matter, though her heart gave a little tug.

"What if you fall in love with him?"

"There is no time for that," Terese assured her.

"Love doesn't need time; it needs only two senseless souls."

"Andrew looks like a senseless soul when he's around you," Terese teased.

"I loved once and I'll never make that mistake again," Megan snapped.

Terese knew better than to question Megan about her past. No one did, but she had hoped that perhaps Andrew's interest in Megan might help heal whatever wounds she had suffered and give her another chance at love.

"Andrew is tenacious and considerate of you," Terese said.

"He is too tall!" Megan blurted.

Terese saw fear in Megan's eyes, but she shuddered and it quickly faded away. However, Terese felt she had another piece to the puzzle that was Megan. It wasn't Andrew she avoided; it was his size.

"Andrew seems gentle enough," Terese said, hoping to help Megan see the man differently. "And he's lean."

"With muscles," Megan emphasized. "Have you seen the size logs he's lifted? Why, I bet he can squeeze the life from a man with one hand." She shuddered again. "I want nothing to do with him."

"As you wish," Terese said.

"And you would be wise to be careful yourself," Megan warned, raising her voice. "Men are not truthful creatures."

At that moment Andrew popped his head in the open door. "I am," he said proudly. "I would never lie to you."

"So say you now," Megan challenged.

Andrew hesitantly peered inside the cottage as if waiting to see if Megan would order him out but when she didn't, to Terese's surprise, Andrew ducked his head to fit through the open door and entered.

"I would always be truthful with you," Andrew assured Megan.

"Then start now," Megan said, continuing her challenge. "Why do you follow me around?"

Andrew's cheeks blushed. "I like you."

"Why?" Megan demanded and snapped the branch in her hand.

Andrew grinned. "You're a tenacious little one and fearless. I admire you for that." Andrew's grin faded. "If there's something you don't like about me maybe I can change it."

Megan stared at him for a moment then said softly, "You're too tall."

"Oh," Andrew said, looking deflated then suddenly

brightened. "I could hunch down when I'm beside you."

And he demonstrated, looking positively ridiculous, though he had Megan laughing.

Terese quietly slipped out of the cottage, the pair not noticing her departure and that she had to contain her laughter at the sight of Andrew making a fool out of himself to win Megan's chilled heart. A heart that Terese believed Andrew had been defrosting all along.

She strolled the convent grounds, stopping to speak to different people along the way. While Lachlan had been generous in offering everyone a home with the clan Sinclare, Frances and Henry expressed interest in possibly making a home here with the women, both having spent their lives in the area and not wanting to leave it.

Gelda expressed the same to Terese when she had stopped to admire her freshly sowed garden. Gelda and her family much preferred to make Everagis their home if that was possible.

Terese wished the same for herself, that Everagis could remain her home, but where it was a certain possibility for the others . . . it wasn't likely to be for her.

Her passionate mood quickly dwindled to one of concern not only for herself, but for the other women. She had to keep her feelings for Lachlan in perspective. She would enjoy him here and now, know intimacy for the first time with him, but never forget that there was no future beyond that.

Rowena caught up with her as Terese approached the common house.

"You look concerned," Rowena asked while keeping her smile bright. "Do you feel all right?"

"Better but weary."

"From your wound or your thoughts?"

"A bit of both, I think," Terese said and wasn't too successful in forcing a smile.

"You should rest your wound and your thoughts," Rowena suggested. "I could make you a brew if you'd like."

"I would like that," Terese said and was grateful she had such good friends and would always have them. They would be there for her long after Lachlan was gone and that she must also remember.

Terese cupped the mug in her hands as she walked down the narrow hall to her room. She had instructed Rowena that if she didn't wake for supper not to disturb her. She closed the door to her small quarters where a narrow bed and chest vied for room and sat on the bed.

She almost changed her mind. Her body, and damned if her heart hadn't joined in, wanted to see Lachlan. But she had to stay in control. She couldn't surrender completely to him. If she did, in the end she would be hurt.

Once she finished the brew, she laid on the bed to rest, but when she closed her eyes all that she saw was Lachlan, all that she felt was Lachlan's touch, all that she breathed was the earthy scent of him and all she wanted was . . .

"*Lachlan*," she whispered as she drifted to sleep.

* * *

Terese woke with a start from a dream well before sunrise. She threw off the wool blanket and swung her legs off the bed, shaking her head at the dream or to rid herself of it, which she wasn't certain.

Her father's hardy laugh continued to echo in her mind, so pleased was he that he had gotten his way. He had married her to a man of his choice and there she had stood in chains.

Terese shivered and hurried into her green wool skirt and yellow blouse, she tied her shawl around her waist wanting it on hand when she walked to the hill to watch the sunrise. She slipped sandals on, combed her hair, and just as she began to braid it she stopped and stared at her wrists. The idea of being chained to a stranger for the remainder of her life suddenly made her all the more determined to remain free of her family.

Alyce was dead and she would stay dead. She would get involved with no man, but she would enjoy Lachlan while he was here, then send him on his way and worry over it no more.

Her door creaked opened and Piper peeked her head in. "Good, I was afraid I'd have to wake you."

"A problem?"

"Someone wants to see you," Piper said. "*Now.*"

"Septimus?"

"How did you know?" Piper asked.

"Something he said to me when he and his men came to our assistance."

"I'll go change into my nun robes."

Terese stood. "That won't be necessary."

"Why?"

"Septimus knows we are not nuns."

Piper was full of questions, but Terese was eager to have done with this meeting and promised later she would tell all. They left without waking anyone and traveled a shorter distance into the woods than Terese had expected.

Septimus stepped out of the dark, the full moon spotlighting him. "You've had time to heal. Now I want answers."

Terese nodded to Piper and she moved away, swallowed by the dark shadows to wait nearby.

"First I have something to say," Terese said sharply and didn't give him a chance to argue. "Your leader knew from the time I entered your camp that I was no nun. He knew Everagis was no true convent. He was also aware that the clans had sent scouts. What is going on?"

Septimus smiled. "And what makes you think this?"

"You said it yourself when you mentioned the game I played. Your leader has known all along. How long has he kept a watchful eye on Everagis?" She held her hand up when she saw that he was about to argue. "Don't waste my time denying it, or I will take my leave and you will be left to explain to your leader why you returned with no answers."

"He was right," Septimus grinned. "He said you'd be either a formidable adversary or worthy friend."

Terese nodded. "So, your leader wisely decided I would make a better friend."

"He felt you would *serve* him better that way."

Terese stepped forward and with nostrils flaring and her tone sharp as a sword she said, "I serve no one. You tell your leader that it will be a *partnership* we share or *nothing*."

Septimus chortled. "I don't think you're in the position to bargain."

"Oh, but I am," Terese assured him with a chilling grin.

"And why is that?" he asked still amused.

Terese stepped closer, her whisper harsh. "I know your leader's secret."

Septimus startled, though quickly recovered. "That might prove a problem."

"Not so," she disagreed. "We both have much to gain by our silence."

"That is true."

Terese turned around slowly in a circle as she spoke. "I know you are there. I know you can hear me. We share a camaraderie few understand. Let our original agreement stand and our secrets will forever remain buried."

"So be it," said a deep voice from the darkness.

"When do the warriors leave?" Septimus asked.

"When the messenger who was sent returns."

He nodded. "We will keep a watch over Everagis and if you are in need—"

"I will reach out to you," Terese said with a promising nod. "One more thing."

Septimus waited.

"What of the warring clans?"

Septimus grinned. "That will be settled in the next few days and will be a problem no more."

Terese understood. "If your men should need care—"

"I know where to bring them," Septimus concluded and after a slight bow disappeared into the dark.

Piper was at her side before she summoned her and wisely she remained quiet until they were a distance away.

"I don't understand," Piper finally said, slowing the pace.

"You don't need to," Terese assured her.

"You spoke of a secret."

"It is between the leader and me."

"Does it place you in more danger?" Piper asked anxiously.

"Any secret has its danger."

"You do not intend to share, do you?" Piper asked.

"I cannot, for I gave my word, as you all did to me," Terese reminded.

"I understand," Piper said. "But I fear the danger this will place you in while trying to protect us."

"It is necessary."

Piper merely nodded. "We better hurry. The sun will rise soon and Lachlan will expect to join you on the hill."

No more words were necessary between them. Terese knew that Piper would say nothing of this meeting. It would be Terese's decision when and what she shared with the other women.

It wasn't the women Terese was concerned with;

it was the secrets that she continued to accumulate. Sooner or later, secrets had a way of being discovered.

As much as she didn't wish to see Lachlan leave Everagis, she knew it would be safer for all when he did. The thought had her hurrying her pace even more and when she and Piper approached the edge of the woods, the sun was just about to break on the horizon.

Terese left Piper and sprinted across the field and up the hill where Lachlan was waiting. He turned and smiled.

And she ran into his arms.

Chapter 13

Lachlan hugged her waist and felt his heart swell with the kisses she lavished over his face. But it was a twist to his gut that he got when he saw the look of sorrow in her blue eyes, and he felt a sudden sadness as if she were saying good-bye to him.

The thought tore at him, the pain unbearable and he yanked her against him. With a fiery glare that was meant to mark her, he claimed not only her lips, but her as well.

Her surrender sealed the exchange for him. She submitted to him willingly, eagerly, and that told him that she wanted to be part of him as much as he wanted to be part of her.

Their kiss trailed off to smaller kisses until their lips simply brushed and they rested foreheads to each other.

"I thought you might not show up this morning," Lachlan said.

Terese rested her head to his shoulder and her hand to his chest. "Why?"

"I was told last night that you took to bed early and

were not to be disturbed. I thought perhaps that you changed your mind about *us*."

"I needed to think," she said, taking his hand and leading him to their favorite spot where with an arm around her waist he lowered her and himself to the ground.

He ran the back of his hand down her cheek and lightly across her lips, and she turned her face into his touch.

"You have a gentle and patient way about you."

"Not all that patient," he said with a glint of a grin. "But tell me what troubles you."

He saw that she hesitated and it disturbed him. He took her hand. "We are friends, Terese, and always will be. I trust you and wish for you to trust me." He felt her ease slightly away from him, not far, barely a fraction, but it was a distance nonetheless. He would have none of it and tucked her closer against his side. "Don't," he warned softly. "Stay beside me. You belong there."

Her smile though sweet, was sad. "I'm not sure where I belong."

"I can only imagine. Being sent away by someone you thought loved you, having to assume a different identity to remain safe, and learning to be a warrior to protect yourself and others. It cannot have been easy. But trust me when I say I will not hurt you. I would *never* send you away and I *will* always protect you."

"Why? We are but friends who will pass in the night and then be no more."

This time the pain struck his heart and gave him worry, for she spoke the truth and yet, he didn't like the sound of it. It took a moment for him to respond and even then he wasn't sure of his words.

"Think of no time beyond this time. Nothing else matters, nothing else exists, except you and I, and here and now."

She smiled slowly, though he saw that sadness still tinged her blue eyes.

"No time beyond this time," she repeated softly.

Again a pain struck his heart and he worried, for what if it was the old god's love arrow piercing his heart? What if he was falling in love? What if Terese was the woman meant for him? He had no idea what he would do.

They talked as they did each morning, debating opinions, laughing and kissing and deciding that they would share a private noonday meal and later, much later they would share much more.

With promises and plans made, they parted to see to their responsibilities. But noon brought a far different plan then either of them had expected.

Terese was ready and waiting for Lachlan well before the assigned time. Rowena had packed a generous food basket and Terese knew the perfect spot to take him. It was near the stream but secluded. The sun had remained bright in the sky and her cheeks flushed pink with the thought of spending time alone with him.

No time beyond this time.

Terese intended to remind herself often of those words, to simply enjoy the here and now and not worry beyond the moment. She deserved this time, this pleasure and she would have it without regret, though guilt was another matter.

They were friends who could trust as he had reminded her again and again. But she wasn't being completely honest with him and that bothered her. She had rationalized the situation over and over, and concluded the same each time. There was no way she could confide the truth to him. She would lose her freedom and that she refused to do.

No time beyond this time.

Those words would be her saving grace, and she would think on them often and long after he had gone.

Shouts and cries startled Terese out of her musing and she rushed out the door of the common house to see everyone running to a group of people entering Everagis. Terese quickly joined them.

"These people are fleeing the battle between the clans and the mercenaries," Megan explained quickly when Terese caught up with her as Megan helped a partially crippled old man to the common house.

Andrew appeared and took charge of the old man. "Where do you want him?"

Megan pointed to the large tree near the common house and then turned to Terese. "There are about five who have injuries. The others are exhausted and hungry."

"Then let's take care of them," Terese said, but before she reached anyone Piper popped up in front of her looking fretful.

"One of the mercenaries has been injured," Piper whispered. "Septimus and a few of his men wait in the woods for us to tend him."

"Wait for me in the usual spot while I gather what we need," Terese instructed and looked around for Rowena. She would need one of Rowena's healing baskets to take with her and while all looked to be in use, one would need to be spared.

Lachlan's unexpected approach and battle-ready expression stopped her in her tracks.

"I leave Andrew and most of the other warriors here to protect everyone. Boyd and Evan go with me," Lachlan said.

"Why?" Terese asked. "The battle doesn't concern you, and what can three men do against so many?"

Lachlan ginned. "Such confidence you have in me."

She bristled, knowing full well the sizeable force of the mercenaries. "It is *concern* I have for you."

He took her hand. "I am not foolish. I wish to track the mercenaries and see if I can find their camp and hopefully spy upon it."

"This is about your brother Ronan, isn't it?" she asked.

"I need to know if he is among them and needs freeing."

"If he is?" she asked, shaking her head. "You have so few men to be able to help him."

"Again, I am not a foolish warrior," Lachlan reminded. "I have coins to offer for his release and if not . . ." He shrugged. "I send word to my brother Cavan and he will lead a force of men here to free our brother. I wouldn't be surprised if some of Angus Bunnock's men joined him. It would be his way of showing gratitude to our clan for helping him and having his own men ascertain that his daughter was dead and buried on hallowed ground."

Terese blanched and her legs grew weak. That couldn't happen; her father's men would recognize her and forcibly return her home.

Lachlan slipped his arms around her. "You pale and shiver. What—"

She hugged him tight. "I don't want anything to happen to you . . . *to us*."

He kissed her gently. "Nothing can ever happen to *us*. I promise you that."

She watched him disappear among the mayhem and knew he had given her a promise that he didn't know he would not be able to keep. If he ever discovered the truth, they would no longer be friends.

Terese pushed the worrisome thought from her head and found Rowena, secured a healing basket, and joined Piper with less worry of discovery since Lachlan had already taken his leave. His men paid her movements no heed, too busy scouting the perimeter of the convent.

It didn't take long for Piper and her to reach the injured man and at first glance both of them knew that he would need more care than either Terese or Piper could give. And his formidable size would be a problem. Piper could stand behind him and not be seen.

Terese looked at Septimus. "We need to get him to Rowena. She is the only one skilled enough to stitch such a severe wound and tend him if he is to have any chance of surviving."

Septimus didn't argue. "Two of my men will get him there for you."

Terese nodded and then did something she didn't want to do but knew she had no choice. "Tell your leader that Lachlan of the clan Sinclare and two of his men are tracking your group. He intends to spy on you."

Septimus nodded. "He was right. You are good to have as a friend rather than a foe."

Terese felt like no friend betraying Lachlan, but her survival depended on it. And she didn't fear for Lachlan's safety, for she knew the leader would never hurt him or his men.

"Piper will keep you informed of your man's condition," Terese said.

"Your help is greatly appreciated," Septimus acknowledged with a bow of his head.

"You don't seem the kind to be a mercenary," Terese couldn't help but say.

"There was a time none of us were," he said and with another bow of his head, turned and left.

It was late evening when quiet returned to Everagis. Everyone was settled and fed and the injured had been cared for and were resting comfortably. Rowena continued to tend Talon, the wounded mercenary. His leg injury had required thirty stitches and she now sat with him, worried that he would develop a fever. Though his size and rough features would have most fearing him, he was grateful and polite to Rowena. Once again Terese wondered over the origin of the mercenaries.

Terese lingered around the grounds later that evening in hope of Lachlan returning. When it grew late and exhaustion finally took hold, she gave up and, disappointed, went to bed. She woke with a start when it was still dark and anxiously threw on her skirt and blouse. With hurried though quiet steps she made her way up the narrow hall into the large room of the common house and rushed to the door. She halted, her hand on the metal latch, and took a deep breath.

She knew Lachlan had returned and waited. She sensed his presence. How? She could find no sensible answer. She only knew that he eagerly waited for her as eagerly as she wanted to go to him.

She opened the door slowly, for a moment thinking perhaps this was all a dream and then she saw him.

He stood with his arms folded across his chest, a slight pitch to his stance, and the half-moon spotlighted a charming smile on his handsome face.

She felt her breath catch, her heart flutter, and her flesh tingle. She wanted this man, needed him and so without further thought, guilt, or regret she ran to him.

His arms spread wide and she ran into them. They wrapped lovingly, protectively and strongly around her and for a sheer moment she felt as if she had arrived home. The thought near buckled her legs.

"I knew if I stood here long enough that my mere presence would wake you."

She kept the tremble from her laughter, though it was no easy task, for it rippled through her entire body. "You did wake me." She hesitated almost afraid to give voice to the truth. "I could feel you."

"My magic worked," he whispered. "For while I stood here, I envisioned touching you."

"Where?" she dared ask.

His hand slipped slowly beneath her blouse and she knew he waited to see if she would stop him.

When she didn't, he whispered, "Here."

She startled when he gently scooped up her full breast in his cool hand and ran his thumb across her nipple until it hardened at his will. Her already weak knees almost gave way, especially when his lips and teeth began to nibble along her neck and up along her ear, sending a myriad of tingling sensations rushing over her flesh.

"That's just the start of where I plan to touch you," he murmured and continued nibbling.

This time her knees did waver, but his arm caught her firm around the waist.

"You'll sleep with me tonight," he said softly.

It wasn't a question or a command. It was simply what they both wanted, and he knew it just as she did.

"I will be yours tonight," she said willingly.

"And every night, and day and morning and afternoon and—"

She giggled for he punctuated each reference with a

nibble and a kiss. "Have you the stamina?" she teased, feeling as insatiable as he.

He released her and staggered backward with a hand to his heart. "You wound me, woman."

She laughed and sauntered over to him. "I heal all wounds with a kiss."

He grinned. "I have a lot of wounds."

Her voice was low and whispery. "Show me."

He tapped where his hand rested at his heart. "Here."

Her hand reached in his shirt and slowly spread it open. Then she splayed her hand on his chest, her body further titillated by the warmth of his flesh and his hard muscles. She had no experience with intimacy, though she wasn't ignorant of it, she and the other women talked about men and sex. The women who were familiar with it advised those that weren't that it came more naturally than one would expect and to trust your instincts when the time came.

She found that her instincts were much more aware than she was and so she freed them and followed their lead, which was why she did not pause when she felt the urge to kiss his wounds and make them all better, so very much better.

Warm and delicious, that was how he tasted and the need to nibble at his flesh and sample his nipple with a light flick of her tongue caused a jolt to them both.

Lachlan grabbed hold of her arms and forced her an arm's-length away. "We need to go to my cottage now."

She nibbled at her bottom lip missing the taste of him.

"Stop that," he ordered with a gruff groan.

"I like the flavor of you," she whispered. "I'd like to taste more."

Lachlan's groan turned deep and urgent, and he grabbed her hand and pulled her along behind him as he marched off.

Unfortunately, they didn't get far.

"Terese!"

She knew from the frantic call there was a problem and being it was Rowena, it could mean only one thing. There was a problem with the mercenary. She stopped, forcing Lachlan to halt, though he did so with an annoyed grunt.

"I need your help," Rowena said.

"Can't someone else help?" Lachlan asked a bit sharply.

"I'm sorry," Rowena said with sincere regret. "I need Terese's help."

"Whatever for?" Lachlan demanded.

"That doesn't concern you," Terese snapped. "If one of the women needs another we do not bother to ask why. We are there."

"Let someone else be there," Lachlan argued.

Terese yanked her hand out of his. "No. When I am needed I go without question."

Lachlan grabbed hold of her arm and pressed his cheek to hers to whisper harshly, "I need you."

"And I you," she assured him, "but first I must see to this."

"You make me wait?" he challenged.

"I am worth the wait," she murmured in his ear and felt him shiver.

"Then I will wait no matter how long it takes," he assured her, his tone more tempered.

She kissed his cheek. "I will do my best to make it quick."

He grinned. "I on the other hand will not be quick."

Terese laughed as he reluctantly released her and she hurried to Rowena

He called out, "I'll wait at the cottage."

She acknowledged him with a wave and followed Rowena into the house, asking quickly, "What's wrong?"

"Megan suffered a wound early yesterday and foolishly ignored it, too busy tending others."

"Is it bad?"

"It wouldn't have been if she let me see to it right away. It already shows signs of poisoning."

"We can't let that happen," Terese said and the two women immediately went to work on Megan. It took longer then either woman expected, Terese busy bathing the wound with a special brew that would hopefully flush away any poisons, while Rowena mixed a paste to be applied. Another brew was prepared to help Megan rest. Just when they thought all was done, Talon roused with a slight fever and the two women went to work on him.

It was near dawn by the time Terese was free to

take her leave and at first she thought it was too late, Lachlan would have never waited for her. Tired as she was, she was more curious so she crept silently through the convent grounds and just as quietly eased open Lachlan's cottage door.

The only sound in the one room was the crackle and snap of the fire in the hearth. As she approached Lachlan where he lay on his side in bed, she saw that he was asleep. His chest was bare and she admired his sleek muscled lines and grew curious when she noticed how the blanket rested low on his hip, meaning he was completely naked beneath.

Instead of passion striking her, a yawn did and she knew she was too tired to do anything but sleep.

"Damn," she whispered, annoyed yet again that they had lost the chance to be together. She was about to turn and leave when she heard.

"My sentiments exactly."

She looked and saw his eyes open and her heart gave a quick catch. "You waited."

"I've slept on and off, each time hoping when I opened my eyes you'd be there."

"And now I am here . . . but—" Another yawn demonstrated what she was about to reluctantly tell him. She was tired.

"I am as tired as you," he said," though I'd love you to sleep beside me."

He eased the blanket back just enough to invite and not tease.

She smiled at his thoughtfulness and his invitation

and without hesitation she joined him, though she kept her clothes on. She rested her back to him and he in turn wrapped her solidly in his arms.

"I'm glad you came even though you were tired," he whispered and kissed her cheek.

"And I'm glad you waited," she murmured as they both drifted off to sleep together.

Chapter 14

L achlan watched Terese sleep. She purred like a contented kitten and he smiled. She felt good in his arms, so good that he wanted to keep her there, not let her go. Not now, not ever.

He rested his head back on the pillow and drank in the scent of her hair that simply intoxicated him, but then everything about her made him drunk with joy. These feelings were strange to him; while he enjoyed many women none had the affect on him that Terese did, and right from the start.

Lord, but he thought he would suffer for his unholy thoughts about a nun and how relieved he was and pleased, ever so pleased, to discover that she was simply a woman, though *simply* did not describe Terese.

No, she was complex, courageous, thoughtful, beautiful, and . . . *his*.

He shook his head. He had always reserved his opinion on women after he bedded them, not so with Terese. He cared for her more than he wanted to admit. He truly enjoyed time spent with her and it mattered not what they did. They could sit in silence and watch the sun rise or set, it didn't matter; it was being with her that made the difference.

He had found himself looking forward to each and every day because he would see her, talk with her, laugh with her, tease her, and kiss her. He loved kissing her. She tasted so sweet, and she was as hungry for him as he was for her.

Damn, could he be falling in love?

He had no plans to fall in love, but then Cavan's wife Honora had warned him often enough that love arrived in its own time. He, however, had objected, insisting he would be spared love's burden. Had he tempted fate?

He buried his face in her wheat-colored hair and blessed fate, for the heavens had been generous to him. He grinned, thinking he sounded like his love-besotted brothers, and he almost laughed aloud envisioning their responses to his predicament.

She stirred in his arms and began to stretch her limbs, moaning as she surfaced from sleep. He gave her room and enjoyed the view, watching her arch her back, her round breasts almost greeting his face. She raised her legs in a lazy stretch and rounded her ankles, hearing a crack or two. A huge yawn preceded her eyes fluttering open and once she caught sight of him peering down at her, she startled and crumpled into herself as if trying to hide.

"Forgot where you were?"

She nodded, her eyes wide.

He smiled. "You are beauty and grace when you wake in the morning."

"Truly?" she asked astonished.

"My word on it," he whispered and was about to kiss her when his door crashed open.

Andrew rushed in. "Megan is—"

He blanched. "Sorry I interrupted, but . . ." He looked to Terese and she bounced out of bed.

"Has Megan grown worse?"

"She has a fever. She's burning up," Andrew ranted.

Terese fled the cottage without a backward glance.

Lachlan shook his head and glared at Andrew. "How bad *truly* is it?"

"Rowena told me Megan had a fever."

"And that she was burning up?"

"Fevers do that," Andrew said in his defense.

"So you assumed Megan was burning up," Lachlan said and got out of bed to dress quickly.

"What difference does it make, Megan is ill."

Lachlan placed a hand on Andrew's shoulder. "I know you're beside yourself with worry, but you stole Terese from me."

"Would you not have done the same if it were Terese ill with fever?"

Lachlan nodded slowly and led Andrew out of the cottage. "Let's go see how Megan is, though I must ask. What would you have done to me if it was you in bed with Megan?"

Terese was panting and had a stitch in her side by the time she reached the common house. She entered to an empty room and immediately grew concerned.

This was the time the women would be gathered for the morning meal with more than one busy preparing the food.

She made her way down the hall fearful of what she would find, and when she heard a shrill cry from Megan's room she ran the last few feet.

Terese entered to find Rowena, Hester, and Piper crowded in the small room all laughing and sharing the morning meal with Megan, who was sitting up in bed and looking her usual rosy self.

Piper bounced to her feet, holding her bowl of porridge tight. "What's wrong?"

Terese sighed. "Nothing, though Andrew—"

"That big idiot arrived here looking for Megan," Rowena said. "And as soon as I mentioned fever, he turned deathly pale and took off running."

Terese smiled. "He's worried senseless. He believes Megan is about to meet her demise and had me believing it as well. *Burning* with fever, he told me."

"He truly is worried about me?" Megan asked.

"Like a fool in love," Rowena said.

"I agree," Hester piped in. "The man is besotted."

Piper added her agreement. "He follows you around like a love-sick pup."

"I haven't noticed it," Megan said, though a hint of a smile told otherwise.

"Then you're either blind or a fool," Hester said.

Megan's expression turned hard. "I was a fool once; I will be one no more."

The women turned quiet and then Hester spoke.

"Perhaps it's a man's turn to be foolish in love with you."

Hope sprang in Megan's face though only briefly. It vanished as fast as it had appeared. "I will not be hurt again. The last one almost killed me."

The women remained quiet, not knowing Megan's past but knowing, from the way she had been badly beaten when they found her, she had suffered greatly at the hands of a man. A man who had claimed to love her.

It was Piper who suggested, "Why not give Andrew a chance?"

Hester added her opinion. "He seems like a good man."

Before Rowena or Terese could offer their own thoughts, a rapid pounding sounded at the door, followed by two more bursts until it suddenly stopped.

Terese laughed. "I bet Lachlan grabbed Andrew's hand before he could pound again."

The women all grinned and suddenly made excuses to take their leave.

"What are you doing?" Megan demanded with a note of panic.

"Giving you time to get to know Andrew," Hester said and scooted out the door, followed by Piper. Terese was about to take her leave, Rowena having already gone to answer the door, when Megan grabbed her hand.

"I'm afraid," she said.

Terese sat on the bed beside her. "What have you

got to lose by getting to know him? You are safe here. No one will let any harm come to you." She smiled. "Andrew cares for you and would kill anyone who dares to hurt you."

Megan pulled Terese closer to her and whispered, her voice breaking with fear, "A man told me that once and I believed him. I trusted him. I loved him." Tears filled her green eyes. "He kept me isolated, beat me senseless, and nearly killed me."

Terese took firm hold of her hand and listened.

Megan choked on her tears as she said, "I had no choice. I had to do it. I had to kill him."

Megan burst into tears and Terese wrapped the sobbing woman in her arms, her own eyes filling with tears for the horror Megan must have suffered.

"You did what you had to do to survive," Terese assured her. "It is over now and done, has been for years. He can hurt you no more. Unless . . ."

Megan turned wide, frightened eyes on her.

Terese pushed the dark curls off Megan's forehead. "Unless you allow the fear he instilled in you to stop you from finding and loving a truly good man."

"I don't know if—"

"Give Andrew a chance," Terese encouraged and laughed. "Good lord, the man offered to shrink himself down when you said he was too tall, and he's forever there to help you and not once has he raised his voice or spoken badly to you."

"I am safe here," Megan said wiping away the last of her tears.

"You know not a one of us would let any harm befall you. You may still have trouble accepting it, but you are safe here and will remain so."

Hester peeked her head in. "Andrew would like to see you to ascertain for himself that you are well and not burning up with fever." She giggled. "He's beside himself with worry, Megan. You have to put him out of his misery."

Terese looked to Hester. "What of Talon? He is only two doors down."

"Rowena went to sit with him, since he seems to fancy her company," Hester said. "I told her I'd let her know when Andrew was gone."

"I could go outside and visit with him," Megan suggested.

"No," both women said.

"Rowena said at least two, maybe three days, off that foot," Terese said.

Megan threw the blanket off her. "Then just get me to a chair near the hearth in the common room. It's not wise for us to take a chance of Talon being discovered."

"She's right," Hester said and Terese agreed.

The two women supported Megan with their shoulders under her arms, lifting her off the ground, their heights a good four to five inches over her petite one.

As soon as Andrew saw her he went to her aid, scooped her up, and plopped down in the chair near the hearth with her in his lap. He swiped the blanket out of Hester's hand before she could cover Megan's legs and he tucked it in securely around her. Then with his arms around her he insisted she tell him what happened, he wanted to hear it all.

Hester grinned at Terese and disappeared behind the curtain to the women's living quarters where Terese was sure she would wait to give the all-clear signal to Rowena. While Terese took hold of Lachlan's hand and walked out of the cottage, the pair in the chair never noticed anyone's departure.

"Tell me that I am right about Andrew, that he is a kind, good man," Terese said as they walked over the convent grounds.

"That would depend," Lachlan said.

"On what?" she asked anxiously.

"If I must include this morning's incident when he intruded upon us at the most inopportune time," he said with a grin.

She laughed. "Under the circumstances I think you should forgive him."

"I will only forgive his foolish actions because he is a man in love."

Terese stopped. "You truly believe that Andrew loves Megan?"

"I know he does," Lachlan confirmed. "I have never seen him make a fool of himself for any woman, therefore, he must be in love."

Boyd shouted for Lachlan and gave an impatient wave.

"Something must be amiss," Lachlan said and gave her cheek a peck. "I will return as soon as I can."

"It seems we both promise that."

Lachlan cupped her chin. "A promise, that I assure you, will be kept."

"Go, I will see you later," she said, though her heart ached when he took off. Time was growing short for them and while there was no talk of love between them and certainly no necessity for it since it could never be, she couldn't help but wonder how it would feel to truly be loved.

Don't think about it. The warning pierced her thoughts, shattering the notion.

Terese shook her head and hurried off to see to the daily chores and the visitors that were becoming more and more permanent residents of Everagis.

Night brought with it a steady, gentle rain. It was good for the crops and though a few shelters were a tight squeeze for some, at least all were in out of the rain. The day had kept Terese and Lachlan busy with little time to spare for each other.

Meals were prepared and shared, those healing tended, the night chores finished and everyone tired for bed, though not Terese. She paced the floor of the common room feeling as if her flesh was on fire. The last hour she could think of nothing but Lachlan, the feel of his mouth hot against hers, his hand cupping her breast, his mouth nibbling her tender flesh. She shuddered with the memories.

She wanted him, good lord, how she wanted him.

All she had to do was go to him as she had this morning before dawn. So why did she hesitate?

Thunder struck and she jumped then wrapped her arms around herself. She knew why she hesitated. She knew that this was it. Once she went to him she would seal her fate. They would couple and she knew without a doubt it would be wonderful, and she would not want it to end. She would not want him to leave. She would want more and that was not possible. She had repeatedly warned herself against such senseless thoughts, but they would creep in and she couldn't help but think what if . . . *what if?*

"Go to him and accept what is or keep your distance," she whispered to herself. "Those are your only choices."

She had thought she had settled this battle that brewed within her, but she hadn't. Would she ever?

You cannot have more and you know it. She silently chided.

Take what you can. Take it now and don't look back. No regrets. Only memories to enjoy when he is gone. Go now to him. Go now and lose yourself in him. Forget who you are and love him.

Terese refused to argue any longer with herself. She ran to the door opened it and saw that the rain had turned heavy. She didn't care. She had to do this. She had to do this now or she never would.

She shut the door behind her and ran, and began to cry. Her tears joined the rain that rolled down her face. Why she cried she wasn't sure. Perhaps it was for the young woman who had thought her father would let her choose a man to love, or for the young girl who had dreamt of finding love, or simply because life was nothing as she thought it would be.

But here at this moment life was hers for the choosing and she chose to love Lachlan if only for a brief time.

Through the rain and her tears she saw a figure approach. The dark shadow startled her and she slowed her pace, wiping at her eyes to see more clearly. It apparently did the same, holding back until the other could be identified.

One cautious step, two, and then she recognized at the same moment Lachlan did and they ran eagerly to each other, wrapping themselves in a tight embrace while their kiss served not to appease their hungry passion but rather to enflame it beyond reason.

Lachlan grabbed hold of her face. "Nothing. Nothing stops us, do you hear me?" he said, like a madman bent on finding sanity.

"Nothing!" she repeated with the same intensity.

He gripped her hand and hurried her along, the rain pelting them. When they reached the cottage door, he began to strip her bare.

"I want our clothes left here so that all know tonight I made you mine and we are not—*not* to be disturbed."

Terese agreed, beginning to strip him bare and when they stood naked before each other, Lachlan scooped her up and whispered, "Tonight, I make love to you."

Chapter 15

Terese shivered when she heard the click of the door even though she was wrapped snugly in Lachlan's arms.

"You're chilled," he said with concern.

"No," she was quick to say. "I'm warm and comfortable in your arms."

"That's because you belong there." He kept her cradled in his embrace as he walked her over to the fireplace. "The heat will dry us some."

The heat of the flames toasted their bodies while Lachlan continued to rain kisses along her face, neck, shoulders, and finally her breast; her nipples budding to life as he teased them with his tongue.

He lifted her and carried her to the bed and her hands went in search of him as his did to her. They were soft touches, exploring touches and touches that tantalized. His touch was often followed with lingering kisses and her passion soared as his lips continued down her body.

"Your taste intoxicates," he whispered and then tasted some more.

She welcomed not only his kisses but his nibbles and nips that fired her body with a heated passion that had her moaning and writhing with pure pleasure.

"Your tongue is talented," she said giddily when his lips reached for hers once again.

"Ah, but there's more, so much more.

His suggestive remark sent a frenzy of desire shooting through her and she said, "Show me."

Lachlan grinned. "With pleasure."

He started at her neck and worked his way down, slowly tasting her as if she was an exquisite wine that needed to be savored to fully enjoy. He drank deeply of every inch of her and when he spread her legs apart to delve into her sweetness she startled and he chortled and . . .

Terese was screaming out with pure pleasure and as he moved over her, he whispered, "That's just to start, as I promised you there's *much, much* more."

And she wanted more, she wanted everything he could give her and then some. She welcomed him, her arms going around him, her body rising up to greet him.

"I want you," she said softly.

He brushed her lips with a kiss. "And you shall have me forever and always."

For now, she reminded herself. *For now*. And tears formed in her eyes.

"No, love, no tears." He soothed and kissed at the corner of her eyes. "This is good. This is right and I will *never, ever* hurt you. You have my word on that. Trust me, always trust me. I will *never* fail you."

She wanted to believe. She wanted to hope, but then hope had died a long time ago for her. But she had this moment, this time with him and she would enjoy it.

"I have never known such pleasure, such utter joy as I do here with you."

He grinned, that charming grin of his and it made her smile.

"I will make sure that you always know pleasure and joy with me, and in a moment I'm going to make you mine forever and always."

"I'd like that," she whispered, for she truly would like to be his forever and always, though again, it could never be.

He kissed her then and touched her, here, there, and everywhere setting her flesh on fire, her skin tingling with a heat that ached for relief. He slipped full over her and captured her hands, she gladly locking hers with his and then he slipped gently into her.

He took his time, though she rather he didn't. The deeper he got the deeper she wanted him until she rose up to meet him forcing the final thrust that had her moaning with the sheer joy of it.

He set the rhythm and she joined in. It was so very natural, so very good, so very right, and she lingered in the budding sensation that grew and grew until she was digging her fingers into his back and begging for . . . something.

It came like a flood that engulfed her, swallowed her and left her barely able to breath. She gasped and clung to him as ripple after ripple vibrated through her body and she felt when his body did the same, and he held on to her as she did to him.

He kept her at his side when he slipped off her and she was glad of it for she didn't want to separate from him just yet. Though their bodies were damp, this time with perspiration, she wanted to feel every inch of his flesh beside hers.

He was a magnificent creature, not lean or large, which made him perfect in shape and form, muscled but naturally so, though he was endowed with a sizeable manly organ and that gave her a chuckle.

"I amused you?" Lachlan asked with a laugh.

Terese was blunt and gently cupped him in her hand though he was more than a handful. "My thought was of your size."

"And you find that amusing?" he asked with a teasing poke to her arm.

She giggled and jiggled him in her hand. "I find you endowed beyond expectations."

"Be careful, he'll respond to your charm," he warned playfully.

She returned his playfulness. "I haven't worn him out?"

"You have a long way to go for that."

"Promise?"

"I'll do better then that, I'll show you all night long," he said.

"Promise," she repeated with a soft franticness. "Promise me you'll show me all night and all the days we have left together."

He looked at her strangely then took hold of her

face. "*All* the days we have left together I will make love to you."

He kissed her and she felt tears well in her eyes. She didn't want him to see and so when their kiss ended she rested her head on his shoulder and forced not one tear to spill. She wouldn't let him see her cry, wouldn't let him know her pain. She would love him while she could and then they would be no more.

Lachlan kept his promise; they made love throughout the night, the thunder punctuating a climax or two and the steady rain falling outside a soothing melody. Sleep was stolen between bouts of lovemaking and then there was the talk, she encouraging Lachlan to share his family memories and she envious of his close family ties.

It was a night she would never forget, and she had no doubt she would recall many times long after he left. And she looked forward to every memory they would make before his departure. She wanted a storage house of memories to keep and enjoy.

Sunrise wasn't far off when Terese woke and smiled when she saw how content Lachlan was wrapped around her. She could get used to this and that's when her smile faded, and she decided it was best that she wasn't there when he woke.

She had reminded herself on more than one occasion to keep things in perspective and she had to make certain she did just that. He would leave, she would be alone, and she would miss him badly enough as it was. She didn't need to miss waking up beside him.

She eased out of bed and then realized she had no

clothes. They were outside on the ground probably still soaking wet, since the rain only stopped an hour or so ago.

"You're not sneaking away are you?"

Terese turned with a start to see Lachlan on his side, elbow bent, head resting on his hand, smiling.

"I have no clothes."

He grinned and she had to smile.

"A wise choice I made last night to strip you of leaving me."

"Is that what you did?" she asked extending her arms out and unabashedly displaying her nakedness.

"A damn gorgeous sight to wake up to," he claimed wholeheartedly.

She dropped her arms and headed for the door. "The sun has yet to rise. I can hurry to my quarters before anyone sees me."

He was at the door blocking it before she reached it.

He ran his finger over her breasts, down her stomach, and slipped slowly down between her legs. "For my eyes only."

She did the same to him, starting at his chest, swirling in circles down along his stomach to take hold of him in her hand. "It looks like someone else has risen before the sun."

"He always does."

"Always, not just for me?" she asked and gave a slight squeeze.

Lachlan rolled his eyes. "From now on only for you."

How she would love that to be so, but she wasn't foolish enough to believe this to last, for now, however . . .

"He's all mine? Promise?"

"I give you my word."

"In that case, I think I'll kiss him good morning," Terese said.

It wasn't long before Lachlan scooped her up and rushed her to the bed, and there they stayed well past sunrise.

Chapter 16

"Lachlan. Lachlan. Lachlan!"

Lachlan jolted and turned to stare at Boyd.

"Have our warriors gone completely love-sick?"

"I was thinking," Lachlan defended.

"Of Terese, no doubt. Andrew has completely lost his senses over Megan. Evan spends all his time with Piper in or out of the woods, and now Kyle is witless over one of the young women that arrived at Everagis the other day. You have all gone mad."

"Or are you simply jealous?" Lachlan suggested, which only served to agitate Boyd all the more.

"No one has caught my fancy."

"I see the way you watch Hester," Lachlan said, looking over the work the men had done to extend the small stable area.

"She's not interested, I've tried."

"You're not sincere."

"No, I'm not," Boyd admitted, "which she pointed out with a jab of her finger."

"Bonnie, that sweet lassie you favor, will see to your needs when we return home."

"Which will be?" Boyd asked anxiously.

"Want to leave already?"

"This place doesn't suit me. It's too remote and too damn quiet."

"I find it peaceful," Lachlan said.

"Because you're as love-sick as Andrew. You mark my words, he's not going to want to return home with us. He'll want to stay here with Megan."

"Megan can go with him."

Boyd snorted a laugh. "Not a one of these women will leave here. They've made it their home and they're not going anyplace. A man who loves any one of them better realize that, or he's in for a big disappointment."

One of the men working on another cottage called out to Boyd.

Boyd waved to the man, but before leaving he said, "You know there's really no reason for us to remain here. A messenger can deliver the church's decision to these women. We can be on our way whenever we please."

"The women need protecting," Lachlan argued.

Boyd began drifting away. "Open your eyes, Lachlan. They can protect themselves."

Lachlan grew annoyed, since he knew Boyd spoke the truth. It was no longer necessary for him and his men to remain at Everagis. He could take his leave anytime. The truth was, he wasn't ready to leave.

After last night and this morning, he knew that there was much more between him and Terese than he had ever planned on. And he wasn't about to walk away before he gave it a chance to take root and grow.

He'd be an idiot not to admit to himself that he was falling in love with Terese and had been since almost the beginning. Love had struck him and it wouldn't let go, and he believed Terese felt the same way. However, he didn't wish to rush her and there was the problem that Boyd had pointed out. Not a one of the women would leave Everagis, and he couldn't stay here. He needed time to resolve these issues the best way possible.

It was easier for his men. Andrew or Evan, or anyone of the other single men could remain here if they chose to, but he had an obligation to clan and family. And then there was his brother Ronan. He and his brothers would not rest until Ronan was found.

His brow frowned with deep ridges at the thought of Ronan. He worried over what was happening to him. Had he healed? Was he being treated well? And why? Why hadn't he been able to return home? He had so hoped to learn something from the mercenaries in the area, but so far that had proved unsuccessful, Evan being upset over not being able to pick up a trail or a scent.

"Something troubles you?" Terese asked, approaching him with an outstretched hand.

He grinned, recalling how just a few hours ago she had stood stark naked in front of him. It had pleased him to know that she didn't feel vulnerable in front of him, but rather that she trusted him. That was good. They were good and would only get better together.

He took her hand. "Your beauty chases away any troubles."

"Tell me," she urged and stroked his brow. "You looked so very upset."

"I was thinking about how upset Evan is that he can't find even a hint of a trail to the mercenaries' camp."

"Perhaps they have left the area."

He shook his head. "I don't believe so. From what the people who have arrived here tell us, the mercenaries have claimed land and intend to stay. And as I have said, one of the clans will decide it will be better to bargain with the mercenaries, having them as friends, which will settle the matter for all."

"And those that have lost homes?"

He kissed her softly then answered, "Will find a home here at Everagis. Your village grows, haven't you noticed."

She nodded slowly.

He tapped her brow. "Then why the frown?"

"I wish you to find your brother."

"Believe me when I tell you we will. My brothers and I will not stop searching until Ronan returns home."

"Ronan may not be the Ronan you know when he finally returns home."

Lachlan nodded. "True enough. Cavan was not himself when he first returned, but with time and his wife's love, he is himself again. Once Ronan is home with family he will do fine."

"You miss your family?"

"I do," he admitted. "They are a loving bunch. We laugh often, talk much, have our share of disagreements, may even be known to throw a punch or two on occasion, but we're always there to help each other whenever needed. That's why Ronan knows we look for him and will find him."

"I'm sure he does," Terese said.

Lachlan slowly wrapped his arms around her. "I think you and I should take a stroll to my cottage."

"And why is that?"

"We have things to discuss."

"What things?" she asked smiling.

"I'll tell you when we get there."

"I have chores to see to."

"They can wait," Lachlan said and whispered, "this is much more important."

"How can you be so sure?" she asked as he held her close to his side and began walking toward his cottage.

"Because if I don't strip you of your clothes soon and lose myself in you, I'll go stark raving mad."

"You would survive," she insisted, though she continued walking with him.

"No, I would not," he declared adamantly.

"I am not that necessary to your survival."

He stopped a few feet from his cottage. "You're everything to my survival, Terese, and I believe it is the same for you. Tell me you do not wish, want, need to walk through that door with me and make love. Tell me and I will let you go do your chores."

She stared at him for a moment and when she turned

to walk away, he felt his heart drop and his passion crash. But then she giggled and switched directions running straight for his cottage.

"I'll get there before you," she challenged.

His passion soared and he ran with the determination of a man eager to make love. He scooped her up in his arms just before she reached the door and hurried her inside, shutting the door firmly behind him and then depositing the both of them on the bed.

Clothes soon found their way to the floor and naked limbs were wrapped around each other, gentle laughs and nibbles mixed and hands explored.

Lachlan loved the feel of her smooth, silky skin. It reminded him of the softness of a newly blossomed rose petal and was just as fragrant.

"You smell so good," he said wrapping his arms around her middle and resting his head there.

"Rowena's soap. It's a special blend," she said, running her fingers through his dark brown hair.

"I could stay wrapped around you forever."

"You're welcome to."

His heart swelled with her remark, for she told him that she didn't wish to part from him, which meant she just might be falling in love with him. And with that sense of joy filling him he began to make love to her.

He took his time, exploring her naked flesh with a delicate touch, lingering his kisses in places he found sensitive to her and loving every little moan that slipped from her lips.

He refused to let her do anything this time. This

time his pleasure would come from pleasuring her. He brought her to climax with intimate touches then forced another one from her with the magic of his tongue. Then he entered her and brought her to a climax that had her reeling and him exploding, his body shuddering from the tremendously satisfying sensation that continued to ripple far beyond what he had ever experienced.

They lay spent against each other, their breathing erratic, not able to speak. But their fingers locked tightly and held on firm, both letting the other know they had no intentions of letting go.

Terese smiled broadly as she walked, a spring in her step, toward the common shelter. Her body never felt so good, so satisfied, so alive. She hadn't wanted to leave Lachlan. She would have loved to linger, but she had chores to do and Lachlan had things to see to, and it wouldn't be right to spend the entire day in the cottage, just the two of them. Everyone would talk, not that they probably weren't already, and that was why she was glad to be so far removed from clan and family. Here she was free to love and not be judged. Here couples handfasted, joining together the old way, since clergy was far and few between. Here was her home.

It was a beautiful and glorious day, and she wouldn't let anything destroy it for her. She would relish the joy of it all and think on the pleasure yet to come.

She laughed softly.

"Someone is pleased."

Terese looked to see Hester approach and she could see by her expression something was wrong. She didn't want anything to be wrong, not this day. She wanted this day to continue with smiles and tingles and never-ending passion.

She raised her hand before Hester could say anything. "Just give me a moment to tuck away my happiness for safekeeping."

That caused Hester to smile. "There's no problem. We all would like to have a meeting tonight. It has been awhile since we've had a chance to voice our concerns."

"You're right," Terese agreed. "It has been too long since our last meeting, but why the bleak expression?"

Hester walked alongside Terese as they continued toward the common shelter. "Things are changing around here and I fear losing those I think of as sisters."

"None of us intend to go anywhere," Terese said. "Everagis is our home and somehow I think we will keep it. However, to make certain that we always do have a home I intend to speak with our recent friends and see if they can provide us with a parcel of land should we need it so that we may keep the friendship that already exists between us, providing them with our healing skills and a portion of our harvest."

"Wise choice, but then that is why we look to you to lead us," Hester said. "I don't know what we would do without you."

"You would survive," Terese said firmly. "You would have to; you would have no other choice."

"Yes, you've taught us that too, but I'd much rather have you around."

"And I'd much rather be around," Terese confirmed.

"What excuse will you give Lachlan for tonight?"

"I'll think of something."

"You are happy with him," Hester said.

"More so than I imagined," she admitted.

Hester shook her head. "It seems to me that love is more madness than anything else."

Terese laughed and nodded. "I agree. Love does seem maddening."

"And yet you embrace it?"

"I don't think you have a choice once you fall in love. It grabs hold and has you in its clutches and suddenly nothing makes sense anymore."

"And when it finally disappoints?" Hester asked.

Terese took hold of her hand. "We survive."

Hester smiled. "Thanks to you I survived. I watched your face as you spoke to the innkeeper. He blanched with each word you spoke and quickly accepted the bag of coins you gave him. He released me right quick after that. I always wondered what you said to him, but I never had the courage to ask."

"Until now."

Hester nodded.

Terese grinned. "I told him if he didn't accept the coins I offered for your release that one night soon or perhaps months from now, he would be paid a visit by a bloodthirsty Bunnock warrior and never see the light of day again."

"And he believed you, a woman?"

Terese chuckled. "He believed me a Bunnock warrior who had the point of her dagger poking in his gut hard enough to draw blood."

"You truly are a warrior," Hester said.

"I am what I have to be as are you, Rowena, Piper, and Megan. We have all tasted the bitter side of life and now finally we get to taste the full rich flavors of life. And I for one intend to enjoy."

"Then we'll keep the meeting short tonight," Hester offered.

"Now, that I appreciate and I assure you so will Lachlan."

The two women laughed and entered the common room to see to chores.

Chapter 17

The meeting never took place. Another injured mercenary was brought to Everagis that night and the women worked endlessly on him, but unfortunately could not save him. It left them all upset, though oddly enough it was Talon, the recovering mercenary, who praised the women for their efforts and insisted that he would tell his leader how hard they had worked to save the man.

Terese noticed that Rowena went directly to Talon when they had finished and had shed tears on the large man's shoulders. His thick, meaty hands had stroked her back and he had soothed her with gentle words. It was obvious that Talon cared for Rowena as she did him.

It looked like love had descended on Everagis and had yet to let go.

While Rowena was comforted by Talon and Hester and Megan saw to cleaning up, Terese and Piper went directly into the woods to take the news to Septimus so that he and his men could see to burying their comrade.

She had decided to be honest with Lachlan and tell him that the women were holding a meeting as they usually did to discuss matters of importance to Everagis. Surprisingly, he had understood and remarked that the meetings were probably one of the reasons that Everagis had prospered. However, he did insist that he would be waiting for her, no matter what the hour.

Septimus was waiting nearby and wasn't surprised by her news.

"I didn't think he could be saved, but I had to try."

"You must always try," Terese encouraged. "You never know, sometimes miracles happen."

Septimus snorted. "I stopped believing in miracles a long time ago."

Terese didn't argue with him. He obviously had faced difficulties that had left him scarred as so many of them had been. Hopefully, in time he would heal. But at the moment she had another problem that continued to haunt her and the only way that she could settle it was . . .

"I need to speak with your leader,"

"He isn't here," Septimus said.

"When will he return?"

Septimus shook his head. "I don't know."

"I must speak to him," she said anxiously.

"Why?"

"That is my concern."

"He speaks to no one," Septimus said.

"He'll speak to me."

"Such confidence."

She ignored his sarcasm. "Let me know when he returns."

"What makes you believe I will follow your edict?"

She grinned. "Because your leader ordered you to."

Terese was exhausted by the time she and Piper returned to Everagis. Piper went straight to bed while Terese saw that everyone was settled and safe for the remainder of the night.

She found that Rowena slept beside Talon, while Megan slept alone. Hester had waited up for her.

"I was worried," Hester admitted.

"There was nothing to worry about. Septimus hadn't believed the man would survive."

Hester yawned. "Then I retire in peace."

Terese had thought to retire to her own bed, but she had promised Lachlan she would see him tonight. She knew he waited to make love, yet she merely wanted his arms wrapped around her. Much as how Rowena and Talon slept, wrapped safely together.

She hurried her steps to his cottage and entered quietly so as not to wake him if he should be asleep. She was surprised and disappointed to find his bed empty. She considered returning to her own quarters, but she was tired and she longed for his arms around her.

She shed her garments and crawled into his bed naked, snuggling beneath the blanket and hoping he would return soon.

Lachlan reached down and tenderly rubbed a silky strand of blond hair between his fingers before he eased it off Terese's cheek. He was relieved to see her there. He was tired, no exhausted, more from his endless and, it seemed fruitless, search for his brother. When Evan excitedly informed him that he thought he had picked up a track that he believed would lead them to the mercenary camp, he followed him, with considerable enthusiasm and hope. Unfortunately, it had taken them nowhere.

He hadn't a chance to inform Terese of his sudden departure, since he hadn't wanted to interfere with her meeting. He knew that she would come to him later and they would make love throughout the night.

But now?

He simply wanted to sleep. He felt exhausted and empty. Would he ever find his brother? The question and endless disappointment irritated him. However, finding Terese in his bed gave him a sense of peace, and all he wanted to do was crawl beneath the blanket and wrap himself around her. He stripped off his clothes and slipped under the blanket, easing against her. She was so soft and so warm and there was the scent of her; earthy and fragrant.

She turned in his arms. "You're home."

Her words hit him in the heart, for to her he was home, a place of belonging and love. And he felt the same; he was home here in her arms. While it filled him with joy, it also frightened him, for he repeatedly worried that she would not leave Everagis and he could not remain here.

"I'm home," he said and kissed her cheek.

Her lips sought his mouth and she kissed him softly and sweetly and it was enough to spark his passion. He returned the kiss and soon their hands were roaming, touching, and their bodies drifting closer and closer until the only way they could get closer was . . .

He entered her slowly and their rhythm was gentle and loving as if their need was to never let each other go. Their passion built slowly, steadily, strongly until they both cried out in an explosive climax and collapsed wrapped around each other.

They snuggled in each others arms too tired to talk and so content that sleep claimed them instantly.

Lachlan woke with the scent of Terese filling his nostrils and he turned to nestle around her only to find her gone. He sprang up in bed and looked around the room, thinking she would be there somewhere, but it was empty; he was alone.

He didn't like the sensation that rushed over him, almost as if she left him, ran away, and he jumped out of bed and hurriedly dressed in his shirt and plaid. Last he remembered they had been wrapped around each other after a quick but loving coupling. He never expected her to be gone when he woke. She often woke him in the morning, her hand laying claim to him and enticing him, not that he needed that much tempting. He was more than willing at any time of the day or night.

Even last night when he had been too tired and crawled into bed, once she had turned in his arms and kissed him, her hard nipples brushing across his chest; he had sprung to life.

He had expected to talk with her this morning. There were things he wished to discuss. Being it was well past sunrise she wouldn't be in her usual spot on the hill. More than likely she'd be busy with chores and so he went in search of her.

Gray clouds hovered overhead promising rain sometime today and though rain was needed to nourish the seeded fields, he much preferred the sun. He stopped to speak with Boyd, letting him know that once the shelter the men were working on was finished, they were to do no more.

Boyd smiled and slapped his thigh. "Damn, we're headed home soon, aren't we?"

"Just do as I say," Lachlan said and headed to the common shelter. He had no designated departure time set, but he knew that soon, very soon he would need to discuss it with Terese, at least the possibilities. And the thought scared the hell out of him.

What if she refused to go with him? He couldn't believe that a possibility. He sensed that she loved him and after last night he believed it even more. In two or three weeks at the most, he should be able to set everything right so that she would be looking forward to returning home with him, especially when he asked her to marry him.

The thought still set his heart to thumping madly and his stomach churning like he had drunk too much ale. He hadn't thought love would claim him just yet. Truthfully, he hadn't thought love would claim him at all. He had planned on eventually picking a woman who would suit his needs and wedding her.

Now, however, he could see the benefits of loving the woman you wed, and he felt lucky to have found the perfect woman for him.

He even understood his brothers' attachment to their wives, though he'd never admit that to them. They would tease him unmercifully and that he could do without.

"Lost in your thoughts?"

Lachlan swung around and grabbed Terese around the waist, drawing her near for a quick kiss. "I don't like when you leave my bed before I wake."

"I have chores and duties to attend to," she said, hooking her arm in his to walk alongside him.

"Aren't I chore enough for you?"

She leaned in to whisper in his ear, "You are no chore; you are a pleasure."

His passion lit and flamed like a dry log whose heat spread rapidly throughout, though he attempted to contain it.

"Keep that up and I will drag you back to my cottage and keep you there the remainder of the day."

"Promises. Promises," she teased.

Thunder rumbled overhead and Lachlan glanced up at the gray sky that would undoubtedly shed rain soon. "The weather accommodates my need. Everyone will seek shelter from the storm. What else will there be to do then? . . ." He allowed her to imagine the rest.

"You tempt," she said.

"I invite," he corrected, thunder rumbling along with his words.

She let his arm go. "We shall see."

He tried to reach out and grab her, but she laughed and took off insisting she had chores to do. He watched her disappear into the common shelter and once again glanced up at the darkening sky.

"Don't fail me," he warned and stumped off to find Evan.

Lachlan entered his cottage, shaking the rain off. He had been lucky to be nearby when the downpour started so he wasn't soaked only damp along the shoulders and hair. A few minutes spent by the fire would take care of that.

He turned and stopped, staring at the small table spread with food, and was that a jug of ale he spied? He then looked to see that the bed was made with fresh linens and a fine green wool blanket folded down.

He sniffed the air. That was mutton stew, he was sure of it and then noticed the cauldron that hung over the flames. And there was a loaf of black bread on the table, not to mention tarts and sweet bread.

Lachlan looked around, not that Terese could hide anywhere; the room was too small. Was this a gift, a feast for him alone? He certainly hoped not.

The door suddenly opened and Terese popped in, rain dripping off her and holding a bunch of wild onions in her hand.

"I forgot these for the stew," she said with a shiver.

Lachlan smiled and went to her. "You did this for us?"

"It's raining," she grinned. "What else is there to do?" She sneezed.

Lachlan reached out to her. "We need to get you out of those wet clothes."

She skirted around him. "First I need to get the onions into the stew or the flavor will suffer."

She went to the table and in seconds had the onions chopped and dumped in the stew. Then without thought she stripped off her clothes and hung them over a chair in front of the fire to dry.

Lachlan savored her every movement. Her body was exquisite, narrow waist, rounded hips that would surely serve her well when birthing. The thought startled him and grabbed at his heart. Was he really thinking of children with Terese? He grinned. Yes, he could easily see her rounded with his child, and he would love her even more.

Damn, but he did love her. How, when, where it had happened, he didn't care. He only knew that he loved her down to his very soul and he'd let nothing, absolutely nothing stand in their way.

He stripped before he went to her and wrapped himself around her.

"I wondered how long it would take you to join me." Her hand settled over his arms.

He nibbled at her neck and nipped teasingly at her ear. "Was I fast enough?"

"It's slow and gentle I'm looking for, since the stew has time to cook yet and the storm looks as if it's here to stay for a good while."

"Then we have all the time in the world," he said and believed it so, since he intended to spend the rest of his life with her.

He took hold of her hand and tugged her along to the bed. They settled beneath the folded blanket, though it was only their calves it covered. They lay on their sides facing each other. Their hands began to explore ever so gently and lovingly.

"I will never grow tired of touching you," he said between nipping at her lips and then settling a kiss on her that turned more heated than he had planned.

Their passion took control and soon they were hungry and eager for each other. Their touches turned more demanding and their kisses more fiery. They both didn't want to wait, couldn't wait and they joined quickly; Lachlan slipping over and in her.

It was magical between them, but then it was always magical between them. Each time was special, different and more than satisfying. And he never wanted this to end between them. He wanted to love like this forever with her, and he knew it would be so. He knew their love was strong enough to make it so.

Before he slipped off her, with his breathing still labored he whispered in her ear, "I love you."

He rolled off her onto his back and lay there spent and content. He could hear her breathing had yet to calm, and wasn't concerned when she did not immediately return his declaration of love. She would in time; he was sure of it.

He wanted her to declare her love when she was ready, not because she felt obligated. She would need to choose her time to tell him what he already knew, and he would be patient. He wanted to savor the moment as she did now, though she could be pleasantly surprised.

He turned on his side toward her, hoping to receive some comment from her and disappointedly saw that she was asleep, a slight purr pouting her lips. A pang of frustration struck him. Now he wondered if she had even heard him declare his love.

He could wake her, but he really didn't have the heart. He'd let her sleep and when she woke they would eat and afterward make love again, and then he would tell her again, after their breathing had calmed, after she was once again fully rational, after she was completely satiated from making love . . . he would tell her that he loved her and wanted to marry her.

Chapter 18

Terese sat at the head of the table in the common room deep in thought while the other women took their seats. Her heart ached and she felt close to tears but she kept both contained as she had when she heard Lachlan whisper in her ear, *I love you.*

She had feigned sleep, though she had wanted to leap up and throw her arms around him and tell him the same. But she couldn't, she had always known it wasn't possible no matter how many times she dared daydream or hope for a miracle. She knew in her heart that in the end she would have to bid him farewell.

Later after they had eaten, she had taken control of their lovemaking. And she made love with him as if it were their last time, which she feared it was.

She savored every kiss, every intimate caress, lingering until she had driven them beyond reason and in their loving insanity they had joined like two lovers who could not get enough of each other or like two lovers' last night together forever.

She wanted to cry at the aching thought, but she reminded herself that she could no longer allow this to continue. It would grow only more difficult not only for him, but for her to say good-bye.

Tears choked at her throat with the thought of never seeing him again, never talking with him, waking beside him, loving him. What a fool she had been to start this. She had thought she could easily keep it all in perspective and what did she do?

She went and fell in love with him . . . madly and deeply in love with him.

After they had made love, she had feigned sleep once again fearful of him not only repeating his declaration of love, but of her losing all sanity and blurting out her love for him. She had then waited until she was certain he was in the thick of sleep, and had snuck out of the cottage.

Once at the common shelter she gathered the women for a meeting.

"What's wrong?" Rowena asked softly, knotting the tie of her night robe.

Terese glanced around at each of the women, and from the looks of concern she suspected that they all were aware of her plight.

Hester reached her hand out to her. "It's time for the warriors to leave, isn't it?"

Terese was glad she phrased it as she did, for the thought of hearing aloud that it was time for Lachlan to leave pained her heart.

"I don't want Evan to leave," Piper said tearfully.

Terese had been so concerned with her own heartache she had forgotten about the other women who would possibly be affected by the warriors' departure.

"He's only just kissed me," Piper admitted. "And I liked it. And he doesn't make fun of my connection to the woods; he shares it with me."

"Andrew hasn't kissed me yet, though I know he wants to," Megan said. "He's patient with me and so gentle." She chuckled. "And he makes me laugh and . . ." She choked back tears. "Lord, I never thought I'd care for another man ever again, but I find I do care for Andrew and would love to know him better."

"And you, Terese?" Rowena asked. "How do you feel about Lachlan?"

A tear finally spilled from one eye and she let it trail down her cheek. "I never thought I'd have the opportunity to meet a man to love, but I could easily love Lachlan. He's charming, brave . . ." She laughed. "And a mighty fine lover."

The women grinned.

Terese turned silent and the women waited, the laughter and grins fading.

She swiped the tear off her face and her words were abrupt and stern. "Lachlan loves Terese, not Alyce." She looked first to Piper then to Megan. "I know that neither of you would leave Everagis, but you both are welcome to invite Evan and Andrew to remain here if you wish. It would give them time to see if they would want to make a permanent home here with each of you."

"You should have the same for yourself," Megan protested.

"How I wish that could be so, but we all know it cannot," Terese said. "Lachlan cannot remain here. He has a duty to his clan and his family. And I cannot go with him, for then my father will—"

Hester interrupted. "Lachlan loves you; it's obvious. He can request your hand in marriage from your father, and surely your father would agree."

Terese shook her head. "Lachlan isn't interested in Alyce. He has referred to her as a shrew, and do you really think he would want to wed me once he learned that I have been lying to him all this time?"

"But he has spent time with you," Piper said. "Surely by now, he knows you are no shrew."

"I cannot take the chance," Terese said. "If I admit my true identity and Lachlan doesn't want me then my father will send men for me, and I will be forced to wed a man of my father's choosing."

"What will you do?" Hester asked.

Another tear slipped from Terese's eye. "Tomorrow I tell Lachlan it is time for him and his men to leave."

"He will protest," Hester warned.

Terese fought the ache in her heart. "I will do whatever it takes to get him to leave."

Tears glistened in all of the women's eyes.

"We will be here for you and help anyway we can," Rowena said and the other three women nodded.

"I know," Terese said forcing a smile that never surfaced. "And I will need your help when this is done, for my heart will break in so many pieces that I wonder if I will survive the pain."

* * *

Lachlan was upset to find Terese gone when he woke. She had done that a few times now and it disturbed him. He felt as if she was running from him, and he didn't like the thought.

He was also annoyed that he had never gotten another chance to tell her that he loved her and wished to marry her last night. He wanted this settled, for he was eager to take her home and introduce her to his family. He knew they would be surprised but pleased and that his two brothers would tease him unmercifully, but he looked forward to it, for they would truly share in his joy.

His one disappointment was not being able to discover anything about Ronan, but with the mercenaries remaining in the area, he felt certain Cavan would send a group to further scout the area and make contact with the group.

The thought of doing it himself had crossed his mind, but he considered the circumstances and the amount of men he had, and he had decided that the task called for more warriors than he had available.

He would take all the information to his brother Cavan, and he would decide on how to proceed.

Now he simply wanted to find Terese and start the process that would have them returning home, marrying, and spending the rest of their lives together.

Evan nearly crashed into him when he stepped out of the cottage.

"Can I stay, sir, can I stay?" Evan repeated nervously while bobbing up and down around him.

"What?" Lachlan asked, but before Evan could say anything Andrew popped in his face.

"I'm going to remain behind for a while to make sure the women are safe," he said.

Lachlan shook his head confused. "What are—"

"Damn, I'm a happy man," Boyd said, slapping Lachlan on the back.

Lachlan backed away from the three of them. "What the hell are you all talking about?"

They all turned silent.

"What's going on?" Lachlan demanded.

Each man looked from one to the other as if they were trying to decide who would speak up.

"Someone better tell me and fast," Lachlan warned.

Andrew was the brave one. "You better talk with Terese."

Lachlan felt a jolt to his gut.

"Andrew's right," Boyd agreed. "It's best you speak with Terese."

Evan nodded. "She's at the common shelter."

Lachlan stormed off, his gut warning him that something was amiss, terribly amiss. And when he walked through the open door of the common house, Hester and Rowena made a hasty exit, leaving him alone with Terese.

"Tell me," he said sharply.

"It's nothing really and the others should not have said anything before I spoke with you," she said casually. "It's just that I feel it is time for you and your men to leave."

"Why?"

"You have done all you can for us, and there truly is no reason for you to remain here, and I know many of your men wish to return home."

She seemed so cold, so unattached to her words, as if she cared not at all and was simply dismissing him.

"What of *us*?" he asked bluntly.

She shrugged. "What of us? We have enjoyed each other as we intended. Now it's over."

Lachlan took a quick step toward her. She didn't flinch or jump, she remained stoic where she stood.

"You're going to tell me that I mean nothing to you? That what we shared meant nothing?"

"Of course it did," she said and gave his arm a pat. "We spent a lovely time together, and I will remember you always. You know how it goes. You've bid good-bye to women before."

Lachlan felt as if she had slapped him hard in the face and he grew angry. "You're telling me that you have no feelings at all for me? This has been nothing more than a tryst you easily cast aside?"

"I care for you."

"You love me," he insisted, "as I love you. I don't know what this game is you play with me, but I'll have none of it."

"We both knew this time would come."

There she was. He finally heard her, the woman he loved and who loved him. Her tone was soft and concerned, and he was sure her voice had trembled.

He reached out to her, but she backed away from

him. "Don't do this to us. Don't be afraid to let me love you or for you to love me."

She chuckled. "It's nothing like that—"

"It damn well is," he shouted and she jumped.

"Raising your voice and getting angry will not settle this matter," she warned coldly.

"There is nothing to settle," he said, his anger not as defined. "We are in love and we will get married."

"No, we won't," she said adamantly. "You and your men will leave here at dawn tomorrow. We will provide you with all the provisions you require, and we will thank you for your generous help and that will be the end of it."

"You truly can't mean this."

"I can and I do," she said emphatically.

He remained silent for a moment and then said, "If that is what you wish."

"I do," she said with a jut of her chin.

"Then I will do as you wish and since what we have shared means nothing to you, then you won't mind sharing one last night with me."

She paled. "I don't think that would be wise."

"Why? I mean nothing to you. Unless of course you are lying to me and send me away for a different reason," he said sarcastically. "Then I would need to find out what you lie about."

"This will serve no purpose."

Lachlan slammed his hands flat on the table. "It will serve a damn good purpose. Make love with me tonight and then afterward tell me . . . look me in the eyes and tell me you want me to leave, and I will leave."

"If that's what it will take," she said with a shrug. "Now I have work to do and you have men to get ready for morning departure."

Lachlan went to step outside then turned around. "I don't know what this is all about. I don't know why you deny the truth. If you fear something then I wish you would tell me and I will fight your fear for you. I love you, Terese. I love you like I never thought I would ever or could ever love a woman. You are part of my heart, and I know I am part of yours. Don't do this to us. Don't throw our love away. Please don't throw it away."

Terese waited until he left then barely made it to the door to close it, her legs trembled so badly. She braced herself against it and began to weep. She wished she could scream out her pain, pound at the door, run after him and beg him; beg him to love her—Alyce Bunnock the shrew he had been sent to bring home.

She couldn't take the chance that he would reject her, and so she sat there crying silently and that was how Hester found her after shoving against the door to open it.

Hester immediately sat on the ground beside her and wrapped her arms around her. "Perhaps you should tell him the truth."

"And what if he rejects me, what then do I do?"

"It might be a chance worth taking."

"I don't know," Terese cried. "I feel as if I'm being torn in two, but I wonder how bad the pain would be if I told him, and he walked away from me? And then it would only get worse for my father would tear me away from Everagis and everyone here. Whichever way I look at it I suffer."

"Then tomorrow it will be done; he'll be gone," Hester consoled.

Terese closed her eyes for a moment and when she opened them fresh tears began to fall. "He insists we spend one last night together."

"You cannot," Hester said, upset for her.

"He insists that if I truly don't love him, it won't bother me and that if I can look him in the eyes after we make love and tell him to leave, he will."

"Oh lord, no, Terese," Hester said, tears filling her eyes. "How will you ever be able to do that?"

Terese shook her head, her tears continuing to fall. "I don't know. I love him so very much. I don't know where I will find the strength to do it."

The two women sat hugging each other while tears flowed freely, one heart hurting for the friend whose heart broke in two.

Chapter 19

Lachlan snapped and barked orders at his men and not a one made a comment. He was more than angry; he was furious. He couldn't believe that Terese thought so little of the time they had spent together. And there was no way anyone would ever convince him that she didn't love him.

He shook his head, not able to make sense of this turn of event, but confident he would change her mind this evening. He had to; he couldn't imagine returning home to Caithness without her. It wasn't about making love with her. It was more about making her admit how she truly felt about him, about them.

"You don't mind that Evan and I remain here?" Andrew asked, approaching Lachlan.

"How many times have you asked me that?" Lachlan snapped. "And how many times must I continue to say no, I don't mind."

"I'm sorry."

"There's no need to be," Lachlan assured him curtly. "You need time with Megan as Evan does with Piper.

If it doesn't work out you're welcome to return home. If it does, then I'm happy for you."

"That's not what I'm sorry for," Andrew said.

Lachlan understood. "Terese will see reason before it's time to leave."

"Megan tells me that Terese will never leave Everagis. Never. It is her home."

Lachlan turned a vicious scowl on him. "I am her home as she is mine. She will realize that and come to her senses." Lachlan turned and stomped off.

"Leave him be," Boyd advised with a hand to Andrew's shoulder. "He has never had a woman deny him anything. It will take time for him to accept this."

Andrew shook his head. "It makes no sense. You can see how much Terese loves him and he her. Why would she deny the obvious?"

Boyd grinned. "Learn now that women are not sensible creatures, and they work hard to drive men crazy. Keep that in mind when dealing with women and you may, just may keep your sanity."

Just before sunset Terese went to the stream, washed and donned fresh clothes, a dark blue wool skirt and a white linen blouse. She towel dried her hair, though it remained relatively damp, and slipped on a pair of sandals.

Her mind and stomach had been in chaos since this morning. She hadn't eaten a thing all day and nor did she want to. How she would get through tonight, she didn't know. Part of her ached to spend this last night with him and the other part wanted to scream out the unfairness of it all. But then she should be used to that; it seemed to be the way of things for her.

Piper popped out of the woods looking distressed, and for a moment Terese was caught between hoping something would save her from this night and praying nothing would stop her from making love with Lachlan one last time.

"Is something wrong?" Terese asked, waiting for fate to decide.

"No, I just feel this is so unfair to you," Piper said.

Relief flooded her though was quickly replaced by apprehension. "Do not worry about me," Terese said, gathering her things.

Piper was quick to help, folding things into the basket. "We all worry about you as you do us."

Terese handed her the basket. "Please take this to my quarters. It's time for me to say my good-byes to Lachlan."

Tears pooled in Piper's eyes. "I would die if I had to say good-bye to Evan."

"Trust me, Piper, you would survive."

Tears slipped down Piper's fair cheeks. "But would it be worth it?"

Those words haunted Terese as she made her way to Lachlan's cottage, and she took a breath before she knocked, wondering if this was a wise thing to do. Before she could change her mind Lachlan opened the door, took her hand, and tugged her inside.

"I had Rowena prepare us some food. Are you hungry?" he asked.

She shook her head, much too upset to speak let

alone eat, though she did smile. She couldn't help it. His charming smile was contagious and his handsome features were so pleasing to the eye, and he spoke with such concern and tenderness.

Lord, but she was going to miss this man.

Lachlan slipped his arms around her waist. "Talk with me, Terese. Tell me what's wrong."

She didn't trust keeping her eyes on him for she feared she would surrender to tears and be lost. So she rested her head to his chest, which made matters worse, since she heard the confident beat of his heart.

He rested his chin on the top of her head. "Whatever it is we can work this out."

She closed her eyes and tried to determine if he meant it, if they truly could work this out.

"I recall Alyce Bunnock saying something similar to me about her situation when I met her. She had hoped someone would see reason and help her. Do you think you would have helped her?"

"She was a woman who sealed her own fate," Lachlan answered, "and I had a duty to her father. I would have tried to help her as best I could, but in the end I would have had no choice but to return her to her father."

"What if she had loved someone else, say, you for instance, and wanted a life with you?"

"It seems an unfair comparison. Alyce was not a woman I could love. She was nothing like you."

"You don't know that," she snapped.

He forced her to look at him. "I do know that. Alyce had a duty to her father and clan, and she should have realized that and done what was necessary. I would have never gotten involved with Alyce."

She had her answer more clearly than she would have cared to hear it.

"Alyce means nothing to me; you mean everything to me."

I am Alyce, she wanted to scream at him, but instead she kissed him. She needed this night done. She needed *Terese* to love him one last time.

"Make love to me," she said softly.

"We need to talk first," he said between kisses.

"Later," she whispered.

He wrapped his fingers in her hair and tugged her head back so that his lips could claim hers in a kiss that warned her he would never ever let go. And she let him believe it, for tonight, just tonight, she needed to believe it as well.

He carried her to the bed and stood her in front of it to slowly remove her garments, teasing with a kiss or touch all the intimate spots he was so very familiar with and she reveled in each and every one.

His clothes followed and with a firm arm around her waist, he took her down on the bed with him, stretching out over her, their bodies flat against each other while he kissed her senseless. And he continued rendering her senseless as he made love to her.

It was remarkable to her that their lovemaking continued to be more and more enjoyable as if it were anew for them each time they came together. His kisses and touches never ceased to enflame her and make her hunger for him.

His lips and sensuous nibbles continued to find places on her body that sent endless shivers pulsating through her until she thought she would simply go mad with pleasure.

And he knew, oh how he knew where to touch at just the right moment and bring her to climax, only to coax another climax from her as soon as she thought she was spent, and then he would enter her and make her want him all over again.

Their night continued much the same, endless kisses, caresses, and climaxes. Neither tired, neither wanting to stop. They loved tirelessly, Lachlan reminding her over and over again how much he loved her.

Much later they lay wrapped in each others arms, Lachlan caressing her back.

"I can't wait for my family to meet you. They will want to plan a big wedding feast and—"

Terese sat up, not minding that her breasts were bare and her rosy nipples still rigid from their lovemaking. "I'm not going home with you."

He laughed. "I am your home as you are mine."

She wanted to cry at the truth of his words. Instead she laughed. "Everagis is my home and always will be."

Lachlan jolted up. "Stop this nonsense."

She jumped out of bed and reached for her clothes. "It is not nonsense. Accept it and go home."

He yanked the clothes from her hands. "You are my home."

She grabbed the clothes from him and scooped the

others off the floor. She needed to get dressed, cover her nakedness, for suddenly she felt much too vulnerable being naked in front of him.

She slipped them on fast and then faced him with a toss of her head. "No, I am not your home. Everagis is my home."

Lachlan raked a frustrated hand through his long dark hair. "That's not true and you know it. I love you and you love me."

She shook her head and laughed. "That is what you believe."

"It is the truth; you can't deny it."

"Go home, Lachlan. Go home and live your life."

He grabbed hold of her arm as she turned to walk away and yanked her against him. "Tell me, damn it. Tell me you don't love me. I want to hear you say it."

She felt her heart break, the pain stabbing at her chest, trying to rob her breath, and she answered before she didn't have a breath left in her. "I don't love you. I never have."

Lachlan released her so suddenly that she stumbled.

She decided to continue her attack, for she feared if she didn't he would try to work his charm on her, and she was much too susceptible to it.

"You were enjoyable while it lasted, but now it's time for you to leave. I don't wish to spend the rest of my life with you."

Lord, forgive me for such a blatant lie.

He stood naked with a look of shock and vulnerability that broke her heart even further.

"We had a good time. Take the memories and enjoy them."

"I don't believe you," he muttered, shaking his head.

"Don't make this hard, Lachlan. Don't make me say it again."

"Say it," he demanded. "Say it again."

"I don't love you," she shouted, the pain so intense she thought she would die. "Go home. I don't love you."

She turned then and ran out of the cottage before he could stop her, and she didn't stop. She ran into the woods and kept running and running wanting to outrun the pain, mindless of the branches scratching her arms or her destination, until finally out of breath, she stopped.

Terese dropped to the ground and wept, alone with her heartache.

"Terese."

She turned to see Piper standing behind her almost as breathless as she was.

"I saw you and followed," Piper said between breathes.

"I don't know where I am," Terese cried.

Piper leaned down and wrapped her arm around her. "That's all right. I do. Come on I'll take you home."

Home. Did she truly know where it was anymore?

"Rowena could use your help," Piper said.

"What's wrong?" Terese asked, standing without help from Piper.

"A young woman large with child arrived at Everagis a couple of hours ago in labor. She's having a rough time of it and Rowena fears losing her."

Terese wiped at her tears. "Then we best help her."

"Are you sure you're all right?" Piper asked.

Terese shook her head and wiped away fresh tears. "No, I'm not. Let's go. Duty always calls."

Hester entered the room where the woman labored to birth her babe and addressed Terese. "Lachlan and his men are ready to leave. He asks for you. Would you rather I make an excuse?"

Terese stood. "I will not be a coward now that it is at the end."

She bravely walked out of the common shelter with Hester by her side, Megan remaining with the woman. Rowena joined the two, though she and Hester stayed their steps when they drew close to Lachlan to let Terese have a moment with him.

"We thank you and your men for all you have done for us. We will be forever grateful," she said to him and it hurt to see that he didn't wear his usual charming smile because of her.

"Andrew and Evan will remain for now. No doubt you will see Sinclare warriors again. I will not be one of them," Lachlan said, "though I will recommend that the church turn this land over to you and the others so that you may remain here at your *home.*"

That he should do that for her when she had been so cruel to him broke her heart all the more. "That is generous of you."

"Not really," he said curtly. "It's simply the cost of your pleasure."

Terese felt the slap as if he had delivered it straight to her face. She didn't respond since part of her felt deserving of it, for she had hurt him badly. She watched him ride away and forever disappear out of her life.

"I love you, Lachlan," she murmured. "You take my heart with you, for I shall never give it to another."

Chapter 20

Lachlan sat in Cavan's solar, a tankard of ale in his hand, staring at the cold hearth. He'd been home near two weeks and he felt worse then he had when he first arrived. He intended to forget Terese, put her out of his mind and get on with his life as she had so coldly suggested. But no matter how hard he tried, he couldn't stop thinking about her. She was there in his every thought and dream refusing to let go, or was it he who refused to let go?

"Lachlan!"

He jumped and the ale sloshed over the sides of his tankard. He sat straight in his chair and looked to his brother Cavan, a large, formidable man with the same dark piercing eyes of all his brothers except Ronan. Ronan had their mother's green eyes. "I was lost in my thoughts."

"Which is where you have been since your return," Cavan said with concern rather than anger.

Artair settled in the chair next to him. "What haven't you told us?"

"Nothing," Lachlan said, hoping Artair would leave

it at that, though knowing that was unlikely. He was the most practical of all the brothers, reasoning situations until he drove you mad, though he curbed his sensibility with his wife Zia.

Cavan leaned his arm on the mantel, shaking his head. "That's not true. Something troubles you. We know it; we all know it, and damn it our wives will not leave us alone until we find out what it is."

Lachlan had to laugh, though it wasn't a robust one.

"Zia believes it involves a woman," Artair said.

"Honora agrees and surprisingly mother has said nothing," Cavan said and suddenly his eyes turned wide. "You confided in Mother?"

"When requested, our mother keeps things to herself," Lachlan said.

"Zia and Honora consider you their brother and they worry over you. Please, for their sake, and I beg you for ours"—Artair looked to Cavan, who nodded vigorously—"tell us what is wrong."

Perhaps it was the need to shed the pain for he blurted out, "I fell in love and she rejected me."

Thankfully, they looked on him with empathy not pity and before either of them could offer condolences or advice, a knock sounded at the door.

Cavan bid the person to enter and surprisingly it was Bethane, Zia's grandmother. The woman was tall and slim with an ageless beauty and wisdom that a rare few attained. She was here to help Zia birth her babe, which wasn't due until the end of summer, a little over two months away.

"I bring a message from your mother," Bethane said with a smile. "Angus Bunnock has arrived."

"He wasn't due until tomorrow," Cavan said and looked to Artair then Lachlan. "We need to greet Bunnock. I am sure he will want to speak with you, Lachlan. Then later we shall talk."

Artair gave Lachlan's shoulder a squeeze before he stood and followed Cavan out the door. Lachlan stood slowly, placing his tankard on the nearby table, and when he turned to leave he came face-to-face with Bethane.

She took his hand and with a smile said, "People aren't always who we think they are, and yet upon a closer look you will see that she is the one you believed her to be."

He felt a bit dazed when Bethane released his hand, and she slipped her arm around his to walk out of the room, which he sensed he couldn't have done without her help.

She left him once they reached the great hall. He shook the dazed feeling from his head and joined his brothers as they greeted the burly man who had entered the room with two stout warriors on either side of him.

"Angus, you are most welcome to Caithness," Cavan said. "I only wish the circumstances were different."

"Aye, but I should have known Alyce's stubbornness would be her demise," Angus said with more annoyance than sorrow.

"It was illness not stubbornness that took your daughter," Lachlan said, feeling the need to defend the dead woman.

Cavan shot him a look that warned him to watch his tongue then turned to Angus. "My brother Lachlan—"

"The one who made the journey for me," Angus said and went to Lachlan and slapped him hard on the back. "I am grateful." He sniffed the air. "You have had a feast prepared, Cavan."

And with that they all settled on the benches to feast on the generous amounts of food on the tables. Angus sat with the Sinclare brothers, while his men didn't even sit before grabbing for the food on the other table.

Angus wiped his dirty hands on his already grimy shirt then scratched at his thick beard. "How is your mother? You know she's a good woman and deserves a good man to look after her."

The three brothers exchanged glares, and if Angus knew them well enough he would have recognized this as a warning to go no further.

"I'm right here, Angus Bunnock," Addie Sinclare said loudly as she emerged from the shadowy corner with a platter of sweet bread and handed it to Lachlan, who placed it on the table.

"You're still a beauty, Addie," the old man claimed.

And she certainly was. Fifty-three years had not robbed the woman of her natural beauty. She was tall and slim with red hair spattered with gray that she wore piled on her head, though several soft waves managed to fall around her face, and her brilliant green eyes continued to sparkle with the vibrancy of the young.

"But not foolish enough to shack up with the likes of you," she said boldly, though with a smile.

"You're breaking my heart, Addie," Angus declared. "You know I always loved you. I'd make you a good husband."

Addie's smile faded. "I had a good husband and there is no one who can replace him."

Lachlan smiled and saw that his brothers did as well. They were proud of their mother's courage and the love she still carried for their father, though he had passed over a year now.

"I was sorry to hear about Tavish," Angus said, offering his sincere condolence. "He was a good friend and a good man."

"Thank you," Addie said, "and I am sorry to hear about Alyce. She was a—"

"Shrew," Angus said. "No one wanted her."

"She was a beautiful woman just like her mother," Addie defended. "I often envied the skill she had in braiding her long blond hair and how she had taught Alyce to do the same with her identical hair. And Alyce had the most beautiful blue eyes. They reminded me of the sky on a gorgeous summer day."

Lachlan felt a punch to his gut. "Alyce had long blond hair and blue eyes?"

"That she did," Angus said. "And your mother's right, my daughter may have been a shrew, but she was a beautiful shrew."

"Was she tall?" Lachlan asked anxiously.

Angus nodded. "A good eight inches over five feet.

Lachlan near growled his annoyance. "A born leader?"

"Like her father," Angus boasted. "Could sit a horse as good or better than most men and could handle a sword like a man, though she had a mind of her own. She did and wanted things her way, always her way. Wouldn't listen to me, wouldn't obey me, fought me no matter what I said to her." He slammed his fist on the table. "And had the gall to fight with me in front of my own men and tell me I was a fool."

"You can be a fool, Angus," Addie said.

He grinned. "See, you saying it doesn't sound bad." He cringed and shook his head. "But Alyce screeched it." He mimicked her, his voice pitched high. "You're a fool, an old dumb fool if you think I'll marry a fool of your choosing. I'll die first." He shook his head again. "And she did, though it's strange. Alyce was always strong as an ox, never getting sick."

Lachlan felt a double punch to his gut. Could it be? Could Terese actually be Alyce Bunnock? It would explain so much. He didn't know whether to be angry or relieved. Had she been trying that last night they spent together to confront him with the truth when she asked if he would help Alyce? Or had she simply wanted her way as Alyce always wanted and played him for a fool?

Lachlan braced his arms on the table and looked at Angus. "Tell me more about your daughter."

Much later that night Cavan and Artair sat in the solar with Lachlan.

"Are you sure you want to do this?" Cavan asked.

"I must," Lachlan said.

"Not so," Artair disagreed. "It is for Angus to deal with."

"No," Lachlan argued. "It is mine to deal with and my decision is made. I ask that you both respect and accept it."

"As long as it is what you want," Cavan confirmed once again.

"It is for the best," Lachlan said, "besides we need to make contact with the mercenaries and see if they know anything about Ronan. How many men will I take?"

"Same as before, plus Bogg," Cavan said.

Lachlan nodded realizing his brother's plan. "Bogg was once a mercenary."

"He will find out what we need to know," Cavan said. "Are you sure you wish to leave so soon?"

"It took me two months to return home. I've been home for two weeks and it will take me two months to return again. I will miss the birth of your daughter." Lachlan shook his head. "You've got me believing that Zia and her grandmother know that she will have a daughter."

"It's been that way for generations, but Zia assures me our next child will be a boy," Artair said with a smile.

A gentle knock interrupted them and Addie entered. "I wish to speak with Lachlan alone."

Though the solar was strictly the laird's domain,

Lachlan knew Cavan would not deny his mother, and he and Artair left, closing the door behind them.

"I miss your smile," Addie said, taking the seat beside his and placing her hand on his arm. "Tell me this decision of yours will bring it back."

"Oh mother, what I'm about to do will bring me so very much happiness," he said and grinned from ear to ear.

Terese looked over the lush fields. The harvest would be plentiful this year. There would be enough to store for winter and more than enough to share with the mercenaries. In a couple of months, around November, meat would be cured and stored for winter and Septimus promised that his men would supply them with more if necessary.

Andrew and the other men were busy building more cottages, though Andrew worked most diligently on the one he and Megan planned to share. They spent all their time together and Terese had never seen Megan so happy. That they were in love was undeniable, and Terese was so pleased for her.

Piper and Evan were inseparable and already had a cottage of their own. Piper had asked that she be able to confide in him about the mercenaries for it was getting more and more difficult to hide the tracks from him. And she didn't want to continue to lie to him.

Terese had given her permission after they had all discussed it at a meeting, and though the women were concerned for Piper as to how Evan would react to the news, they needn't have worried. He was more excited about Piper showing him how she had concealed the tracks from him, then the news itself. The two were meant for each other.

Rowena was also in the throes of love, Talon having returned time and time again to see her after he had healed and returned to the mercenary camp. His stays at Everagis grew longer than his returns to camp until finally Septimus threw him out claiming that a love-sick pup was useless to him. Talon now spent his day building a cottage for him and Rowena.

Terese grew melancholy, thinking about Lachlan. Actually, there hadn't been a day that had gone by since his departure over four months ago that she hadn't thought about him. She missed him terribly, especially at night when she crawled into an empty bed. She ached for his arms to wrap around her and to feel his body planted against hers.

She shook the thoughts from her mind or else she would cry. She had been doing a lot of that lately, and it annoyed her.

Terese turned hearing someone approach, and smiled. It was May, or at least that's what the women had named her since she arrived in May in the throes of labor the last night Terese had spent with Lachlan. She'd had severe bruising around her neck and had been unable to speak. So far her voice had not returned. But she had given birth to a beautiful baby boy who everyone fussed over. Though only a few months old, the lad laughed and smiled and rarely cried.

Since May couldn't speak, the lad had yet to receive

a proper name so he was often called little darling, sweetie, sweet stuff or any other endearing name that came to mind.

May was good at using her hands to make herself understood, since she never attempted to write anything, Terese assumed that she didn't know how.

"Is the little one sleeping?" Terese asked.

May nodded and then proceeded to communicate with her hands.

Terese watched and then asked, "Are you telling me people approach?"

May nodded vigorously.

That's when Terese spotted Hester approaching her on a run, and a sense of dread washed over her.

"May's told you riders approach?" Hester asked anxiously.

"Riders?" Terese repeated the sense of dread growing. "Do you know who?"

Hester reached out for Terese's hand, but she pulled away. "No, don't tell me . . ." She shook her head. "It can't be. He told me he wouldn't return." She grabbed hold of Hester's arm. "Tell me it's not him."

"I'm sorry," Hester said. "Lachlan will be here any moment."

Chapter 21

⁂

Terēse's hand went to her stomach. She had been able to hide the slight roundness thus far, the only ones who knew that she carried Lachlan's babe were Rowena and Hester. It wasn't that she didn't trust Megan or Piper, she just didn't want to put them in the position of lying to the men they loved. And she supposed she had feared Andrew or Evan might decide to contact Lachlan. What did she intend to do when she couldn't hide her expanding stomach any longer? She had no idea, though now she had a bigger problem to worry about.

Why had Lachlan returned?

May had gone her way and Hester walked with Terese to the center of the village.

"You cannot notice the bulge to my stomach, can you," Terese whispered to Hester.

"The apron you wear does a good job of concealing the slight bump," Hester assured her.

"Lachlan cannot remain here long," Terese said with a tremble of worry.

Hester squeezed her hand. "I and the others will not

let anything happen to you. You saved each of us at one time or another and now we will do the same for you."

As if the women heard, they appeared one by one until Megan, Piper, and Rowena stood around Terese, waiting with her as the riders approached. Others in the village joined the women, all realizing friends approached and eager to greet them.

He was a bit of a distance away when she saw him riding tall and regal in his saddle. He didn't have to get any closer for her to see that he was handsomer than she remembered him. The summer sun had sparked his brown hair with touches of gold and he appeared broader in the shoulders and chest, or perhaps he appeared more formidable because she felt vulnerable.

She remembered the babe then nestled safely in her stomach and knew she would do whatever was necessary to keep him safe, even resurrect Alyce Bunnock.

Lachlan came to a stop a few feet away from her, Andrew and Evan being the first to greet him and his men. His eyes strayed to her now and again, and she sensed his return had something to do with her.

"He knows," she whispered for only the women to hear.

"Nonsense," Rowena said.

"How could he?" Piper asked.

"It doesn't matter," Megan said.

"She's right," Hester agreed. "It doesn't matter. Your home is here and here you'll stay."

While he approached them with a lazy gait, his dark eyes told a different story and Terese knew trouble brewed.

She decided to take control from the start. "You told me you wouldn't be returning. What brings you back?"

"No greeting, glad to see you, missed you?" Lachlan asked with a teasing glint.

"Speak your piece, Lachlan, for I have no time for your playful charm this day." Though truth be told it was difficult not to smile at his teasing charm, or get lost in his good looks, or want to desperately melt into his strong arms.

"You're sounding like a bit of a shrew there, *Terese*."

"Is it a *shrew* you're looking for?"

"So Angus Bunnock tells me and a beautiful one at that, long blond hair, blue eyes that match the summer sky." He glanced up at the sky and then back at Terese. "And Angus tells me that Alyce never got sick and was a born leader. Sound familiar?"

"We all helped bury Alyce," Megan said with a sharp tongue.

"I'm sure you did," Lachlan said. "You buried her so good that no one would question."

"There's nothing to question," Rowena insisted.

"I think differently," Lachlan said and looked directly at Terese, "and so does her father. He's sent me to confirm that it is his daughter who rests in the grave. Her height being a good indication if it is her, for Alyce stands at least eight inches over five feet."

"This is church land," Megan declared. "You have no right to disturb a grave."

"This is no longer church land," Lachlan informed the startled women. "And I have permission from the laird who now claims it."

Terese was no fool. She knew exactly who the new laird was. "Everagis now belongs to the clan Sinclare?"

"Is this true?" Andrew asked with a smile as he approached from behind Lachlan.

"It is." Lachlan nodded. "And Cavan has appointed you leader."

Terese stopped Hester with a hand to her arm when she stepped forward to protest.

"This is wonderful news," Andrew said excited, though tempered it once he saw how the women glared at him. He wisely remained behind Lachlan, his mouth clamped shut.

Lachlan looked to the sky. "There's enough light left to dig up the grave."

Terese pushed past the women to stand only inches from Lachlan. "You haven't come to dig up the grave. You have come to confront me."

"Tell me the truth," Lachlan said.

"You already know it," she challenged.

"I want to hear from you."

She knew somewhere deep in her heart that she wouldn't be able to maintain this ruse forever. Someday, somehow, someone would learn the truth and her charade would be revealed. She had taken a chance and for a while it had been good. Now she would face the consequences of her actions, and the only thing that mattered to her was the babe that she carried.

Terese tossed her chin up and with a spark of defiance said, "I am Alyce Bunnock."

Andrew reacted with a gasp and Evan, who approached, stopped dead in his tracks. The women, however, closed ranks around Alyce.

"Your father wants you home," Lachlan said.

"My father can go to hell," Alyce said sharply.

Lachlan grinned. "Perhaps he should, but presently he has the power to order you home."

"Why? To wed someone I don't want to wed?" she asked, her tongue remaining sharp, mostly in fear of what would happen when her father discovered her pregnant.

"What has been decided is in your best interest," Lachlan said.

Alyce laughed then assaulted him with a prickly tongue. "My interest is best decided by me."

"You know you will return with me, so why fight it?" Lachlan asked, much too confident to her way of thinking.

Megan stepped forward. "Alyce remains here with us."

"Afraid not," Lachlan said.

Megan looked to Andrew.

Andrew appeared perplexed and torn. "Perhaps it would be wiser for Alyce to remain here."

With a sharp snap of his head, Lachlan looked to Andrew. "Our mission was to retrieve Alyce Bunnock and return her home. Do you suggest that I ignore our laird's edict?"

Andrew looked helplessly to Megan.

Megan turned sorrowful eyes on Alyce.

"Enough," Alyce said. "I will not have you pitting people against each other."

"Then what will you do to settle this?" Lachlan asked.

Alyce felt her heart grow heavy. What choices did she have? She certainly couldn't wed another man when she carried Lachlan's child, and yet Lachlan did not want Alyce. So what were her choices? She didn't know.

"What does my father want of me?" she asked.

"For you to wed the man of his choice," Lachlan answered.

His words were cold, as if he did not care what happened to her and it broke her heart.

"Will you do it?" Lachlan asked.

"Why can't you tell her father that you couldn't find Alyce and let her live her life in peace here at Everagis?" Rowena asked and the other women nodded in agreement.

"Cavan will be sending more men here to establish Sinclare prominence and eventually someone would realize the truth," Lachlan said. "But that's beside the point, Angus Bunnock wants his daughter wed, and he will stop at nothing until he has seen it done."

"He's right," Alyce said. "My father rules with an iron fist and will have his way no matter what the cost to me."

"It's not fair," declared Piper.

"Fair or not, Alyce returns home with me," Lachlan said.

Hester stepped forward. "You will not take her from us. This is her home."

"Not anymore," Lachlan said coldly.

"She belongs here," Rowena said with a shake of a fist.

"Not any longer," Lachlan said.

The women gasped.

Even Andrew and Evan seemed alarmed.

"If you think I'll go willingly you are wrong," Alyce said. "You will need to restrain me the whole trip and then some."

"You are already restrained," Lachlan said.

"What do you mean?" Alyce asked, not liking the sound of it.

"You have been wed by proxy to a man of your father's choosing."

The women cried out while Alyce felt her whole body go numb. While she wanted to deny it, she knew all too well that her father had the power and privilege to do as he pleased and so he could rightfully wed her to whomever he chose.

Nausea gnawed at her and her knees grew weak, but she revealed none of her worries, instead she remained strong and in command.

"So you, like others, do my father's bidding," Alyce said caustically.

"I do no man's bidding," Lachlan said with a defined anger in his dark eyes.

"Yet you are here to take me back."

"I am."

"And why is that?" she asked.

"Simple. I have come to take my wife home."

Chapter 22

L achlan knew she heard him clearly, though undoubtedly his words took time to settle in and all the while she shook her head. He hadn't meant to shock her, or perhaps he did. He was still angry with her, not for sending him home, but for not trusting him enough to confide the truth.

She was more beautiful than he remembered and somehow more vibrant. There was a color, a glow to her that he hadn't recalled, or perhaps he was more deeply in love with her than he remembered. Whatever it was, he was glad to be here and relieved to know she would be returning home with him.

"We should speak of this in private," he said, wanting to discuss so much more with her.

"Why?" Alyce challenged. "You've just said everything. I'm your property now."

He expected her to lash out at him, though he hadn't expected it to feel like a punch in the gut. If she truly knew him, she would know that she was anything but his *property*.

Time, however, would have her understanding that,

but time was a slim defense to claim against the hurt he saw in her eyes.

Keeping patience in tow, he said, "We need to talk."

"So you can give me orders?" she declared defiantly.

He had to smile, for he could see that Alyce had a stinging tongue, but in all honesty it was in her own defense. So how could he fault her for it?

"So we can speak reasonably," he countered.

Alyce laughed caustically. "Reasonably you say when you know full well I wanted no part of marriage."

"Give me—"

"The same chance you gave me?" she questioned sharply.

He tried to maintain his patience, but she was sorely tearing it to pieces. "This may be a—"

"Disaster for sure," she claimed.

He was beginning to wonder the same, but then he looked past the storm brewing in her blue eyes and once again saw her heartache, and knew he was right. She loved him and somehow, some way he was going to make her see just how much he loved her.

"Disaster or not, we belong to each other," he said.

For an instant he heard the catch in her breath and caught the hope in her eyes before she challenged, "You mean *I* belong to you."

"No less than *I* belong to you."

"You think me a fool?" she asked with a hint of uncertainty.

"Do you wish to be?" he asked, hoping she'd see the stark truth of his query.

"I will not go with you," she said defensively and the women tightened the circle around her.

He expected her to protest and knew there was but one response. "You have no choice. You are my wife."

"And must follow your orders," she said as if she had just proven her argument.

"Again I ask that we talk in private," Lachlan suggested.

"No," Alyce said bluntly. "There is nothing more to be said between us."

"I disagree," he protested strongly.

"It matters not to me. I have nothing more to say." With that she turned and walked away, the women holding fast to where they stood so that Lachlan could not penetrate their protective shield.

He watched her disappear into the common shelter and shook his head. This was going to prove much more difficult than he had anticipated, but then he wasn't as familiar with Alyce as he had been with Terese.

He shook his head even harder and silently berated his own foolishness. There was no Terese; there was only Alyce. The woman who was finally allowed to emerge from her shell and be who she truly was, the woman he knew as Terese.

How did he get her to recognize herself and accept her true nature? How did he make her understand that she was the woman he loved, and her name was simply that, a name?

Time and patience were his only adversaries in this skirmish and he had an abundance of both. In time she would see the truth: that he loved her beyond reason and that was all that truly mattered.

Alyce collapsed in the chair at the table as soon as she entered the common room. She had feared her trembling legs would betray her long before that and was surprised and relieved to have kept a steady gait in spite of worries.

She rested her head in her hands, her elbows braced on the edge of the table. She could not, or perhaps she did not want to believe that she had been wed against her will. She had often wondered why she fought what she knew was her duty and the only answer that ever surfaced was that she knew that was not her destiny.

Her destiny was to live and love as she chose.

But isn't that what she had gotten, the man of her choice? The man she loved. The man she missed? The man she wanted to spend the rest of her life with? The man whose child nestled safely in her stomach? The man who claimed to love her?

But if he did love her then he knew her and if he truly knew her, he would not have forced this marriage on her. He would have requested she wed him and left the choice to her.

The door creaked open and she knew the women would enter one by one and offer their support, but it would do little good. She was wed and would now have to obey her husband. The realization hit her hard and tears gathered in her eyes. She wiped angrily at them, annoyed that she grew teary-eyed much too easily lately. She had seldom shed tears; to her it was a waste of time, action proved much more satisfying. But what action could she take now; she was stuck.

She looked up, glad to be able to talk with the women who were like sisters to her and was shocked to see Lachlan standing there.

"I don't want to speak with you now," she said firmly, then stood and turned her back on him. She braced her hand on the rough-hewn mantel to help keep her legs steady. Damn, but she continued to feel weak-kneed around him and that annoyed her all the more.

"I understand why you lied."

She rounded on him with wide glaring eyes that glistened with unshed tears. "You understand and then wed me without my permission?"

"I thought—"

"No," she said shaking her head and her hand at him. "No, you didn't think, not for one minute."

Lachlan scratched his head and smiled. "Actually, I thought it was quite chivalrous of me."

"So you wed me out of sympathy?"

He laughed. "You truly think that?"

"Why else would you wed me?"

He shrugged, smiled, and crossed his arms over his chest. "I don't know, maybe because I love you?"

Why did he have to tempt with his charming smile? And why did his muscled chest invite, reminding her of the many times she had pillowed her head on it morning and night? She could almost hear the strong beat of his heart and the wildness of it after they had made love. Damn, damn, damn him for reminding her how much she missed and loved him, and she felt all the more unreasonable. "If you truly loved me you would have never wed me."

He shook his head. "That makes no sense."

"It makes perfect sense," she argued. "You would have returned here and asked me to wed you."

"And chance you denying me?"

"Aha," she accused, shaking a finger in his face.

He grinned. "I knew you'd be stubborn and prickly about it."

"And you wed me knowing it would irritate me?" she asked exasperated, especially with his smile. It was the smile she loved that always managed to charm and tantalize.

"Someone had to be sensible."

"Now I'm not sensible?" She threw her hands up in the air.

"Not when it comes to love," he confirmed with a chuckle.

"You think you have this all under control, don't you."

"Yes."

"Well, you don't," she said. "And do you know why?"

"No, but I have a feeling you're going to make it clear."

She walked over to him and poked him in the chest. "It's simple. You, my dear Lachlan, have yet to deal with *Alyce Bunnock*."

He grabbed hold of her wrist and swung her around so that her back was pressed to his chest and he wrapped his arms around her, locking her against him, and whispered in her ear, "I look forward to it, *dear wife*."

"You are not my husband," she declared more weakly than she intended, his familiar scent tinged with earth and pine teasing her nostrils and senses.

"I have the papers to prove it."

"They mean nothing to me," she said sadly, for they didn't. A proxy had signed where her signature should rest.

"In time—"

"Time will matter not," she said, her sadness remaining, but her spark returning.

"Give us a chance," he said and nuzzled her neck.

"Why should I?" she demanded.

"Because I love you and I believe you feel the same about me."

She attempted to deny it and found herself unable to speak. She struggled with the truth, for she did love him, but he had hurt her by marrying her. He had been well aware why Alyce had been sent away, and why she had gone to the extreme and faked her death.

She closed her eyes against the torment. If she simply accepted Lachlan as her husband all would be well, after all she did love him. Why then did she feel so very betrayed by his actions?

He should have allowed her the choice. She had sent him away claiming she didn't love him and as soon as he had discovered her true identity, he had wisely surmised the reason for her action.

With that assumption, he wed her without thought

to how hard she had fought to make that choice herself. So then how could he claim to truly love her?

"I need to consider this," she said and eased out of his arms, he reluctantly releasing her.

"That's all I ask," he said with a smile.

"Is it?"

His smile remained, though he tensed. "What do you mean?"

"You returned to Everagis, declaring it Sinclare land, making Andrew, in a sense, the laird here and with expectations of me returning home with you. You changed my life completely without consulting me, and then you tell me you love me."

Lachlan rubbed the back of his neck. "My only excuse is that love has made a witless fool of me."

"That excuse will not do, for I know you are no witless fool, love or not."

A rap on the door before it swung open interrupted Lachlan's response.

"I need to speak with you," Piper said and Alyce knew something was amiss for Piper would not have disturbed them otherwise.

"Please excuse us," she said to Lachlan and waited with a defiant glare for him to refuse and claim that as her husband he had a right to remain.

However, Lachlan bowed respectfully and walked out shutting the door firmly behind him.

A few moments after the latch clicked shut Piper spoke, though kept her tone low. "I've discovered that Lachlan has brought a man named Bogg with him and that his orders are to penetrate the mercenary camp and find what news he can of Lachlan's brother."

"I need to share this news with Septimus and alert him to the changes here at Everagis."

"You'll be leaving us, won't you?" Piper said teary-eyed.

"I don't see what other choice I have. Lachlan is my husband, though I will attempt to delay my departure as long as I possibly can."

Piper smiled. "Good, for I do not want to see you go. None of us do."

Alyce couldn't trust herself to speak of leaving Everagis and the women who had become her family any longer, for she already felt the tears building in her eyes and was annoyed.

"Make the arrangements for us to meet Septimus late tonight when all are asleep."

Piper turned to leave.

"Don't let Evan know."

Piper nodded and left.

Alyce plopped down at the table again, her feelings mixed and her thoughts confused. Had she been handed a gift only to refuse it? Was she being stubborn and shrewish?

She sighed and shook her head, receiving no clear answers.

There were many reasons why she should accept the gift presented to her and be grateful, but there was one that haunted her.

Lachlan had fallen in love with Terese. She had to know if he could love Alyce Bunnock.

Chapter 23

Alyce was tired, her legs ached and her body sweaty. With Lachlan at Everagis, she and Piper couldn't take the chance of meeting Septimus at the usual meeting place. Precaution was definitely called for and so she and Piper had walked a distance to meet with him, and then of course there was the return trip.

They were near to home and while she preferred bed and sleep, there was one thing more she ached for . . . a dip in the river. She needed to wash the sweat from her, let the cool water cleanse every inch of her. If she were lucky perhaps it would even wash away her worries.

Piper went on ahead with a promise to return with fresh garments for her. Alyce stripped out of her clothes, grateful for the waning moon that let the night keep much of its darkness. She felt shielded by the night shadows and without concern eased into the river plunging beneath and surfacing with a contented sigh.

She didn't want to think on anything. She simply

wanted the river to work magic and wash her clean of everything. However, her mind refused to cooperate, and she thought about her meeting with Septimus. He was not happy with her news, but her suggestion of how to handle the matter had brought a smile to his handsome face.

It would be beneficial for all if Septimus allowed Bogg access to the camp and then feed him only that information his leader wanted the Sinclares to know.

As usual Septimus praised her intelligence and offered to wed her, claiming she was one of a kind. She of course declined his jest, but on occasion wondered over Septimus. Who truly was he? He was much too refined and his speech too articulate to be a mercenary. Was he like her, hiding from someone?

She would probably never know, for she would meet with him no longer. Piper and Hester would see to that now.

Stop! She silently warned herself. What good was it to think on all this now? She would get no sleep tonight if she continued to wallow in her worry. She let the cool, refreshing water soak her flesh, and she rested her hand to her stomach.

There was just a slight bulge, and she marveled at the thought that Lachlan's child grew inside her. It truly was a miracle and one she had not expected to ever experience. Not for a moment did she regret that she carried his child. From the first day she had realized it, she had been filled with joy. How lucky she was that she would always have a part of Lachlan with her. He couldn't have given her a greater gift.

How he would react to the news, she didn't know and she didn't plan on telling him just yet. There were other things to consider first.

She startled at a sound not familiar to the night then realized it must be Piper returning; and as she rose up in the river wringing her hair, she saw the shadow that approached was much too large to be Piper.

Alyce stopped waist high in the river. "Who goes there?"

"Your husband."

Alyce swore beneath her breath and added several more silent oaths to it when she finally caught full sight of him at the river's edge. He wore his plaid and his sandals and no more. His chest was bare, his muscles taut, his skin smooth, though she knew exactly where scars had marred his flesh, for she had caressed every-one of them and forced him to relate the tales behind them. Several had been earned through brotherly adventures and skirmishes when he had been young. Lachlan had chuckled with pride when he had told her, and she envied him once again his loving family.

Her family now.

The thought concerned her. Would they like her or think her a shrew as her family thought of her?

"Alyce."

She startled once again still not accustomed to him referring to her by her given name, but spying the bundle in his hand meant he had to have spoken with Piper. And she didn't know what excuse Piper had given Lachlan for their nightly escapade.

She was about to walk out of the river but instead

froze, worried that he would notice the slight round of her stomach.

"Leave my clothes and turn around," she demanded sharply.

He laughed. "I don't think so."

She slapped her arms across her chest covering her breasts. "I do not feel comfortable naked in front of you."

"Why? What has changed?"

"Everything," she said curtly.

"I disagree. You're simply being obstinate."

"And it will do you good to get used to that," she said then ordered: "Put the bundle on the ground and turn around."

"No," he said firmly. "We are husband and wife. We have no secrets, which makes me ask, where were you tonight?"

"Piper must have told you," she said, not wanting to be caught in a lie.

"You're shivering," he said, avoiding her remark and waved her out. "You'll catch your death. Come out of there now."

"Put my clothes down and turn around," she insisted.

"Do as I say," he ordered.

"You dare dictate to me?" she challenged.

"I dare to love you," he said and dropped the bundle to the ground, quickly shed his plaid and sandals, and stepped into the river.

She backed away, slipped on a rock, and was about to fall beneath the water when his hand reached out and caught her. He had her in his arms instantly, her body pressed firmly against his.

She felt not only her own desire surge between her legs but also his. And damn if she didn't want him to bury himself deep inside her and make her forget, if only for a while. However, she fought against surrendering, fought her own rising passion.

"We stand naked in each other's arms and that is the way it will always be . . . we hide nothing from each other; we trust and we love and then nothing can ever come between us."

How lovely to think that could be so, but there were things between them; her secrets and his lone decision.

She felt the sudden change in him just before he took a step away from her, though his one hand took firm hold of her wrist. She knew then that he had felt the bulge in her stomach and wasn't surprised when his hand moved gently over it.

"Our child," he said with such gentle reverence that she almost fell into his arms in tears.

She merely nodded, unable to take her eyes from his; they were filled with such joy and love.

"Why didn't you tell me?" He shook his head. "Did you ever intend to tell me?" He shook his head again. "Tell me now. Tell me what you intended to do."

She shivered.

"Damn," he muttered and scooped her up and carried her out of the river.

He took the towel her clothes were wrapped in and

briskly dried her off, though was ever so gentle when he came to her stomach and she smiled inwardly. He didn't get dressed himself until he saw that she was fully clothed and had stopped shivering, only then did he slip his plaid and sandals on.

She thought he would demand an answer to his query then, but instead after wrapping her soiled clothes in the towel he took her hand and walked her through the woods. She was surprised that he knew where he went and in the dark, but soon they were both walking through the door of his cottage.

Once the door shut he turned to her. "Tell me now."

"I don't know," she answered honestly. "I had no plans. I didn't know what I would do."

"Did you once think of telling me?"

She smiled though it faded quickly enough. "I dreamt of telling you, but it was no more than that . . . a dream."

"Didn't you think of me?" he asked with a thump to his chest. "How I would feel? What I would want?"

"Did you think of me when you made the decision to wed me without asking?" she accused.

"That's different."

She laughed. "It's always different when it comes to a man's opinion."

He shocked her when after a pause he said, "I'm sorry. You must have worried over what you would do."

She was too stunned to reply. She had expected him

to rant at her, perhaps even shake his fist, but never had she thought he would apologize.

He smiled then, though not that charming grin he so often wore and that could entice. No, this smile made him look like a young lad overjoyed with a gift he had just received.

"I'm to be a father," he said proudly. "This is wonderful. We are wed and we are to have a child."

She walked away from him so that the table was between them. "This changes nothing."

Now there was that famous charming smile of his. "Come now, Alyce," he coaxed with a swagger as he rounded the table. "All has turned out well."

With his approach, she inched away from him. "All has turned out in your favor."

"You can't tell me you don't love me. I know I'm not wrong about that," he insisted.

"I do love you; I will not deny it."

"Then why be obstinate about it?" he asked and eased closer to her.

"Obstinate?" she repeated, stepping further away from him and noticing that they had almost made a complete circle around the table. "I'm being obstinate when you show up—"

"Wait," he interrupted. "Let's phrase it correctly . . . when the man who loves you and who you love shows up."

"That's even better," she said. "The man I love and who loves me shows up, tells me we're wed and that I will be returning home with him, never once considering that I do not wish to leave *my* home."

"Truthfully, *home* is where we both are."

"Then you are home," she said with a broad smile and a wide sweep of her arms.

"For the moment," he agreed, "but I have obligations to my family and clan. And don't tell me you don't understand that."

She did all too much, for this marriage to Lachlan settled her obligation to her father and clan. "My father must be delighted with our match."

"He was very happy when I requested to marry you and accepted my offer immediately, and just as fast made the arrangements."

"Probably worried you'd change your mind," she said, knowing her father probably beamed with pleasure. After all, their union brought together two powerful clans.

"I assured him I wouldn't," he said. "I told him that I intended to keep you forever."

"He must have gotten a good laugh from that."

"I would never let him insult you or our love like that," he said seriously.

She sighed heavily. "Why did I have to fall in love with you?"

"Because I'm irresistible?"

She laughed softly and then yawned. "I'm too tired to argue anymore tonight."

"We haven't argued; we've discussed," he said and wandered over to her, slipping his arms around her. "You need sleep. You'll be busy tomorrow."

"No more than usual."

He caressed her back. "With only two days before we leave I thought you'd have much to do."

She was startled out of her sleepiness and quickly stepped out of his arms. "What do you mean two days before we leave?"

"Cavan needs me to return immediately and my family is eager to meet you, so we leave for home in two days."

She spoke with a sharp and direct tongue. "You may be leaving in two days, but I'm not." She turned to leave, but he grabbed her arm. She glared at him with such a fiery warning that he released her hand as if he'd been burnt and she stormed out of the cottage.

Chapter 24

Lachlan knew this wouldn't be easy, but in the last two days he had gotten a taste of why Alyce Bunnock had been labeled a shrew. She snapped and barked at him and his men and no attempt he made to assuage the situation helped.

She had made every excuse not to spend a moment alone with him. All her time had been spent with the women she had, out of necessity, forged a sisterhood with, which made this parting all the more difficult.

He had maintained his patience with her, reminding himself that this was not an easy thing he asked of her. It would take time for her to adjust, and he was confident that once they had time alone together, and she became aware that being wed to him meant that she would retain the freedom she so strongly desired, she would be content.

Until then . . . he jokingly reminded himself not to strangle her.

They would be leaving in a couple of hours and Lachlan knew this would be the most difficult time for her and the other women. He wished there was something he could do to ease the pain of their parting, but he knew there wasn't.

Lachlan kept out of her way, seeing to last minute details and saying his own good-byes to Andrew and Evan.

"She's going to be missed," Andrew said, casting a quick glance to where Alyce stood with the other women. "She truly is a strong woman who leads with confidence and wisdom."

Evan nodded. "Piper insists that Everagis won't be the same without her."

"Show them that because of Alyce's leadership Everagis has grown and will continue to thrive," Lachlan said. "Make them see they do this in her honor."

Andrew smiled. "The people would be pleased to know that." His smile disappeared. "But what of you?"

Lachlan grinned. "Have you ever seen me incapable of handling a woman?"

"That's true," Evan said.

"Maybe so," Andrew admitted, "but you've never loved a woman the way you love Alyce."

"That's true too," Evan said.

Lachlan patted each of them on the back and maintained his grin. "Faith, me lads, faith."

Andrew's smile returned. "You're going to need plenty of it."

Alyce kept a brisk and confident tone with her good-byes, though tears pooled in her eyes. She refused to shed them, for if she did, they would all be crying like fools and she didn't want the women to remember her that way.

"You'll all do well, and I will return to visit," Alyce assured them.

"Promise?" Megan asked, fighting her own tears.

"You have my word on it," Alyce said and saw that Lachlan approached. The time was here; she truly was leaving her home and family.

"He comes for you," Hester said sadly.

Alyce gave the slim woman an exuberant hug and whispered in her ear, "You must be the big sister now. Watch over them as I would and love them all as I do."

"I will and thank you, thank you so very much for all you have done for me and the others."

Alyce turned to the pint-sized Piper next and with a quick hug and a kiss to her cheek, she said, "You are an amazing wonder in the woods. I would never have survived them without you. Love and be happy with Evan, you deserve it."

Piper was so choked with tears that she could only nod her head.

It was Rowena's turn and the two hugged and smiled, and Rowena whispered, "You take care of yourself and the babe."

"And you have a good life with Talon," Alyce said and turned to Megan.

Megan threw herself into Alyce's arms and cried. "I will miss you. You have been so good to me. You gave me my life back."

"You took your life back," Alyce said and looked around at the women. "We did well. We faced adversity together and grew stronger. We built a home with hard work and plenty of love and welcomed with open arms those who needed the same. Continue the good we have done and Everagis will continue to prosper along with all of you. And know that you all will remain in my heart."

She turned quickly and walked away, her heart feeling as if it were breaking in pieces and didn't stop when she reached Lachlan, she walked past him to the waiting horses and, without anyone's help, mounted the mare Lachlan had ready for her and rode off without looking back.

Lachlan caught up with her a few moments later, which she had no doubt he would. She waited for him to chastise her, but he didn't. He simply brought his horse alongside hers and rode in silence beside her.

His men caught up with them, a few moving in front to take the lead and the others trailing behind.

The ache still bit at her heart, though she knew it would fade. Her heart had pained her when her father had sent her away. She had felt betrayed, but eventually she healed. Did she really have any choice in the matter? She could either make the most of what life dealt her or surrender to what? Misery? Anger?

No, she had refused to do that. She had forged a new life with new people and now it seemed that she was about to do that again. And once again against her will. Would she ever truly be able to decide her own fate?

But if she were honest, hadn't she decided her fate when she had fallen in love with Lachlan?

"If you grow tired, let me know and we will stop and rest," Lachlan said.

She turned and stared at him for a moment before turning away from him to look straight ahead. There was love there in his eyes for her. It shined like a radiant beacon that reached out to her with tender concern and empathy and oddly it helped ease some of the ache from her heart.

"I am sorry I have caused you such pain," he said.

His sincere concern continued to help heal her hurt, and she felt a twinge of guilt for the way she had been treating him, though not enough to forgive him.

"In time—"

She didn't let him finish. "I do not wish to speak of it."

"It would be better if we discussed it."

"I don't wish to discuss it."

He opened his mouth and she interrupted him again.

"If you intend to tell me I'm being obstinate, you're wasting your time."

He smiled and she wanted to smack it off his face, for he had used it as a weapon against her these last two days. No matter what she had said or done; he had smiled. But then why wouldn't he; he knew he would have his way.

"I know and you know that you're obstinate. There's no need to remind you."

"Then what did you intend to say?" she asked curious.

"Anything that would allow for a conversation without argument."

"I told you I didn't want to talk," she reminded him.

"We always talked," he reminded in turn. "I often wondered how we found so much to talk about. We never lacked for conversation unless of course we were making love."

She didn't fight or prevent her smile. He was right. They had talked endlessly and had never grown bored with each other. Truth be told, she missed that time with him.

"I've missed talking with you," he admitted.

While she wouldn't admit the same, she said, "We had good talks."

"We could have them again."

She threw his own words back at him, though felt a shrew for doing so. "In time."

He simply changed the subject. "How are you feeling?"

"Fine," she answered curtly and turned her attention to the road ahead.

"The babe hasn't made you ill? Cavan's wife Honora suffered some illness when she carried the twins, though Zia, Artair's wife, suffered not a day and will probably have delivered the babe before we reach home."

"Please tell me we will not be living with your family in the keep," she said.

He gave a low laugh. "I knew that might be a problem so I left orders for a sizeable cottage to be made ready for us."

"Close to the keep?" she asked.

"No, a distance."

"By woods?"

"We live surrounded by moors," Lachlan said.

"Desolate land," she claimed with a shiver.

"Beautiful land, if you look at it differently."

"I prefer the woods."

"There's a small cropping of woods not far from the keep, though most stay clear of it, claiming it's enchanted; Honora being the exception. She frequently visits there. I'm sure she'll take you there if you wish."

"This is all so easy for you," she said suddenly angry. "You return to a loving family to live as you choose and you expect me to do the same. How rude of you!"

She snapped the reins to ride past him, but he grabbed hold of them and forced her mare to hold firm.

"You will remain beside me," he ordered sternly. "You can snap at me and disagree with me, but when I give an order regarding your safety you will obey."

She sneered. "I have and will continue to look after myself."

"That is no longer necessary," he said sharply. "That is a husband's responsibility."

"I didn't ask for a husband."

"Well, you have one."

"Not by my doing," she reminded.

"That makes no difference. You're stuck with me."

"We're stuck with each other.

Lachlan shook his head. "Not true. I chose to wed you. No one forced you on me. I didn't even know you carried my child at the time, so that wasn't a consideration. I wed you because I love you, therefore, I am not stuck with you."

Her heartache had taken on a different pain and she voiced it. "I wish I had the same right to choose."

"I believe love made the choice for both of us."

"I don't doubt you love me, but I wish you would understand me," she said.

"I think I understand you better than you realize."

She disagreed. "I don't believe so."

"Then perhaps it is you who needs to understand me."

A shout from one of his men had him riding off, leaving her to ponder his remark. She believed she understood him. Was it possible she didn't? Was she missing something?

She had two full months before they reached his home, perhaps there would be epiphanies along the way.

The disagreeable weather made for a miserable journey. Rain haunted them as well as constant gray skies. They were caught in more than one downpour and had to seek what shelter they could.

Alyce spent much of the journey alone since Lachlan was constantly busy seeing to all the problems caused by the weather. The small cart that carried essentials got stuck in mud more often than not and some of the horses had to be directed around thick mud holes. By evening when camp was finally settled everyone except those on watch slept.

It was a grueling journey and one Alyce couldn't wait to see end. She was tired and irritable and at times angry and not even sure at what. One day it was her father her anger settled on, then another time it was Lachlan and sometimes she was angry with herself. She berated herself for refusing to accept her marriage to Lachlan and be happy, after all she loved him. What more did she want?

As selfish or shrewish as it might sound, she wanted her life, her way. Everagis had given her a taste of freedom and she loved it. It hadn't only been difficult and painful to say farewell to the women, it had been heartbreaking to leave Everagis. She felt as though she had left a part of herself there, a part she'd never get back again.

Her musings were interrupted by shouts and she halted her mare. It was raining hard, the ground turning muddier and her cloak soaked through. She saw the men dismount and begin to lead their horses, which meant a mud hole ahead. She didn't wait for help, though she knew Lachlan expected her to. It would only hold them up some more and she wanted this journey to end as fast as possible.

She dismounted and her feet sunk into the thick mud. She shook her head and took the reins to lead her horse.

"Slow and steady, girl," she said and with some difficulty they moved along.

They were doing fine when suddenly she heard a shout from behind her. She turned to see that one of the men had lost control of his horse, the animal's one hoof having become stuck in the mud. She was frantically trying to free herself, but she only managed to bury herself more. The man's angry shouts didn't help and were beginning to upset the other horses around him.

Alyce couldn't stand watching the man's stupidity and after consoling her horse and tethering her to a branch; she went to take control of the dangerous situation.

"Stop shouting," she ordered the man.

"Get away from here," he yelled and waved her away, which frightened the already frightened horse more. "Go! I know how to handle this idiot animal."

Alyce booted the man in the leg, grabbing the reins from his hands as he went tumbling into the mud. "You're the only idiot animal around here."

He wiped the mud from his face, his eyes flashing wide and he made ready to get up.

Alyce made a tight fist and shook it in his face. "Try it. Just try it and I'll knock what teeth you have left out."

She didn't wait to see what he would do; she turned to help the horse. First, she calmed the mare with a soft voice, so the mare would stop fighting and digging herself in deeper. Then she gently tugged on the reins and the horse slowly inch by inch began easing herself out of the mud.

Alyce was familiar enough with animals to know that if the horse wasn't free soon, she would panic again and sink even deeper. She needed a good shove to help her take that last step.

She continued talking to the mare while bracing her hands on her chest. She pushed easy at first and then she urged the horse to backup putting all her weight into pushing against her.

"You can do it," she encouraged and urged, "Go. Go. Go." And she shoved hard against the mare's chest and with one sudden step the horse was out, and Alyce fell facedown in the mud.

Chapter 25

Lachlan couldn't believe his eyes and wiped the rain from his face twice to make certain it wasn't an apparition he witnessed. His pregnant wife was attempting to free a horse, and not even her horse, from the mud when she suddenly fell forward.

He hurried as fast as he could, though the thick mud slowed down his steps. He cursed and muttered as he watched her face disappear into the muck. By the time he reached her she was struggling to get up.

Grabbing her under the arms, he yanked her up and turned her around. He was struck silent by her laughter and the brilliance of her wide eyes that resembled bright moons in a pitch black sky.

"Did you see that? Did you see what happened?" she said through her laughter.

"I certainly did," he snapped. "And it was a foolish thing to do. You could have been hurt."

Her laughter dwindled. "But I wasn't, and the horse is free and I—" She poked his chest with a muddy finger. "Got to play in the mud."

"You fell in the mud," he corrected.

"It's the way you perceive it," she argued with laughter. "Besides I knew perfectly well what I was doing unlike your idiot warrior who caused the problem."

"It wasn't your concern," Lachlan said and almost smiled, for while she was covered in mud there was an appeal to her that Lachlan had a hard time ignoring. Perhaps it was her tenacious ability to find humor and courage in adversity.

"Don't even think of restricting me from helping a poor animal in distress," she said, mud and rainwater flying off her hand as she shook a finger at him. "Your dictate will fall on deaf ears." She hefted up her mud-soaked, rain-drenched cloak and skirt and headed to her horse.

Lachlan followed on her heels. "My concern is for you and the babe."

Alyce didn't answer until she reached her horse and had the reins in her hand. "Don't for once think that I would do anything to harm our child. He is nestled safe inside me and I will keep him that way. I will always protect him, with my life if necessary."

"By falling in the mud?" he accused.

"Mud provides a soft, protective cushion." She shook her head. "Don't you think I considered that before I took action? How can you claim to love me when you don't truly know me?"

"I could claim the same, since you knew full well your actions would upset me."

"Then perhaps neither of us knows each other."

"Then it's about time we learned," he said and took hold of her waist to swing her up on her mare. "Now stay there until we make camp."

He didn't wait to hear her protest. He marched off, though his steps were anything but firm and confident. The mud made him appear the complete opposite and he could almost hear her snicker.

How did he allow her her freedom, when it cost him his sanity? She was a strong, courageous and capable woman, but she was also his wife. While he didn't wish to limit her, he also didn't wish to live with a constant pit of worry in his stomach.

There was no telling what she would do. She was accustomed to being answerable to no one and being in charge. How could he expect her to change her ways in only a few weeks? Angus Bunnock had repeatedly warned him, after the marriage papers had been signed and sealed, that his daughter was much like him, a leader. Angus had wished Alyce had been born a male, for he confided to Lachlan that she would make a better laird than he had. And while Angus had grown angry with his daughter for failing to accept the men he had offered in marriage, he understood why she refused every one of them. But it was his duty to see her wed, while he would have much rather seen her lead.

Lachlan wiped the rain from his face in frustration. This return trip home was not going at all as he had planned. He had thought for sure they would have plenty of time to talk and settle some if not all the problems between them. It didn't look as if that was going to happen.

They would reach home in a couple of weeks and if the weather continued as it had, it would leave them no time to spend together. There were no answers to his dilemma. It would be slow and steady steps for them both and in time . . .

He shook his head. She had warned that time would change nothing but then . . .

He smiled. Alyce truly didn't know how charmingly persistent he could be.

They arrived at the Sinclare keep a tired, frustrated, rain-soaked troop all relieved and grateful to be home; all but one.

Rain followed them right to the front door of the keep, it serving only to help Alyce find fault with her new home. She didn't care for the desolate moors that surrounded the village and tall keep that blended in color with the gray skies. From what she could see of the village, it looked prosperous and well tended, and she was surprised by the flurry of villagers, all with generous smiles, who braved the torrential rain to welcome the warriors home.

She was dismounting when Lachlan's hands closed around her waist and helped her off her mare.

"Let me have the pleasure of—"

"Playing the gentlemen?" Alyce finished.

Lachlan pressed his cheek to hers and whispered, "No, just the opposite. I want the pleasure of touching you."

His seductive whisper sent a shiver racing through her, especially since his remark conjured up visions of his hands intimately roaming her body.

"Tonight, we'll finally have time alone," he murmured and placed his hand in the lower curve of her back to guide her up the steps to the keep.

She got angry at her traitorous body for responding to his suggestive words and simple yet intimate touch and she lashed out at him. "I'm hungry, dirty, and tired."

"I'll feed you, wash you, and with gentle touches lull you to sleep," he whispered.

She attempted to protest, though why she couldn't say, since his offer was excitingly tempting, but he was quicker.

"You can berate me later, preferably while I'm washing you," he teased with a smile. "Right now, prepare to meet my family."

He pushed open the heavy wooden door and they entered the great hall. There was a bustle of activity and it took a moment for them to be noticed. Once they did, the women rushed to them.

"Thank God you're home," a tall, slim woman cried out.

Alyce could see the resemblance to Lachlan and knew the woman had to be his mother.

"We were worried with the weather being so bad," a petite beauty toting a lad not yet a full year in her arms acknowledged.

"I told them you would be fine," a red-haired beauty with startling green eyes and a babe swathed in a blanket cradled in her arms commented.

"You've had the babe, Zia," Lachlan said, thrilled, and peeked at the sleeping child.

"I named her Blythe, after my mother," Zia said proudly.

A man that Alyce reluctantly admitted to herself was handsomer than Lachlan, and definitely his brother, slipped his arm around Zia.

"Your wife looks exhausted. Introduce us so she can sit, rest, and eat."

"My brother Artair, the only sensible one among us," Lachlan said, both men reaching out to lock hands.

"Good to have you home," Artair said and turned to Alyce. "Welcome to the family, Alyce."

Lachlan began introducing each one. His mother Addie, Cavan's wife Honora, and Tavish, the twin named after Lachlan's father. Zia and Artair and a yapping Champion, a loveable dog who came bouncing in the room from what Addie explained was his favorite haunt, the kitchen.

"You need food, a bath, and rest, in that order," Addie said and took her hand.

Addie had Alyce seated at the table before the hearth with food in front of her before she could say a thing, and she didn't hesitate in assuaging her hunger. Besides, she would rather her mouth be full, since she wasn't in the mood to converse with Lachlan's family.

They were his family, not hers, and seeing them content and happy only made her miss *her* family more.

"We are so pleased to have you as part of our family,

Alyce," Addie said, refilling her tankard. "We couldn't wait for Lachlan to bring you home."

"This isn't my home," Alyce said bluntly.

The table turned silent.

"I do my duty as my father wishes," Alyce explained.

"That is good. You will be an obedient wife to my brother," said the strong and commanding voice.

Alyce turned expecting to face Cavan, laird of the clan Sinclare, and ready to speak her mind. However, the impressive height and width of him coupled with the way he tenderly cradled his sleeping son in his arms stunned her silent.

Honora rose to take the child from him and placed him in the cradle beside his sleeping brother.

Cavan went to his brother Lachlan and greeted him with a firm hand to his shoulder. "It is good to have you and your wife safely home." He turned to Alyce. "Welcome to our family."

"I really didn't have much choice in the matter," Alyce said tartly.

"Not many of us do," Cavan said and slipped his arm around his wife as he nestled beside her.

"You didn't wish to wed your wife?" Alyce asked, knowing full well their story and expecting the laird to take insult.

Honora laughed. "Neither of us wished to wed the other, but we found ourselves stuck."

Lachlan playfully poked Alyce in the side beneath the table.

She jabbed him back and said, "And you accepted this fate without question?"

"I had a duty," Cavan said, "and so did Honora, and I thank the heavens everyday that in honoring my duty, I was blessed with the perfect wife."

"I have the perfect wife," Artair challenged with a grin.

"That's true he does," Zia agreed happily.

"I hate to disappoint all of you," Lachlan said and thumped his chest. "But my wife is perfection."

The three brothers raised and clanked their tankards together and gave a roar.

The weight of the journey suddenly descended over Alyce and she found it difficult to keep herself upright. She soon had no choice but to rest against Lachlan and his arm went quickly around her.

"You're tired," he said with concern.

"It's been too long of a journey," Addie offered.

"Especially since she is with child," Lachlan said with pride, though concern remained.

Addie clapped with joy. "More grandbabies. I'm so very blessed."

Everyone else took turns offering congratulations while Alyce was overcome with a longing for her home and her sisters. She wanted their comfort not these strangers, and damn if tears didn't threaten her eyes. She fought them, but she was so exhausted it took the last bit of strength she had to keep them locked away.

Addie stood as did Honora and after Zia handed Blythe to Artair, she stood as well.

"We'll get you washed and settled in bed," Addie said.

That did it for Alyce. She didn't want strangers tending her. She wanted the women who had faced the roughest of times with her and remained strong and ready to care for each other.

Alyce bolted up, tears clearing paths down her muddy cheeks. "I don't need your help, nor do I want it." Hit with a sudden pain, her hand flew to her stomach. Her eyes turned wide, and she didn't know what to do or who to turn to.

Lachlan had her up in his arms in seconds.

Zia was quick to order Lachlan to take his wife up to their bedchamber.

Lachlan hurried out of the hall with his wife in his arms. "Zia is an excellent healer. She will take care of you."

Alyce kept silent until they entered his bedchamber. "Put me down," she commanded sharply. "The pain has passed, I'm fine."

He eased her to her feet. "Perhaps but it is best—"

"I need a bath and sleep."

"After Zia has a look at you," he said calmly, but firmly.

Zia entered just then followed by Addie and Honora.

Alyce was quick to make her wants known. "I don't need your help, a bath and bed is all I need."

Lachlan looked ready to object, but his mother spoke first.

"I'll see to having a bath made ready," Addie said and Honora offered to help, leaving only Zia.

"Have you had pains before this?" Zia asked, remaining by the open door.

"A good healer and friend told me what to expect. I do not need another opinion," Alyce said coldly.

"Zia is—"

"Going to leave you to enjoy your bath and rest," Zia finished. "If you have a question or care to talk I'm here for you."

"That was rude," Lachlan said as soon as Zia closed the door behind her.

"I don't need, nor want their help," Alyce said, guilt stabbing at her. Zia seemed like a good woman as did the others, and she knew she was being prickly but she was annoyed.

"You're not even giving this a chance," Lachlan accused. "I understand your anger and that you miss your home, but it's time to create a new home for you, me, and our babe."

"That's easy for you to say when you have your family around you."

Lachlan rubbed the back of his neck. "Give my family a chance. You may find you like them."

He was right. Alyce knew he was right and yet she would continue to argue with him if she didn't hold her tongue. The need to lash out remained strong, though she knew it would do little good. She should simply accept her fate . . .

She shook her head and almost screamed aloud. She had forged a different life for herself and one she favored. She loved Lachlan, but how could she be someone she wasn't? What now was she to do with her days?

"Go away!" she yelled at him.

"Let me help—"

Alyce groaned, grabbing the sides of her skirt. "Don't you understand I don't want your help? I beg of you. Go away and leave me in peace."

"You are my wife—"

"Not tonight," she said bluntly. "Tonight I sleep alone."

Chapter 26

Lachlan paced in front of the fireplace in the great hall. A fire kept the chill and dampness out, the weather still proving temperamental, though the rain had stopped leaving behind overcast skies.

He had shared breakfast with his family, having intended to see if Alyce would join them, but Zia advised against it. She cautioned that Alyce needed rest after such a strenuous journey.

He heeded her advice and now waited for her to wake, everyone having left him to go about their daily duties.

Champion suddenly pounded in the room followed by his dog Princess, though her entrance was more of a royal prance. Addie followed them in.

Lachlan bent down to what most masters would expect, an exuberant welcome. Not so Princess, she sat regally in front of him expecting him to welcome her, which of course he did.

"Where was she yesterday, Mother?" Lachlan asked.

"Hiding from the storm," Addie explained. "You know how she hates storms."

As if Princess knew they discussed her, she raised her chin as though annoyed that he hadn't realized that.

"It appears that I have two females in my life who want things their way," Lachlan said, rubbing beneath her chin, just where he knew she favored. "Or is that all females, Mother?"

Addie pointed to Princess who had inched closer to Lachlan and was now cuddled against him as he continued to stroke her. "I'd say you have a way with knowing exactly what a woman wants and will soon have her melting to your touch."

"I was always confident of that until . . ."

"You fell in love?" his mother asked.

Lachlan nodded. "Love changes everything."

"It certainly does," his mother agreed.

"You do things you don't expect to do. Act a fool. Worry endlessly. Argue senselessly and yet . . ." He shook his head.

"You wouldn't do without each other for a moment," Addie said.

"Not one moment do I want to spend without Alyce," Lachlan admitted. "Though you probably wonder why when she was not very pleasant to you or the others yesterday."

"Love does not always come easy or gently. Sometimes we deny it, or fear it for reasons we don't understand ourselves, but in the end love conquers even the most foolish heart."

Lachlan stood and hugged his mother. "You always know what I need to hear."

"More of a reminder," Addie said with a smile. "What are your plans for the day?"

"I thought to show Alyce our cottage."

"I think she would like that," Addie said. "You and she need time together."

"I couldn't agree more," Lachlan said and suddenly looked forward to the day.

Alyce obstinately kept her joy to herself. She was thrilled with the cottage that Lachlan had made ready for them. It was much larger than she had expected with a separate room off the common room and a loft, and a garden plot right alongside the house. And it was far enough removed from the keep to afford them privacy, something she yearned for at the moment.

"It will do," she said when truly she wished to throw herself in Lachlan's arms and thank him for this gift.

"I'm glad you like it," he said cheerfully. "It gives us room for a large family of our own, and of course I can always enlarge it if necessary."

His sincere joy had her smiling. With a good night sleep and feeling herself once again she felt safe succumbing to his charm, and besides she loved that about him. The way he could smile and find pleasure in the simplest of things.

"You intend a large family?" she asked.

"Only if you agree."

He gave her a choice and that was unlike most men, but then after last night and meeting his family, she realized that the Sinclare brothers were unlike most men.

Alyce found herself being honest with him. "I wouldn't mind a large family."

Lachlan walked over to her and wrapped his arms around her. "We agree on something."

"Don't get used to it," she teased with a grin while her stomach rumbled loudly.

Lachlan laughed. "Hungry?"

"Actually, yes," she said, though it had been only a couple of hours since she had eaten.

"Then let's get you fed and then we can gather your things from my no-longer-necessary bedchamber and move them here."

She liked the idea, making this cottage their home, though she refused to admit it.

They entered the keep and had the table before the hearth to themselves, the room otherwise empty.

"What do the women do all day?" Alyce asked after sitting at the table and surprised to see a servant girl ready with a pitcher of cider and a plate of bread, meat, and cheese.

Lachlan sat across from her reaching for a hunk of cheese. "Zia is busy at her healing cottage. My mother and Honora sometimes help her but most of the time they are busy running the keep, seeing to the babes and stitching."

"I don't stitch," Alyce said as if she admitted a great sin.

"Honora and my mother, with help from some of the women in the village, do most of the necessary stitching. You needn't worry about it."

But she did, for what would she do all day? She

had loved her busy life, and she couldn't grasp doing nothing. With winter near upon them and the garden dormant, there was no planting to see to. She could string a fine bow, but who here would allow her to do that. She was good at settling disputes, but that was Cavan's duty. She was good at preparing meals, each woman having taken her turn, but here there were servants to do that, and she loved planting and tending the fields, but she had a feeling her kitchen garden would be the only land she would be expected to tend.

The partially open door creaked open more and in walked Princess with a haughty raise of her chin.

"My dog Princess," Lachlan said as the animal walked over to Alyce. "And her name suits her well."

Princess sat in front of Alyce and stared at her.

"She wants a pat," Lachlan explained.

Alyce laughed and patted her head then rubbed behind her ear. "I like her."

"Princess goes and comes as she chooses and expects to be catered to."

"And you oblige her?" Alyce asked.

"How do you deny a Princess?" Lachlan asked and the dog sauntered over to him to sit and lean against his leg.

Alyce's stomach protested again and with it came a kick and none too gentle. Her hand flew to her stomach and her eyes rounded.

Lachlan hurried to her side, his hand covering hers and his arm slipping around her waist. "What's wrong?"

"He's moved before, but he's never kicked me," she admitted with a surprised laugh. "He's strong." She moved her hand so that Lachlan's lay flat against her stomach. "Show your father your strength."

As if on command he kicked again.

Lachlan gasped. "Did you feel that?"

"I certainly did," Alyce said laughing.

Lachlan pressed his cheek to hers. "It feels strange to me and I only have my hand on you. I cannot imagine how it must feel for you."

"Just as strange, but somehow right and comforting," she admitted. Her stomach gurgled again.

"We must feed him; he protests."

They hooked hands and left the cottage, Princess prancing alongside Lachlan, and for a moment Alyce felt as if she were home and the thought warmed her.

Late afternoon found Alyce tired and she retired to the cottage to nap, though only for an hour. She woke with a start and decided to roam the village. The sky had darkened from when she slept and the scent of rain remained in the air. She braided her blond hair and wrapped her green shawl around her to keep the dampness at bay; she made certain to wear boots, the ground still thick with mud in spots

The village was a bustle of activity with all calling a friendly greeting to her. She was offered drink and food, which she kindly turned down. Other women offered newly made candles or plants from their gardens, and one woman insisted she take a beautifully crafted basket to carry it all in. By the time she came upon Zia's healing cottage her basket was full, though of what she wasn't certain.

There was a bench outside for those who waited and she took a seat, grateful to be off her feet. She was growing tired more easily of late and hungrier, otherwise she felt fit. She had no intentions of visiting Zia. She only wanted a moment off her feet and then she'd be on her way.

An older man emerged from the cottage with a smile promising to do as Zia instructed and praising her for always helping him.

"I'm so glad you stopped by," Zia said, her smile growing more generous. "I'll fix us a special brew."

Alyce wanted to run, not ready to make friends just yet.

But Zia had already hooked her arm around hers and urged her inside.

Alyce sat at the table in the center of the room noticing how orderly Zia kept the cottage and the fresh flowery scent that permeated the room.

Alyce decided to be blunt. "I've found it necessary to depend on myself."

"I'm familiar with the feeling," Zia said with a laugh while adding a mixture of leaves to the boiling cauldron in the hearth. "And I'm lucky to have found a man who understands me and lets me be who I am."

"He does?" Alyce asked, sounding confused.

Zia poured the hot brew in the tankards on the table. "Well, it did take a bit of training."

Alyce chuckled, thinking Zia reminded her of Rowena, though not in appearance, Rowena being more buxom and with a fuller figure. It was personalities they shared always smiling and cheerful and caring.

Zia placed a gentle hand on Alyce's arm. "It wasn't easy for me either when I first came here, even though I loved Artair. I left much behind, but I've also found much. Give yourself time and let yourself love. It's the only way you'll know for sure if this is where you belong."

Alyce felt a tear surface and was quick to wipe it away, embarrassed that she would cry in front of a stranger.

"I was a crying fool while I carried Blythe," Zia confessed. "Artair didn't know what to do, poor man. And naturally he couldn't do anything, though he felt he should." Zia shook her head. "Men. They think they can fix anything."

Alyce liked Zia. The more she talked the more she reminded her of Rowena and that made her feel she could trust her. "About that pain I had?"

Zia asked dozens of questions and Alyce answered everyone best she could. Zia praised Rowena's instructions and what to expect and claimed Rowena a fine healer, which made Alyce realize that she could easily befriend this woman.

Alyce was laughing at a tale Zia detailed concerning the birth of the twins, that Honora and Addie had concocted to help her out of a predicament but served to upset the men, when Lachlan suddenly burst through the door out of breath.

Alyce and Zia immediately jumped up.

"What's wrong?" Alyce asked fearing the worst.

"You—" He paused out of breath.

Alyce placed her hand to her chest, her heart beating wildly. "I what? What is it? Tell me?"

"You. You're ill?" Lachlan managed to get out between labored breathes.

Artair poked his head in the doorway with a smile. "I told him it was nothing, but he wouldn't listen. But lord, it does my heart good to see him act so foolish when he swore he wouldn't."

Lachlan shot him an evil look then turned to Alyce. "A few in the village said you were here."

"And he naturally assumed the worse," Artair said.

Alyce suddenly felt dreadful. The fear on Lachlan's face was palpable, and she was sure that if she rested her hand to his chest she would feel his heart pounding. He was truly worried about her and while she had seen worry in his eyes before, she had never seen this depth of fear for her before.

"I'm fine," she said wishing nothing more than to ease his burden.

Lachlan wrapped his arms around her waist. "You're sure?"

"Tell him, Zia," Artair urged. "I can't stand to see the fool suffer."

"We have talked and Alyce truly is fine," Zia confirmed. "I expect she will deliver the babe without a problem."

Color suddenly returned to Lachlan's face and he sighed. "This is good to hear."

"Though, I am hungry," Alyce admitted.

"Again?" Lachlan laughed and took her hand to walk out of the cottage.

Alyce turned her head as she reached the door. "Thank you, Zia." And she scooped up her basket as she left the cottage.

Raindrops fell one by one from the gray sky and Alyce and Lachlan hurried to their cottage. Once inside he took her in his arms.

"You needn't have worried," she said.

"How could I not?" he asked, brushing a kiss across her moist lips.

It sent a shiver through her. It had been too long since last they were intimate and she missed his touch.

"After feeling the babe kick inside you and knowing that a child we made from our love was happily growing inside you . . ." He shook his head. "I would brave the tortures of hell to see you both safe." He kissed her gently. "Good lord, Alyce, I love you so very much."

She tried to respond but his mouth captured hers in a kiss that sent her senses reeling.

Chapter 27

Lachlan desperately wanted to make love to his wife, but her gurgling stomach advised that food was more prudent. He did, however, want her to know just how much he ached for her.

"I want to make love to you, but our babe has other plans," he said after ending their kiss.

She sighed with disappointment and it not only pleased him to know that, but made him want her all the more.

"All you have to do is touch me and I want you," she admitted.

"You sound as if it's a curse."

She nipped at his lips. "A pleasurable curse."

He was elated. Things were going well, slowly but surely, and he was confident they would continue to improve, especially tonight since he intended to make love to *his wife* for the first time.

"One I will inflict on you often," he teased.

She returned his playful teasing. "I will counter it with my own."

"Then I will be on guard."

She brushed her lips over his. "I will storm your defenses."

He nibbled at her lower lip enjoying its plump ripeness. "I may be forced to surrender."

The babe interrupted them with a kick they both felt and they laughed.

"He reminds us that he's hungry," Lachlan said.

"As is his mother."

Lachlan was upset to see that no food had been brought to the cottage, and surprisingly it was Alyce who suggested it was do to the poor weather and that she truly enjoyed the bountiful spread at the keep.

"That hungry are you?" Lachlan teased and Alyce tugged him toward the door.

"Starving!" she claimed.

Lachlan fashioned a tarp of sorts with a winter cloak so that they could make it to the keep without getting soaked; the rain while not a downpour, a steady fall.

They were enjoying the spread the servants provided when Honora and Addie joined them with the twins. Princess crept in alongside Champion, but went directly to Lachlan to lie at his feet beneath the table.

"She's afraid of storms?" Alyce asked and Lachlan confirmed with a nod.

"Addie and I need to see to some mending while the twins play in the sewing room, if you care to join us once we're finished here," Honora offered.

"Alyce doesn't stitch," Lachlan answered, recalling her earlier remark and besides he wanted her to himself.

"Then let us know, Alyce, if there is anything you need stitched," offered Honora.

Lachlan could see that his wife was surprised that Honora had not been offended with her lack of sewing skills. It would be only a matter of time before the Sinclare women won her over and she would feel comfortable with them enough to perhaps even think of them as sisters.

Cavan and Artair entered a bit damp but anxious.

"Trouble brews in the east," Cavan said.

Honora and Addie took the twins and left the hall, while Alyce remained beside her husband.

"You can join the women," Cavan instructed.

"I don't stitch," Alyce said and stood. "But I will take my leave, after all what could a mere woman offer seasoned warriors."

Cavan glanced at Alyce as she disappeared down the hall that led to the kitchen then looked to Lachlan.

He shrugged. "Alyce has a mind of her own."

"Then she will fit perfectly with our wives," Artair said.

Alyce didn't know what to do with herself. She had meandered through the kitchen and was offered all sorts of food while the workers saw to their tasks with a sense of camaraderie.

She managed to make it to the stables without getting soaked and found her mare. Bored with an endless day of nothing substantial to do, she grabbed a brush, but before she got started she saw that the stall could use a good cleaning. She found a pitchfork and got busy. Once her mare's stall was cleaned and the animal brushed and given a ration of food, she decided to do the same for the other horses.

It felt good to be doing something. She hated sitting around and if truth be told, she would much rather be at the table with the men discussing the trouble that was brewing.

She supposed that was why her father had such a difficult time with her. When she was young he had allowed her access to meetings strictly meant for men and it was there she had learned the strategies of battle. However, when she had gotten older and began voicing her opinions, especially the ones that outshone the men, her father banished her with a sound reminder of her place in the clan.

Of course that hadn't stopped her from objecting and frustrating her father even more, but what had he expected after allowing her to taste the workings of leadership?

She wiped the sweat from her brow then leaned on the handle of the pitchfork, her smile wide. The stable looked great and was fragrant with the pungent scent of fresh hay. She smiled, feeling invigorated and not the least bit tired.

Her smile faded when she wondered what she would do with her time tomorrow and the day after and so forth. She had four months until the babe was born, but she had no intentions of sitting and doing nothing.

She left the stable and, with the rain having stopped, once again made her way through the village when she heard a shrilling squeal. She ran toward the sound and watched with delight as a young lad of about six tried desperately to catch a squealing pig.

The lad stopped when he spotted her and, with worry, pleaded, "Please help me catch Henry before he runs away."

His sorrowful dark eyes had her chasing after the pig with him in no time. The chubby animal squealed and snorted and slipped right out of their grasps each time they got near him. Soon she was ready to slaughter the chubby little thing, and when Henry slipped past them again, she was sure she wanted to kill him.

She and the lad ran like wild idiots after the squealing animal as he dodged and darted around cottages, through a few gardens, his backside being swatted with a broom by a couple of irate women.

"Henry's going to get away," the young lad cried as they kept close on his hind legs.

"He is not," snapped Alyce and leaped, her arms spread wide ready to grab Henry as she landed on her side in a mud hole beside him, her arms catching him tight around his fat middle.

"Got you, you damn pig," she muttered and looked up expecting to see the lad happy and saw her husband and his two brothers.

"You truly do like to play in mud don't you?" Lachlan said.

The lad prevented any answer since he ran up and grabbed Henry tight, the pig no longer squealing.

"Bad, Henry. Bad, Henry," he scolded. Henry

snorted. The lad turned to Alyce and sniffled back a tear. "Thank you for catching Henry."

"You're welcome," she said, not moving out of the mud hole and realizing that she probably looked a fright.

"It might be a good idea, Lachlan," Cavan said, "to find something for your wife to do so she stays out of mud holes."

That bristled her temper and she tried to get up only to keep tumbling back on her bottom.

She heard them laugh as Lachlan extended his hand to her. She slapped it out of her way. "I don't need any help." Sheer annoyance got her up on her own, and she glared at Cavan. "And I'll do what I damn well please." She turned to leave then turned around and with a poke at Cavan who backed away to avoid her muddy finger said, "And as laird it's your duty to help your people. It should have been you in that mud."

She gave one last poke that Cavan sidestepped, his foot catching the mud and the next thing he knew, went flying backward. Lachlan and Artair instinctively reached out trying to prevent him from falling. Both lost their footing and joined Cavan in the mud, though they hit it face first.

Alyce stood stunned, looking down at the three men sprawled in the mud.

Zia was suddenly at her side shaking her head. "Playing in the mud, lads? You really should know better."

The three scrambled to get up but could only manage to sit up with the assistance of each other.

Zia looked to Alyce. "I assume you got yourself out of the mud?"

Alyce nodded and smiled. "All on my own."

"Well, lads," Zia said. "It would seem that Alyce is the wiser one here."

"She's the one that got us in here," Cavan complained.

"Shame on you, husband," Honora scolded as she joined the other two women. "Blaming a pregnant woman for your own folly."

Cavan tried to protest. "I did nothing."

"My contention exactly," Alyce said.

"You failed to help Alyce?" Honora asked perturbed.

"I—I—I—" Cavan stumbled unable to find the right words.

Zia wrapped her arm around a muddy Alyce. "Come with us, Honora and I will get you cleaned up."

Honora shook a finger at the three men. "You all should be ashamed of yourself for treating Alyce so unkindly."

Cavan shook his head watching the women walk away. "What happened?"

"How the hell are we to know?" Artair said. "Women make no sense." He looked at Lachlan. "And why the hell are you grinning?"

"This was perfect," Lachlan said and slapped his knee sending mud flying at his brothers.

Cavan wiped the splat of mud off his cheek. "You better explain yourself before I drown you in this muck."

"This incident helped my wife bond with your wives."

"So we are to appear the fools so our wives will get along?" Cavan asked, confused.

"He's got a point," Artair said. "Can you imagine what life would be like if they didn't get along?"

Cavan shook his head. "That won't be good." He jabbed a finger at Lachlan. "But find something to keep your wife busy, so that something like this doesn't happen again."

"Not so easy a task," Lachlan admitted.

"What did she do at Everagis?" Artair asked.

"Everything," Lachlan said. "The women and land flourished because of her. She even taught them how to defend themselves in battle, and disguised as mercenaries they kept the area safe."

"How were they aware of who needed protecting?" Cavan asked.

"Piper, their tracker was like none I've ever known. She knew everything that was going on in the area. She could scent intruders in the air long before tracks were even found."

"Then wouldn't they have known of the mercenary troop long before the warring clans knew of their presence?" Artair asked. "And don't either of you find it curious that the mercenaries never bothered Everagis?"

"Why would they bother nuns?" Lachlan asked.

"Why wouldn't they unless they were paid not to," Artair said. "They are paid thieves and murders, doing anyone's bidding for a price."

"Artair makes sense," Cavan said.

"Artair always makes sense," Lachlan said annoyed.

"You're just angry because you didn't see it your-self," Artair said. "But it's obvious why you didn't."

"Why is that?" Lachlan snapped.

"Love blinded you to the obvious."

"He's right again," Cavan said.

"Are you suggesting that Alyce lied to me?" Lachlan challenged, annoyed that there might be some truth to what Artair suggested.

"She's lied to you from the beginning," Artair said.

"She had to," Lachlan defended, not wanting for a moment to believe he couldn't trust his wife.

"Then if she lied out of necessity, perhaps she does so again," Artair suggested.

Sometimes Lachlan hated Artair's reasoning nature.

"If that's so," Cavan said solemnly, "it could mean only one thing."

Lachlan didn't want to hear or believe what Cavan was about to suggest.

"Alyce could very well know something about Carissa and if that's so, then she could possibly also know about Ronan."

"Why not share it?" Lachlan asked.

"A necessity as I suggested," Artair said, "perhaps an exchange or bargain of sorts agreed upon between her and the mercenaries."

"It makes no sense," Lachlan argued, though truly it did; he simply didn't want to admit it.

"Find out," Cavan ordered sharply, "or I will."

Lachlan nodded, knowing Cavan had suffered

along with Ronan during their capture and would do anything to see him safely home.

"Excuse me, sirs."

The three looked up to see the lad who Henry the pig belonged to.

"Do you need help getting out of the mud?" he asked and held out his small hand.

Lachlan wasn't surprised when he heard Cavan refer to the lad by name, Daniel, since Cavan was familiar with all in the clan. He made a fuss over his generous offer and Cavan allowed the lad to help the mighty laird out.

Lachlan remained sitting in the muck wondering just how long he'd remain stuck.

Chapter 28

A lyce was in the cottage when he arrived freshly washed and attired. While food waited on the table Alyce surprisingly seemed uninterested. She sat in a rocker by the hearth wearing a lovely deep blue linen gown and he silently thanked his sisters-in-law for their generosity. The dark blue made her own blue eyes all the more stunning, and he loved that she had left her long blond hair unbraided.

Her beauty never failed to startle him and he wondered if Artair had been right about love having interfered with his awareness. If he hadn't been so taken by Alyce would he have questioned things at Everagis more?

She and Piper had disappeared often and the explanation was always the same. Someone needed help, but that someone, or specifics of the help, were never detailed. And why hadn't Evan, a remarkable scout in his own right, ever been able to locate a single mercenary track?

Love truly must have blinded him because it was certainly blinding him now, since he wanted nothing more than to lose himself in a night of lovemaking with his wife. Or did he fear what needed to be discussed would not only cause a rift between them, but also damage the trust they had built? Or did trust exist at all between them?

"You're not hungry?" he asked for want of anything else to say.

Alyce shook her head. "Not at the moment."

He walked over to her, scooping up a small bench along the way and sitting on it beside her. "Does something trouble you?"

"Must you always be privy to my thoughts?" she snapped. "Will I have no time to myself?"

While Terese could be forward in her remarks, it seemed Alyce was more biting, almost as if she intended to leave her mark on you, least you forget she bit.

He took her hand and laced his fingers with hers. "Why do you always feel the need to attack?"

She reacted as he expected. She yanked her hand, though could not free it, their fingers laced firmly.

"And why do you always feel the need to run from me?" he asked.

"I don't," she snapped and tugged once again.

"You are tenacious, but I"—he smiled—"am tenaciously patient."

"Are you?" she asked with great concern.

"Have you not seen that for yourself?"

"Where was your patience when you wed me with haste? Where was your patience when you forced me to leave my home? Where was your patience in asking me if I wanted any of this?"

He reached out to touch her face, but she turned away from him. "You told me that you briefly dreamt that we would wed and have a life together. If that is your dream why do you deny it?"

"I wasn't forced to wed you in my dream of a future for us. You asked; you gave me a choice and that meant the world to me."

"Why today? Why now does this disturb you once again?" he asked.

She eased her fingers free of his. "Zia and Honora shared tales of their weddings with me and I realized that not one of the Sinclare wives chose to wed their husband."

"In all fairness one Sinclare husband did not choose to wed his wife, though it did not stop Cavan from falling in love with Honora. And you must admit they are a perfect pair.

"Tell me why this truly disturbs you so much," he urged. "It is the way of things for most. You knew as daughter to a laird you would be expected to wed a man of your father's choice. Why rant against it?"

"My father led me to believe otherwise," Alyce said sadly. "He raised me to believe my life was my choice. He introduced me to the ways of a leader. He let me make choices for myself, encouraged me to make them and then after giving me my freedom, letting me taste the joys of it, he took it away."

Lachlan watched her grow teary-eyed and felt like strangling her father.

"At Everagis I found what I wanted and was content, which was why I knew Alyce had to die, for Alyce would never be free. Terese, however, could live as she chose without repercussions."

"Then I arrived."

She smiled, though it was a sorrowful smile. "And changed everything."

"Truly, though, you got what you wanted, to love a man of your choosing."

"Terese did, not Alyce."

He leaned close and teased her lips with his then said, "You are Terese."

"Terese died the day you returned to Everagis."

Lachlan felt a grasp at his heart as if a hand squeezed it so tight that he could barely breathe. He shook his head. "No, Terese lives in you."

She shook her head.

He took firm hold of her chin. "I am sorry if I have confused you, but one thing that will not change, that will remain constant, is my love for you. Whether I call you Terese or Alyce I love you. Isn't that enough?"

"Is it for you?"

"What more would I want?"

"For me to come to you of my own free will," she said.

"I thought you had done that."

"I did once," she said. "Not so now."

"What do I do to amend this?" he asked concerned.

"That is for you to answer."

"And here I thought to make love to you tonight," he said with disappointment.

Alyce stood and took his hand. "Making love has nothing to do with this matter. Our passionate love gave us our child and for that I will forever be grateful. And I will not deny I love making love with you. I want no other hands on me. I want no other lips to touch mine. I want no other man inside me. I want only you."

Lachlan wrapped his arms around her and kissed her like a man who just realized he was deeply in love. He savored the kiss, her taste so exquisite that he was certain he'd never get enough of her.

"Make love to me," she said softly. "I've missed you so very much."

Lachlan swung her up into his arms and carried her to the bed. He undressed her with loving tenderness, but hastily shed his own clothes. They settled on the bed together wrapped in each others arms and she held on tightly to him.

"Never doubt that I love you, Lachlan," she whispered.

"I never have," he said nestling at her neck.

"Promise me you never will."

He rubbed his cheek to hers. "You have my word."

She moved her hands over him.

He grabbed her hand as it settled around him. "Do that and I won't last long."

"You only have strength for one time tonight?"

"Now you challenge me, woman?" he grinned.

"I love a good challenge."

"You asked for it," he teased, his hands roaming her body, and she sighed with pleasure.

He loved running his hands over her, finding spots that had her purring, sighing, moaning with delight.

He took his time enjoying how eagerly she responded to his every touch and kiss.

He had known from their first time together that it was different, special and everlasting, for he was content with Alyce as he had never been with any other woman. He didn't even think of other women, nor did they catch his eye. He thought only of Alyce and the way she fervently responded to his every touch, as she did now arching toward his hand when it drifted away or moving over him when she wished to take control, and he willingly surrendered.

He felt the fatigue in her body and while he enjoyed her riding him, he took hold of her waist and swung her off him to lie beneath him.

"I will pleasure you," he said with a tempting kiss.

"You always pleasure me," she said with a passionate sigh.

He eased in and out of her, not wanting to rush, but to linger in the heavenly feel of her and she agreed, running her hands over him touching him, encouraging him, loving him.

Naturally their passion heated, their rhythm turning frantic and both burst in frenzied climaxes one after the other until they were left breathless.

Lachlan cuddled her in his arms and as he expected, she was asleep in mere minutes. He didn't mind as long as she was there safe with him.

He never expected to love a woman beyond rational reason, but he loved Alyce that way, and while he believed that excuse enough for his decisions, he could understand why it troubled her.

He hoped she would see that she had her freedom though wed to him, but the fact that he forced a marriage on her shadowed his good intentions. She had been right about the Sinclare brides having no choices, though love certainly had claimed them all, which Alyce had not argued. She did not deny her love for him; it was the choice that mattered.

How did he make this right for them? He wanted Alyce to have what she had always wanted. What her father had led her to believe she would always have . . . a choice.

He didn't know how he could do this, just as he wasn't sure how he would approach Alyce and get the answers he needed about the mercenaries. He wasn't one to give into defeat and while charm was his best weapon, he didn't think that was his best approach with his wife.

He had loved her direct and honest nature and she would expect the same from him. His charm could be saved for more auspicious occasions.

He grinned and cuddled around her ready to sleep and ready do what whatever was necessary to see his wife content with their life.

Alyce was bored senseless. She even had trouble keeping track of time. What seemed like a matter of days had turned into three weeks since their arrival home. She had tried to find things to occupy her time, but hadn't been successful. And when Lachlan was sent away to handle a nearby skirmish she had almost jumped on her mare and joined him. The week he'd been gone had been the longest in her life, and her endless days of nothingness had been driving her quite mad.

While she should be growing accustomed and content with her knew home, it was the opposite. She missed her active life at Everagis all the more, though she had to admit she loved Lachlan more with each passing day.

He was so very good to her, so why didn't that matter more? The question haunted her and as much as she tried, she could not find an answer, and so it continued to disturb her.

Autumn was holding fast, though today proved more summerlike and everyone was busy outside clearing and storing in preparation for a winter that would arrive soon enough.

The splitting of wood resonated in the air and women tended what would be the last harvest of the year. Others dried and smoked meat, and candles hung to dry dotted the village.

Alyce on the other hand could find nothing to do. Everyone had a chore or duty or whatever you wanted to call it, but her. And she was on her own since Lachlan and Artair had been sent to see to a problem with a bordering clan. Cavan was busy today hearing and settling villagers' complaints. Between the ill and preparing her concoctions Zia had not a moment to spare, while Honora contentedly looked after her twins and her niece.

Addie was the only one she hadn't seen about, so when she saw her hurrying along in the village looking upset, Alyce seized the moment and asked what was wrong.

"Four-year-old Lily, the youngest of the Connors, is missing since early morning," Addie said clearly upset.

"I'll help," Alyce offered immediately.

Addie shook her head. "Cavan will send men to hunt for her."

"I learned much about tracking from a friend. I could be of help," Alyce insisted.

"I don't think Lachlan would approve, and I don't have time to argue with you," Addie said and ran to the keep.

Alyce didn't wait. She never had before, accustomed to taking matters into her own hands and dealing with them posthaste. A child needed to be found and she had the skills to find her.

Alyce quickly inquired as to where she could find the Connors farm and after saddling her horse, she hurried off to do one of the things she did best . . . deal with and settle problems.

Mary Connor was beside herself when Alyce arrived and quite upset that more help hadn't arrived with her. Alyce calmly explained that more help was on the way, but that she was an excellent tracker and if Mary would show her where Lily was last seen, she would do her best to follow her tracks.

Mary insisted that her husband Jake and two sons, John and Peter, were already doing that. Alyce remained calm and suggested that another tracker could be beneficial.

Mary agreed and showed Alyce the edge of the woods where Lily had last been seen. There she found small footprints, giving her a place to start. Alyce wanted to begin before any of Cavan's men arrived and disturbed the fresh tracks.

She patted her stomach that had been rounding nicely every week and with fatigue gone and feeling stronger then ever, she said, "Hold strong there, little one, while we go find this lass."

While she disliked the reason that had her tracking in the woods, she felt elated with the task and so very confident that she would find the child. Unfortunately, hours later Lily still hadn't been found and with Cavan's warriors and others joining the search, any tracks that could have proved helpful were now destroyed.

"I've allowed you to help far too long, now go home," Cavan ordered.

Alyce glared at him. "Why should I take orders from you?"

"I'm your laird."

While she wanted badly to challenge him, she knew it wouldn't be wise. Whether she liked it or not, he was laird and she had to obey him.

She held her tongue and turned to walk away but stopped and turned around. "I obey you, Cavan, out of respect for my husband, but don't think to command too often, for you will find I don't do well with orders."

She marched off, a mumble of voices trailing after her and knowing full well she would be the village gossip by nightfall, which was when her husband was due home. She sighed, frustrated that with all Piper had taught her she had been unable to locate a track in the woods. She must not have been as apt a pupil as she had thought.

Alyce was about to mount her mare when she suddenly stopped and shook her head. Piper had taught her too well for her not to have been able to locate a track. If she hadn't found one it could mean only one of two things, either someone had covered their tracks, or she was looking in the wrong place.

She glanced around then looked down at the ground scuffed with too many imprints to make sense of just one, and then it hit her. She recalled noticing one small, solid imprint made by Lily and at that moment it struck her. The young lass could have stopped abruptly and possibly changed direction.

With that knowledge to guide her, Alyce turned and went in the opposite direction.

Chapter 29

"**W**hat do you mean Alyce is missing?" Lachlan asked, having arrived home only minutes ago.

His whole family was in the great hall waiting and visibly upset. He shouldn't be, but he was insanely jealous that Artair hugged Zia and that Cavan had his arm around Honora while his wife was . . .

"What the hell happened?" he demanded.

"The Connor lass went missing," Cavan began. "Alyce was the first to join father and sons in search of the child."

"Alyce would do well; she learned from the best," Lachlan said.

"Not so this time. Lily couldn't be found and with dusk not far off and your wife rounded with child, I thought it best she go home."

Lachlan shook his head. "You didn't order her home, did you?"

"Wouldn't you have?" Artair asked surprised.

"No," Lachlan snapped. "I would have known she was the best chance in finding the child and allowed her to lead the search."

"That's a moot point now," Cavan said. "With dusk settling over the land and not a trace of the child, I called off the search until morning. I saw Alyce's mare as soon as I left the woods, tethered to the same spot as before. I knew she hadn't left and I thought perhaps she went to talk with Mary Connor."

"But she hadn't?" Lachlan asked, though he knew the answer. Alyce would never have given up so easily.

Cavan shook his head. "She was nowhere to be found."

"She must have realized something and went in another direction to search," Lachlan said.

"Without informing anyone?" Cavan asked.

"You forget that where she came from, she was the leader," Lachlan reminded. "She asked no one's permission."

"Aren't you concerned for her safety?" Artair asked.

"Of course I am," Lachlan said annoyed. "But I also know that my wife is more than capable of taking care of herself."

"What if she's hurt?" Honora asked.

"You don't understand Alyce," Lachlan said, thinking that maybe he was truly just beginning to understand her himself. "She's been schooled like a warrior and she added to that schooling while on her own. She will determine the situation and do what is best."

"Then what you're saying is that we just wait for her to return home?" Zia asked.

"For now, but if she hasn't returned by morning, I will go search for her," Lachlan said with a firm nod.

Lachlan with Princess at his side retired to his cottage right after supper, hoping his wife would show up sooner rather than later, but as the night wore on and the candles wore down, he began to worry. He repeatedly reminded himself of what he had told his family, that Alyce could take care of herself.

But he didn't like not knowing where she was and if she was all right. Her being with child didn't help the situation. Otherwise he knew her capable of the task and if he knew her as well as he'd like to believe, she was probably enjoying every minute of it.

With nothing left to him but to wait, he stretched out fully clothed on the bed. He intended to be ready at a moment's notice if necessary. He refused to linger on thoughts of her alone in the dark woods. She was a warrior on a mission and she would succeed.

"I'm praying for your success and safe return, Alyce," he whispered.

But isn't that what he did for Ronan? Pray every night for his safe return? He couldn't compare the two; he wouldn't. Alyce would return to him safe and unharmed.

He fought sleep, twisting fretfully, but sleep finally won and he was soon snoring lightly and though hours passed and he slumbered deeply, Princess's whimpers woke him.

The candles had burnt out, leaving the hearth flame the only light in the room. His eyes adjusted to the dimness and he saw that Princess lay in front of the hearth her head up, her eyes focused on . . . the door.

The latched lifted ever so slowly and the door creaked open.

His wife entered her steps silent, slow, and labored. When she suddenly stopped near the hearth and he saw her grimace, he jumped out of bed.

Lachlan slid his arm around her waist and held her firm as she sagged against him. "Are you all right?"

"A bit worse for the wear, but otherwise I'm fine," she said with a light laugh.

He almost squashed her against him in relief, but refrained, not wanting to add to her discomfort. "What happened?"

"I will tell you it all, but first, I'm starving and I need salve for the many scratches my body has suffered."

Lachlan grew alarmed. "An animal—"

"No," Alyce was quick to assure him. "Bushes and tree branches."

"We'll go to the keep," he said. "I'll get you food and fetch Zia to tend your wounds."

"It's late, I don't want to bother her."

"Zia would be upset that you didn't," he said and he grabbed a wool cloak from the peg by the door and swung it around her shoulders. "Your arms are cold."

Alyce wrapped her arms around Lachlan's waist and snuggled against him as they left the cottage. "You will warm me, feed me, and take care of me and I will tell you how I found Lily."

* * *

Servants were sent to look after the sleeping Sinclare babes as one by one the Sinclares joined Lachlan
and Alyce in the great hall.

While Alyce hadn't wanted to wake them all, she
took a comfort in their presence and eagerness to
hear how she had rescued Lily, and in their pride in
her success. Though the telling was delayed as each
Sinclare arrived and insisted she wait for the whole
family.

Alyce munched on whatever food Lachlan placed
in front of her and drank the brew Zia handed her.
Tiredness crept over her, but a sense of exhilaration remained and she was eager to share her tale, and those
surrounding her looked just as eager to hear it.

Honora was the last to arrive, having made certain
the babes were settled and looked after.

"I have not received word about Lily," Cavan said.

"I assured the Connors I would inform you," Alyce
said. "They were much too happy to think of anything
else."

"However did you find her in the dead of night?"
Artair asked.

"I'd like to know that myself," Zia inquired. "These
scratches resemble someone who has climbed a tree or
scuffled with a prickly bush."

"I did both," Alyce admitted.

"My, but you are courageous," Addie said with
pride.

"Or foolish," Cavan said.

"My wife is courageous," Lachlan said defensively.

"She would never take a chance of harming our child and did what she did because she knew that she could do it successfully."

Alyce winced—Zia cleansed a shoulder scratch deeper than the others—though it turned to a smile soon enough. Her husband believed in her and she loved him all the more for it.

Cavan didn't argue. He seemed to take Lachlan's words as fact for he gave a curt nod. "Tell me how and where you found the child?"

Alyce was only too pleased to do as the laird asked, for it had given her great pleasure to have found the lass and return her safely to her family. "Once I realized that the lone track told a different story, it was easy to find her."

"Different story?" Cavan asked.

Alyce went on to explain. "The track was dug into the ground firm and I realized Lily had made the track by halting abruptly, which meant she had stopped and switched directions."

"Why didn't you see that on your first inspection?" Artair asked.

"I wasn't paying close enough attention. I forgot the most important lesson my friend taught me about tracking. Take the obvious and look for a wrinkle in it. Once I found that wrinkle, the sudden stop, I was able to determine the right direction. Her small footprints weren't easy to detect along the edge of the woods, but once I found them they were easy to follow until the tracks disappeared once more and the only place left to look was . . ."

All heads bent back as Alyce looked up to the ceiling.

"Lily was in a tree," Addie said excited.

"She went after a kitten, didn't she?" Honora asked.

Cavan sent her a how-did-you-know-that look.

"I've helped a few children retrieve their cats," Honora said proudly.

"You climb trees?" Cavan asked incredulously.

"When necessary," Honora admitted.

"I don't need to ask you if you do," Artair said to his wife with a grin. "You would do anything to help a child."

"It is good you know me well," Zia said.

"As should all your husbands," Addie said as if she dared her sons to disagree. "Sinclare women are not timid. They are bold and courageous warriors."

Alyce watched her husband smile at Cavan as if asking if he really wanted to spar with their mother.

Cavan turned to Alyce, a signal for her to continue.

"Lily had followed a favorite kitten of hers into the woods and climbed the tree to retrieve her. She hadn't thought about how high she had climbed being eager to rescue her kitten. Once she had the kitten in her arms, she took a look down and was much too frightened to climb down. She sat huddled in the crook of the massive tree waiting for someone to find her."

"However did you get her down, or yourself up for that matter?" Artair asked.

"Leave the practical question to my brother," Lachlan teased.

Lachlan may be teasing his brother, but Alyce knew he appreciated Artair asking it, for she was certain he wanted to know the same.

"Piper taught me a quick way up and a quick way down," Alyce said.

The men waited and the women smiled.

"I'm not sharing my secret," Alyce informed them, then covered a yawn with her hand.

"You're tired," Lachlan said with concern.

"A sound sleep will do her good," Zia said.

"True enough," Alyce agreed, fatigue consuming every limb in her body.

"Stay here for the night," Addie suggested.

Lachlan startled Alyce when he looked to her and said, "It's your choice."

That he allowed her that pleased her, and she nodded. "Here is fine."

Cavan had a few more questions for her; Zia, instructions for the care of her minor wounds; Artair, a few practical tidbits in dealing with her husband, and Honora requested that Alyce teach her about tracking. And surprisingly Cavan thought it a splendid idea. He even bragged about how skillful Honora was with a bow.

Lachlan finally stood and announced, "Enough, my wife needs to sleep."

Everyone agreed and Alyce was stunned by how fast everyone bid her good night and Lachlan had her out of the room and up the stairs to his old bedchamber. Though she couldn't say she was displeased; she looked forward to crawling into bed.

Alyce didn't wait. As soon as Lachlan closed the door she threw off her clothes and climbed into bed, uttering a most pleasurable sigh as she settled beneath the blanket naked.

"And I thought such passion was meant only for me," Lachlan said as he disrobed and then joined her.

"Tonight it is the bed that satisfies me," Alyce admitted with a quick smile.

"Don't tempt me to challenge the bed, wife," he teased.

"I already know the victor." She yawned and turned to cuddle her back against him and took hold of his arm to wrap around her and place his hand on her rounded stomach. She took comfort in the way his hand would splay protectively over her belly.

"I would be the victor," he whispered in her ear and kissed along her cheek to nip at her lips.

"You and only you," she assured him.

"You are a wise woman."

"I keep telling and showing you that, but you don't listen," she said, her eyes much too heavy to keep open.

"I do listen," he whispered. "And hear much more than you think."

A soft snore told Lachlan that his wife was sound asleep. He had expected as much; she looked exhausted. He was glad to have her finally home and safe in his arms. And while her ordeal had caused him concern, he saw that it had brought her satisfaction.

He could not deny her that, and he would not. He would find a way for her to flourish here and perhaps after time, she would accept Caithness as her home.

Chapter 30

Lachlan gave his wife a few days to recover before he even considered speaking with her about the possibility of her involvement with mercenaries. He expected an argument from her, since she could be confrontational when it came to certain matters. While others might view it as shrewish, he now knew differently. It was Alyce defending her independence. She had fought hard to claim it, and she had no intentions of having it taken from her.

A chilled wind swept across the moors and around the keep. Lachlan took it as a sign that perhaps now was the time to let the sweeping wind blow away the last vestiges of concern between him and Alyce. He wanted nothing coming between them.

Strange, long before meeting Alyce he had not thought of loving the woman he would wed, but having fallen madly in love with Alyce, he couldn't now imagine being wed without being in love. And oddly love wasn't an issue between them. He believed they both always knew they loved each other from the very beginning; even when he had believed her a nun, he could not get her out of his mind. And when at last they could be together, she had not denied her attraction to him. She had made love with him freely and oh so willingly; and her sincere responses had made him love her all the more.

Love, he had been told by many including his family, could conquer anything. However, he had to question that since while he knew his wife loved him, she wasn't as happy as he would have expected her to be. Therefore did love truly solve everything?

"You look deep in thought," Artair said, joining his brother as Lachlan walked to his cottage. "It must concern your wife."

"I can see by your grin that you are enjoying my marital woes."

Artair gripped his brother's shoulder. "You have to admit; you would do the same to me."

"No, I wouldn't and I didn't," Lachlan claimed. "I offered you advice."

Artair nodded. "That you did and good advice at that." He rubbed his chin. "What can I do to help? I may not have your charm, but sometimes sound reason works better."

"My wife isn't happy," Lachlan admitted, though it hurt him to do so.

"Why did you decide to wed Alyce Bunnock?"

"I love her," Lachlan answered as if the question was a foolish one.

"Was that the only reason?"

Lachlan stopped in his tracks. "No. I knew she'd be stubborn about marrying me, so I made it easier for both of us."

"No," Artair said emphatically. "You feared she'd reject you so you made the decision for her. And being you had no doubt she loved you, you assumed all would turn out well."

"Didn't you think the same yourself once?"

"The difference being Zia made her wishes known and refused to comply with my sensible solution," Artair said.

"I can't believe I'm going to ask you this," Lachlan said, shaking his head. "How do I fix it?"

Artair rested his hand on his brother's shoulder. "As difficult as it may be, you give her a choice, or she will never truly be yours."

Zia's cheerful shout had Artair hurrying off and Lachlan continuing his walk to the cottage. He thought he could make Alyce happy, replace her family with a new one. More recently he thought if he could find something that would happily occupy her time all would be well, but he was wrong.

His decision to wed her without asking had been a selfish one. Having gotten a chance to know Alyce through Terese he should have known better. He ran his fingers roughly through his hair, scraping along his scalp in frustration. He had certainly gotten himself into a situation, and now he had to get himself out of it. Was there a chance he would lose his wife because of his own misgivings?

He opened the door to the cottage prepared to talk with her and found it empty.

He stepped outside and looked over the village but saw Alyce nowhere. An overcast sky had joined the chilled day and rain appeared likely. It would be a good day to spend indoors talking. With heavy strides he hurried off to find his wife.

Alyce balanced Tavish on her hip. He was a joyful lad with dark inquisitive eyes that found delight in everything. He was barely a year and already eager to walk completely on his own, though his legs had yet to agree.

"This is fascinating," Honora said with glee as she shifted Ronan from one hip to another.

Ronan, like his twin brother, was eager to be on his feet, but since Alyce was teaching Honora about tracking in the woods, the two lads were stuck in each of their arms. Not that they minded all that much, since both she and Honora would let them walk now and again, with help of course.

"It's being aware and knowing the woods," Alyce said and Tavish graced her with a charming smile that reminded her of Lachlan.

Honora laughed. "I keep telling Cavan that Tavish is going to be like Lachlan and as handsome. He has his smile."

"I agree," Alyce said and gave Tavish a big hug, which he relished since his smile charmed all the more.

"See, he smiles just like his uncle," Honora said

with a lilt of laughter. "And this one . . ." She bounced Ronan on her hip. "He's going to be just like his father, a born leader." She looked to Alyce. "I wonder if you will have a boy or a girl."

"I would be pleased with either since I never believed I would ever have children."

"Why ever so?" Honora asked surprised.

Alyce found herself being more truthful than she intended. "I would rather have led my father's clan."

"I could see that," Honora said so casually that it startled Alyce.

"Truly?"

Honora nodded. "Oh my, yes. You have the instincts of a laird about you. One who commands rather than follows. One who will strategize instead of leaping headfirst. Cavan would be wise to make use of your skills. I will speak to him."

Again Honora startled her. "But will he heed your opinion?"

"Cavan is a fair man and respects my opinions," Honora said. "All Sinclare men are respectful of their wives."

"In payment for forcing marriage upon them?" Alyce said then quickly realized the rudeness of her remark. "I'm sorry. I meant no offense."

"None taken," Honora said while playing tug of war with her son's tiny fingers and a strand of her long dark hair. "I can imagine how you look upon Zia's and my marriage, but believe me when I tell you the choices were ours."

"How can you say that when you were given to

Artair to wed only to find yourself wed to Cavan who had rejected you as a wife years earlier? And Zia had to wed Artair out of necessity, or she would have been condemned a witch. How are they choices?"

"You have grown to know Zia," Honora said. "Do you really think she would have wed Artair if it wasn't her choice?"

Alyce smiled. "No. The woman truly does as she pleases."

"But she considers her husband at all times as he does with her," Honora said. "And why do you think that is?"

"It's obvious. The two are madly in love."

Honora grinned. "Isn't it wonderful?"

Alyce hated to admit, but it was. The pair's passion for each other was palpable. "But what of you?" she challenged. "You had no choice."

"But I did," Honora insisted as they left the woods to follow the trail to the village. "I made the choice to love Cavan and gave him the choice to love me." She smiled. "It didn't take either of us long to fall in love. I cannot even recall when it was I realized I loved him. It was as if we were always in love and we always will be."

"I love Lachlan," Alyce said feeling the need to say it.

"Then let love be," Honora said.

"What do you mean?"

"I discovered, quite by accident, that love is wiser than we are. If we would just let it be, not make demands or imprison it, but simply let love have its way then we finally taste its true joy." Honora smiled. "I have so enjoyed this time with you and Tavish seems to be enamored with you."

The little lad had his head snuggled in the crook of Alyce's neck and his tiny fingers had firm hold of her blouse. His little body was warm against her chest and she loved having him there wrapped in her arms.

"How can you not love the little charmer, or his brother," Alyce said with a smile to Ronan who was half asleep in his mother's arms.

"I hope we can continue our tracking lessons," Honora said.

"I would very much like that," Alyce said.

"There you are!"

Lachlan's shout stopped both women.

"Where have you been?" Lachlan asked hurrying over to them. "I was worried."

"Were you so senseless by our lovemaking this morning that you forgot I told you I was meeting with Honora?" Alyce asked with a teasing glint.

Lachlan was struck speechless.

Honora grinned. "It's so wonderful to see that you have met your match."

"I couldn't agree with you more," Lachlan said with his usual charm and turned to his wife. "And how could I have remembered anything after I appeased your insatiable appetite for me not once, but twice this morning."

"Thrice, husband, not twice," Alyce corrected.

Honora laughed.

"What's so humorous?" Cavan asked, joining them

as Tavish held eager hands out to his approaching father, who scooped him into his arms.

"A debate over the number of lovemaking bouts this morning," Honora said candidly.

Cavan looked aghast. "I can't believe you told them we made love two times this morning."

"Got you beat," Lachlan said with a smug grin. "Three times."

"Four," Artair sang out joyfully from behind them, his daughter Blythe snug contently in the crook of his arm.

With a serious expression Honora looked to Alyce. "We should find out what Zia's putting in Artair's brew and get some for our husbands."

Alyce burst out laughing and Honora joined in.

"Ours sons need their nap," Honora said after her laughter subsided.

"So does Blythe," Artair said and walked off with them, though he teased Lachlan one last time. "I'll see if Zia has any extra brew for you."

Alyce slipped her arm around her husband's and leaned against him. "You need nothing to enhance your prowess. You brought me to pleasure more than three times this morning; you always do."

He kissed her lightly. "You know you just set my loins on fire."

"I was hoping."

He swung her up into his arms and walked to the cottage mindless of the villagers who stared smiling, while a few giggled.

As soon as the door closed Alyce kissed him with

a hunger that surprised her, though it shouldn't have. There wasn't a time she didn't want her husband. He was like a tonic she couldn't get enough of no matter how many times he quenched her thirst.

He kissed her with just as much fervor and slipped along the length of her after he placed her on the bed. They lay side by side kissing, not touching or shedding their garments, simply kissing. Gentle and lazy, frantic and hard, the kisses went from one to another heating their passion with every thrust of a tongue or a simple brush of their lips.

Lachlan rested his hand on her waist and began to stroke along her hip, down her leg and Alyce tingled with anticipation of his intimate touch. She doubted they would have time to shed their clothes for she was wet and throbbing for him already.

She wanted to tell him to hurry and then urge him to take his time. She wanted him badly, yet she didn't want this pleasure to end too soon.

His fingers tugged up her skirt and slipped beneath and she moaned and he teased with slow caresses that seemed to take forever to reach her and . . .

The mournful horn had them both jumping in shock.

"Something's wrong," he said and took hold of her hand to help her up. "We must get to the keep."

Alyce didn't argue, she was all too aware what the sound could signify; an attack.

Lachlan whipped a wool cloak around her before they left the cottage and grabbed his sword. The villagers were in action for battle, women hurrying chil-

dren to the safety of the keep and the men rushing
with swords and bows in hand to man their posts.

A mixture of thrill and fear raced threw Alyce at
the thought of a possible battle. The men would meet
and determine battle plans. Troops of warriors would
be dispatched each with a leader who would see to
implementing their strategy at a precise moment, or
all could be lost. It was a challenge she loved and a
talent of hers that her father had once taken pride in
bragging about.

They entered the great hall, Lachlan having scooped
up a crying young lad no more than three on the way
and handing him over to Addie who was tending the
women and children along with Zia and Honora.

It came as no surprise to Alyce what her husband
ordered next, though her response stunned him.

"Stay with the women," Lachlan said. "You'll be
safe with them."

"I will not. I'll be of no help to them, but I can be of
help to your brothers."

"She's right," Honora said, the twins resting contentedly on each hip. "Take her to Cavan and tell him
I said that Alyce will be more useful to him than to
us."

"Hurry then," he said without protest, and she
smiled.

She and Lachlan had to step aside when they
reached the solar, to give way to two large warriors
rushing one after the other out the open door. She followed Lachlan in, close on his heels, anxious to learn
what trouble brewed.

"What goes on?" Lachlan asked.

Cavan looked up from his desk. "Merc—what is she doing here?"

Alyce didn't wait for her husband to explain, she stepped forward. "Your wife suggested I can be of help to you and I agree."

Cavan stood and slapped his hands on the desk, leaning over in an intimidating pose. "I respect my wife's opinion and so will allow you to join us this *one* time."

"And what if my skills serve you well?" Alyce challenged. "You won't allow me to help again because I am a woman?"

"I have no time to argue with you," Cavan said. "You may remain here for now, however the future will be discussed another time."

"Agreed," Alyce said as if letting him know he had struck a bargain with her that he would have to keep.

"A large troop of mercenaries appears headed this way," Cavan said. "They have caused harm to none so far, but that could be because we are their intended target."

"From what our scouts tell us," Artair said, "a tall man, who rides his horse with distinction and more handsome than you"—Artair paused to glance at Lachlan, though without a grin—"leads them."

"I know him!"

The three brothers turned wide eyes on Alyce.

Chapter 31

"How do you know him?" Lachlan demanded, having heard her clearly but somehow not quite understanding her, or perhaps not wanting to. After all he had made it clear to her that part of the reason he also had been at Everagis was to make contact with the mercenaries in the area to see if they could provide information about Carissa and in turn Ronan.

When Alyce still hadn't answered, Cavan spoke. "Explain," he ordered with the command of a laird who expected obedience.

"His name is Septimus," she said. "And I struck a bargain with him so that Everagis would remain safe."

"A shrewd decision," Artair said.

"A necessary decision," she corrected. "I had people to protect."

Lachlan shook his head. "You knew I wished to make contact with the mercenaries and yet you never told me."

"I couldn't," she said truthfully. "I gave my word

to speak of the bargain to no one in exchange for protection."

While Lachlan knew what it meant to give your word, it disturbed him that she had not confided in him. "But you knew that the mercenaries might be able to provide information about my brother Ronan."

"Your brother Ronan was not among the mercenaries."

"How do you know that?" Lachlan asked.

"I've been to their camp several times."

"While I was at Everagis?"

"That was when I first made contact with Septimus."

Lachlan shook his head. "Wait. Are you telling me that while I was at Everagis you stole off into the woods and made contact with the mercenaries knowing full well I wished to make contact with them?"

"I had a duty to protect my sisters and we were not yet involved."

"They're not your blood sisters, nor are they nuns," Lachlan said raising his voice. "They are simply women, who I have made certain remain protected."

"No!" she shouted at him. "They are women who survived horrible situations and deserved to have a safe haven. And those women and I joined together and made Everagis just that, a safe haven for us. When the mercenaries arrived, did you really expect me to sit and do nothing but wring my hands and expect you to help us knowing your inevitable departure would leave us vulnerable?" Alyce shook her head. "I long ago abandoned the fantasy that a man would rescue me, love me, and protect me. I decided it was up to me to provide it all for myself."

"You could have trusted me," Lachlan said sadly, for it hurt to know that she felt she could depend on no one, but especially him.

"Could I have?" she asked. "Would you truly have understood? You wanted an answer from the mercenaries, while I required much more."

"Have you told us all you know of the mercenaries?" Cavan asked.

"No," she answered boldly. "And I will not, for I gave my word."

"Before or after you became involved with me?" Lachlan asked.

Alyce shot daggers from her eyes at him. "You truly need to ask that?"

"Enough," Cavan ordered. "You can settle your differences in private later. At the moment we need to deal with the present situation."

"I will go speak with Septimus," Alyce said, though it sounded more like a command.

"You will not," Lachlan snapped.

"He is a friend and I will speak with him," she argued. "And settle this matter reasonably."

"He may be a friend of *yours*, but not of the Sinclare clan," Lachlan said.

"I thought I was a Sinclare," Alyce challenged. "Wouldn't that then make a friend of mine, a friend of the Sinclares?"

Lachlan stepped toward her to argue, but Cavan interrupted.

"She is right," he said. "If this Septimus is here to visit with Alyce then we will welcome him."

"He arrives with a troop," Lachlan argued. "Such a heavy contingent speaks more of battle than a mere visit."

"We will send a messenger," Cavan said.

"I will go to him," Alyce insisted.

"You will not," Lachlan ordered.

"You cannot stop me," she argued.

"I most certainly can. You are my wife and carry my child and I will not see you placed in harm's way."

"I can take care of myself," she said, shaking a fist at him.

He grabbed hold of it and yanked her to him. "I don't care. You are my wife and will do as I say."

"Like hell I will."

"Don't challenge me on this," Lachlan warned.

"What challenge?" she snapped. "You can't stop me."

"Try me?"

"Stop!" Cavan shouted. "This is no time to argue. I will send a messenger to the mercenaries and see what brings them to our home. In the meantime we will devise a plan of attack in case it proves necessary."

Alyce yanked herself free of her husband and headed to the door. "Septimus is not here to war with you, and I will not help you make plans to attack a friend."

"We are your family," Lachlan said, stopping her before she could grab hold of the latch.

"Are you?" she asked. "I see that you all trust each

other, and yet not one of you trusts me when it comes to this matter."

"I must protect my people," Cavan said.

"Which is exactly what I did," Alyce said and shut the door hard behind her when she left.

She hurried her steps, mixing with the shadows of the great hall until she reached the kitchen entrance and then made her way through, the cooks so busy they barely noticed her. Once outside she knew her time was limited. She needed to get to her horse and out of the keep before the gates were sealed tight. Local farmers were probably still arriving seeking the safety of the walled village, but soon the gates would be closed tight and she would have no way out.

The wind whipped Alyce's wool cloak around her, and she was glad for its protection. She made it unnoticed to the stable, everyone much too busy to pay heed to her actions and she wished to keep it that way, though it would not be easy. If she could reach Septimus and talk with him she knew she could have this misunderstanding settled before any blood was shed.

Men were much too quick to raise a sword, and though Cavan sent a messenger to Septimus, she knew full well it would read more like a demand and that would not set well with the mercenaries.

And selfishly she had another reason. Septimus would have news of home, and she wanted desperately to hear about her sisters and Everagis.

After her mare was saddled and she had a chance to consider her actions, she realized that if Cavan or her husband did not want her to leave the keep, they would make certain she was unable to. Therefore, Cavan had purposely let her go and there was no reason for her to hide her departure. But why argue over it with her?

She had no time to give it thought, wanting more than anything to see Septimus and hear of home. She rode through the village and out of the open gate assuring those who called frantically to her that she was going to help as many to get to safety as possible.

They certainly would report her departure to Cavan, but then he already knew where she went.

Alyce knew from what Piper had taught about Septimus's scouting tactics that while he led the troop, he would have men scouting a few miles ahead and also along the perimeters. They would know of the messenger's approach long before he arrived, and they were probably also aware of the exact positions of the sentries Cavan had posted. One thing she had learned about the mercenary group was that they were no ordinary ragtag band of men, and she couldn't help but wonder again over their origins.

Once she left the moors, and reached the woods she kept to the edge of the forest knowing Septimus's men would spot her and take her to him and sure enough that was what happened. Two of his men she was familiar with, Dale and Hagen, approached.

She had to smile for they were night and day in appearance, Dale short and stout and Hagen simply large.

Hagen was grinning. Surprisingly, he possessed

all his teeth and not a one was yellow or rotted. His diction marked him more an educated man than a mercenary.

"Septimus advised you would arrive before we reached Caithness. It is good to see you again," Hagen said

Alyce grinned from ear to ear; she was happy to see them. "How is everyone at home?"

"Septimus warned us you would ask at once about Everagis, but he asked that we should get you to camp before we answered any questions or we might never make it there."

She laughed. "He is wise."

"He says it's because he understands women," Dale said, motioning her to follow him, Hagen taking up the trail behind her. "And strangely enough, I bloody well think he does."

Alyce had a string of endless questions to ask, but she knew it was best that she waited and though the ride wasn't long, it seemed like it took forever. Finally, they arrived at the camp and after greeting her, Septimus walked her to a more secluded location at the bank of a creek and sat with her a few feet from the water's edge.

"My sentries are posted well. No one spies on us here," he said.

"Why are you here?" she asked eagerly.

"Why, to rescue you, of course."

"I'm going after her," Lachlan said as soon as he received word that his brave wife rode off to help bring the farmers to safety. He turned to leave the solar and found Artair blocking the door.

Lachlan turned and pounded Cavan's desk. "You knew she'd go to him, and you let her." He shook his head. "If it were your intention all along, why didn't you just let her go from the beginning?"

"I wished to see what she would do," Cavan said calmly.

"You mean you wanted to know if she would obey your orders," Lachlan said.

Cavan nodded. "She impressed me with her many skills, but her one fault is . . ."

"Obedience to authority," Lachlan finished.

Cavan nodded. "She is too accustomed to leading and has no patience for anyone's dictates but her own, though I have seen her acquiesce to you on occasion."

"Not this time," Lachlan admitted reluctantly.

"It was to be expected; she looks on Septimus as a friend," Artair said, having left his post at the door to join his brothers.

"But I am her husband," Lachlan emphasized.

"You'll find that while that holds importance, it also gets in the way," Artair said.

Lachlan shook his head. "I don't understand."

"You're thinking like a husband," Cavan said, "while your wife thought like a warrior."

"She was wise and courageous in bargaining with the mercenaries," Artair said.

"She could have told me," Lachlan said, still feeling the bite of mistrust.

"That would have meant a betrayal to the mercenaries and they would have retaliated, not only against Alyce and her village, but you as well," Cavan said. "As Artair commented, she made a wise and also necessary choice."

"She refused to tell you everything concerning the mercenaries when you asked," Lachlan reminded.

"But she freely told us about Ronan," Artair said. "And she was blunt that she gave her word so therefore was bound to it." He snickered. "You're just angry that she took off to meet a man handsomer than you."

Fury engulfed Lachlan and he raised a threatening fist to Artair. "You're damn right I am. And when I see him I'm going to beat the hell out of him."

"Rescue me from what?" Alyce asked Septimus.

"From an unwanted marriage."

"I appreciate the offer but it isn't necessary," she said, wondering who precisely had sent him. Her sisters had known all too clearly the situation and the repercussions of sending Septimus to Caithness.

"You don't want to give it some thought?" he asked.

While she missed everyone and her life at Everagis, and it still continued to prove a challenge in adjusting to life at Caithness, lately she had come to the realization that she would find it impossible to live without Lachlan. She loved him more than she thought possible and she looked forward to raising their child, and hopefully more together.

"You're thinking about it," Septimus said.

She shook her head and smiled. "No, I'm thinking about why I would never leave him."

"Tell me, so that I can return with your words and let your friends, who worry about you, know you are happy."

She thought of what to share with him and the others, but how did she put into words what she truly felt when she was still realizing it herself? Of course, she could say that she loved him, but the women knew she did. Whatever could she say that would convince them and perhaps even make her fully accept why she truly chose to remain with Lachlan?

"I will tell you before you return home," she said.

"I return now if you are certain about your decision."

"You cannot leave yet," she said, grabbing hold of his arm. "You must stay for a few days at least and meet my new family."

"That's not a good idea," he said.

"You must," she urged. "Cavan, the laird of the clan Sinclare, must know that you did not come here to attack his home."

"I do not care what the laird of the clan Sinclare thinks."

"There will be no bloodshed," she ordered sternly.

"You should be laird. You give orders easily enough."

"Then obey them and meet with Cavan and his brothers."

Septimus stood and held his hand out to help her up. Once she was on her feet he said, "We will camp here. If the Sinclare men wish to meet with me and see that I am no threat to them then let them come here to my camp tonight."

"To expect the laird of the clan Sinclare to come to you would be considered an insult and reason for battle. I will not be part of such nonsense."

"No faith in your new family?" Septimus asked.

"Respect for my new family," she confirmed with a quick nod. "You either do what is right or suffer the consequences."

"You threaten me?"

"I am truthful with you and I expect the same in return," she said. "You either present yourself at the Sinclare keep tonight or tuck tail and run."

"Now that's a challenge that could have serious repercussions."

"No," she snapped, "it is the right thing to do and if you can't see that then turn around and go home without a word from me."

"Not much of a bargain."

"Who said anything of this being a bargain?" she gloated. "You do as I say or go home."

"If you were a man—"

Alyce took a challenging step toward him, "You'd what?"

"My leader was right," he admitted. "You are a woman to respect, but not one to underestimate."

"Wise observation," she said. "I'll expect you at the keep at sunset."

"I don't seem to have a choice."

"I gave you one," she insisted. "Go home or come to the keep."

"The keep it is," he said reluctantly.

Alyce bid him farewell until later, and while Hagen and Dale followed her back to where they had met her, she couldn't help but fret. It wasn't over the meeting tonight, though she knew it would probably prove difficult. It was something Septimus had said.

Tell me so that I can return with your words and let your friends, who worry about you, know that you are happy.

He didn't say your friends who sent me.

Who then had sent him?

Chapter 32

Lachlan sat alone at the table in the great hall. Cavan had the children moved to a safer section of the keep and so the hall was empty, not a person or a sound stirring but him. After Cavan had received word that Alyce had been met and safely escorted to the mercenary camp, and with plans for a surprise attack completed, only to be used if necessary, there was nothing left to do but to wait.

Normally, his patience could handle most any wait, but this wait was proving much more difficult. He understood that Cavan would have never allowed Alyce to ride off without being protected. Lachlan knew his brother would have their best scouts following her, but with Alyce having learned from Piper, Lachlan worried that Alyce could easily outwit them.

However, he trusted his wife's word. Her only intentions were to go and speak with Septimus and once done, she would return. She wanted no bloodshed and neither did Cavan, so this particular matter could be resolved easily enough, or so he hoped. He still felt an itch to punch this Septimus, though knew it would serve no purpose other than to make him feel better.

He saw his mother approach and he honestly was pleased to see her. He had always found it easy to speak with her. She was never one to berate or judge, instead she talked, asked questions and made suggestions, and you suddenly realized a solution to your problem.

"May I join you?" Addie requested with a smile, though she didn't wait for an answer. She sat beside her son.

"Are you here to lecture me?" he asked teasingly.

"Do you need one?"

He shook his head. "I don't know. I thought I was doing well, being a good husband." He shook his head again. "But Artair suggests that being a husband can sometimes get in the way."

"While there is logic to Artair's observation, it is being a husband himself that allowed him to learn that."

"So he didn't really become the all-wise-one until he got married?"

Addie laughed. "Your ability to see humor in life is what makes you so special."

"I always thought I was special," Lachlan grinned proudly.

Addie rested her hand on his arm. "Your uniqueness serves you well. While Cavan concerned himself with everything and everyone, and Artair sought logical solutions, and Ronan tried to be as brave and wise as his older brothers, you stood apart."

"How so?" he asked, touched that his mother thought of him that way.

"You always smiled and always had a good word for someone, always treated others with respect and you were always confident in your decisions." She smiled. "Cavan came to me once when he was about ten and you just six. He wanted to know why everyone liked you better."

"Truly, he did?" Lachlan asked, stunned.

Addie nodded. "He did, and I tried to explain to him that it was your nature and you would always be that way and that he shouldn't fret over it, for he had his own good nature."

"So you told him that I was always going to be liked more than he," Lachlan said with a laugh.

Addie laughed along with him. "I suppose that is the truth of it."

"Cavan is a great leader and respected. I much admire his strength and courage."

"And a leader needs both," Addie said, "for he must make decisions that are not always easy and will not always please everyone and at times may cause him to be disliked."

Lachlan had to grin. "So this is a lecture."

"Nonsense," Addie said grinning. "I wouldn't lecture my grown son, though I will leave you with a reminder."

"Which is?"

"You knew who your wife was when you married her."

"Not so," he said. "I first thought her a nun, then a

woman named Terese, and then I finally learned she was Alyce all along."

"Precisely," Addie said, her smile spreading wide. "I must go. I will see you later."

"Damn," he mumbled after his mother left. Alyce was who she always was no matter what name she went by. He had been privy to her biting nature on occasion, and though it had seemed foreign to him, it was a part of her.

And the woman he had known and come to love was the true Alyce Bunnock. And why was that? It was simply because she was allowed to be who she always was. Her father never truly made her who she was; she was who she was all along, just as he was. And while his family accepted his nature, Alyce's father made her suffer for hers, but regardless, she continually struggled to remain true to herself.

Lachlan felt pride swell near to bursting in his chest that he should have a wife who was a true warrior.

The doors to the great hall burst open and along with the wind Alyce entered. She shut them tight and hesitated where she stood. He couldn't blame her for being cautious, though he was relieved they would get to speak with one another alone before his brothers descended on her.

He started toward her, ready to wrap her in his arms and kiss her until they were both mindless. He cringed and turned when he heard his brother's voice ring out.

"Good, you've returned," Cavan said, entering the great hall with Artair not far behind. Honora was close on her husband's heels, and Lachlan wasn't surprised to see Zia follow. The only one missing was his mother.

Lachlan shook his head when he saw her hurrying in a few feet behind Zia.

Zia went to Alyce's side. "You are feeling well?"

"I feel wonderful," Alyce said with a hesitant smile at first. "The ride in the autumn chill exhilarated me."

"You look great," Honora said. "And I'm envious how the babe has not prevented you from doing anything."

"Yours did?" Alyce asked with interest.

"Enough female chatter!" Cavan ordered and had the women shooting heated glares his way. "We have a serious matter to discuss."

"We'll talk later," Honora said with a pat to Alyce's arm.

They began taking their usual seats at the table in front of the hearth and pitchers of hot cider were soon placed in front of them along with a light fare.

Lachlan stood at the end of the bench waiting for his wife to slide in first, his mother already seated at the other end. Alyce acknowledged his gallantry with a simple nod, though her blue eyes told him much more, and he knew his brother was about to deal with not the shrewish Alyce Bunnock, but the imposing Alyce Sinclare.

"Tell me," Cavan said to Alyce, filling her tankard with hot cider.

Alyce didn't hesitate. "You will receive Septimus and a few of his men tonight just before sunset."

"For what reason?" Cavan asked.

"He is a friend of mine and I expect my family to accept him as such."

"He is a mercenary," Artair said as a statement of fact.

"And that should matter why?" she asked.

"They are not known for being trustworthy," Cavan said.

"I say he is," Alyce argued.

Lachlan remained silent, watching the exchange, enthralled by the liveliness in her eyes. Her resolute nature was one of the things he loved about her.

"There it is," Lachlan said to Cavan. "You have her word on it; that's good enough."

Cavan nodded and before he looked to his mother, she stood.

"I'll see that food is prepared," Addie said and hurried to the kitchen.

"So this Septimus came all this way just to visit with you?" Artair asked.

"No," Alyce said and tore off a piece of black bread. "He came to rescue me."

"What?" Lachlan said, swerving around to stare at her.

Alyce patted his arm. "Don't fret. I told him I didn't need rescuing."

"That he should even think that you do—"

"You did snap me away from my home," Alyce said matter-of-factly.

"You're defending his actions?" Lachlan asked, shaking his head. "I don't believe it."

"You're making something out of nothing," Alyce said.

"A man arrives at my home and claims he's there to rescue *my wife* and I should think nothing of it?" He shook his head so hard that his long hair whipped him in the face. "No!"

"You should be pleased that I have such a concerned friend."

"You have *a husband*," he reminded.

"Who gave me no choice but to go with him."

Lachlan leaned in close so that his nose was a mere fraction from hers. "I cannot wait to meet Septimus."

Alyce smiled. "He looks forward to meeting you." She turned and glanced around to everyone at the table. "I will see you all later; I feel the need to rest."

"Are you all right?" Lachlan asked worried.

"Just tired," she said.

Zia was fast to offer advice. "A nap should serve you well."

"I will see that she rests," Lachlan said and took hold of his wife's arm.

"No need," Alyce said. "Stay and talk with your brothers. I am sure you have much to say to each other. Besides I intend to nap in your bedchamber here in the keep."

"Good idea," Lachlan said, relieved that she would remain close by.

Lachlan wasn't surprised that she pressed her cheek to his before placing a faint kiss on his lips and whispering, *later* before she walked away. He had the overpowering urge to go after her. However, he was surprised when she stopped and began looking over the display of battle plans made with an assortment of pebbles and stones on the table, two over from theirs.

She started shaking her head. "This would have never worked."

Cavan turned as did Artair while their wives smiled.

Lachlan walked over to his wife. "You need to rest."

She brushed him off with a shake of her hand. "Look at this," she said pointing to a grouping of smaller rocks. "Your assumption of Septimus's approach is not logical."

Artair hurried off the bench. "It most certainly is."

"No, look here," she said stressing where she pointed. "You assume he would strike from this point because it is the most common attack point, right?"

Artair nodded. "It truly is the only accessible one."

"No, it isn't," she insisted and began moving the stones around, though Artair protested.

"Let her show us," Cavan ordered.

"Not all battles are fought equally," she said as she maneuvered the stones. "You must consider your foe and his tactics, or you'll find yourself in trouble."

"But you aren't always familiar with your foe," Artair objected.

She looked at him startled. "You should be. Many times friendly clans turn unfriendly and when strangers linger in the area or stranger after stranger show up, then it should be an alert that someone is scouting your home for a possible attack."

"A good point," Artair admitted. "Tell us more."

"My wife needs to rest," Lachlan said.

"This is important, Alyce," Cavan said. "I would prefer to discuss it now, but if you are too tired—"

"You're right, it is important," she agreed. "It needs to be discussed now."

Lachlan was about to object when he saw his wife's face brighten with delight. He could see how excited she was that Cavan actually respected her opinion and he himself was proud of her.

"I feel fine, Lachlan, so no need to worry," Alyce said and then returned her attention to the display table.

Lachlan stood speechless. He had not expected his wife to consider what he thought. Yet she took a moment to assure him, knowing he would be concerned. She had considered him and that not only stunned him, but pleased him.

He, his brothers, and his wife were soon converged over the table, listening and sharing opinions with Alyce's suggestions making the most sense. Soon the stones and pebbles were rearranged and the three men nodded their approval.

"You're right," Artair said. "That is a much better plan of defense and attack if necessary."

"I also suggest you change your sentry stations," Alyce said and detailed where and why.

Cavan continued nodding. "You make good points. I'll see to those changes immediately."

"You are a remarkable strategist," Artair said. "I'd be interested in discussing more with you."

"Another time," Lachlan said, slipping up behind

his wife and wrapping his arms around her waist. "She needs to rest." He was prepared for her to protest, since she appeared to be enjoying herself, but she surprised him.

"My husband is right," Alyce said, caressing her protruding stomach. "His son grows restless, which means he wishes me to rest. Besides I wish to be refreshed for our guests tonight."

"Septimus and his men will be welcomed as your friend," Cavan assured her.

"I know," she said. "If I doubted your intentions I would have never showed you the error of your battle tactics against him."

Lachlan gently urged her away from the table, feeling enough had been said on the matter. But after only a few feet he was surprised when she stopped and turned around.

"Another thing you should be aware of, Cavan. The men you sent to trail me lack in skill, but don't feel bad, Septimus's men weren't much better."

Lachlan scooped up his wife in his arms and hurried from the room before another rousing debate could start between the pair.

Chapter 33

"**D**on't waste your time arguing or chastising me for my actions," Alyce said, slipping her arms around Lachlan's neck after he deposited her feet on the floor in his bedchamber. She favored the feel of the strong corded muscles in his neck and often allowed her fingers to linger there.

"And why is that?" he asked, resting his hands at the curve of her hip.

His simple touch felt more intimate, or perhaps that is what she wanted from him . . . intimacy. Lovemaking with her husband was something she thoroughly enjoyed and something they did often. It had not suffered because of disagreements. Rather it had grown stronger bonding them more closely than ever.

When they made love, nothing came between them. They simply surrendered to each other, and Alyce had never felt so safe and secure than at those moments. It was then she knew how very much he loved her and always would.

"Because it will do you no good," she said and tenderly pressed her lips to his and sighed with pleasure.

"Keep that up and you know what will happen."

"I'm counting on it," she whispered before kissing him with a firmness that left no doubt she wanted more from him.

"You need to rest," he said, concerned after ending the fiery kiss.

"I will sleep better if you make love to me and—" Her hand drifted beneath his plaid, settling around his hardness, and she smiled. "It's obvious you want me."

"I always want you, you witch," he said teasingly. "I look at you and I grow hard."

"And you touch me and I grow wet," she murmured and stroked the length of him.

"Damn," he muttered. "You make me lose my senses."

"I'd rather you lose control."

"It's not nice to challenge me."

"I don't feel like being nice. I feel like—" She whispered in explicit detail what she wanted from him.

He claimed a forceful kiss from her as his hands took firm hold of her waist and hurried her to the bed. Neither bothered removing clothes, both much too eager and ready for the other to bother with such nonsense.

With a quick altering of garments, Alyce was soon guiding him inside her. She loved to feel the silky length of him throb in her hand and know that soon he would rest deep inside her and bring her the most exquisite pleasure over and over.

He groaned when she squeezed him and he in turn nipped at her hard nipple beneath her linen blouse. She groaned, his mouth refusing to let go as he suckled until she thought she would go mad.

She released him and arched up to greet his thrust, crying out in sheer delight. He rose over her, his hands on either side of her head and the passion she saw in his dark eyes excited her all the more.

"Are you all right?" he asked. "I'm not hurting you."

She sighed, grinned, and splayed her hands on his solid chest. "You could never hurt me. You love me too much, as I do you."

"Damn it, wife, I didn't think you could make me any harder and here you go and do it."

She wiggled beneath him. "And oh, does it ever feel *so good.*"

He shook his head with a smile. "Damn, I'm a lucky man to have found you."

She wrapped her legs around him driving him in deeper and with a moan she said, "I claimed you Lachlan Sinclare, and I won't let you go."

Neither spoke after that, they loved hard over and over and over until their bodies were spent and breathless and all they could do was lie beside each other, hands clasped and utterly content.

Lachlan entered the great hall hours later, refreshed not only from lovemaking, but the nap he took with his wife and from a quick wash and a change to a fresh white linen shirt beneath his plaid. He had left Alyce with Zia, who had stopped by their bedchamber to see if she could be of any help. He hurriedly took his leave when Honora arrived shortly after Zia and the three began talking of women things.

Cavan was with Artair in the great hall, which was ready to greet their guests. Tables were crowded with pitchers of ale, wine, and an assortment of foods that would tempt any appetite. It was already tempting his.

He reached for a piece of roasted fowl, his favorite.

"Don't touch that," his mother yelled. "You know your father's rules not to eat before the feast begins." With that she disappeared into the kitchen.

His two brothers grinned as he approached.

"We got the same when we tried to pinch a bite," Artair said.

"You're laird now, Cavan, can't you change the rules?" Lachlan asked, his stomach growling for the roasted fowl.

"Do you want to be the one to tell Mother that Father's rules are no more?" Cavan asked.

"No," Lachlan answered quickly enough and suffered his hunger pains.

"You will do well with Septimus tonight?" Cavan asked Lachlan.

Oddly enough Lachlan didn't smile. "He proves a challenge, since I wonder why he felt the need to rescue my wife."

"I need you to hold your temper," Cavan said.

Lachlan laughed. "Since when do I have a temper?"

"Since you got married," Cavan said.

"No," Artair objected. "It's since he realized just how deeply in love he is with his wife."

Lachlan smiled. "I always knew I was in love with my wife. It was making certain she knew she felt just as strongly about me."

"And does she?" Artair asked.

"Of course she does," Lachlan said, annoyed that his brother should question the obvious.

Artair rested his hand on Lachlan's shoulder. "You'll never truly know for sure unless you free her to make her own decision."

"She is free," Lachlan argued. "She does as she wishes."

"But was it her choice to wed you and make her home here at Caithness?" Artair asked.

"It was her duty to wed," Cavan said. "Lachlan at least loves her and obviously she loves him."

"That doesn't seem to be in doubt," Artair agreed. "But I think Alyce would have preferred to make the choice herself, just as each of our own wives did."

Cavan bristled. "Honora didn't have a choice."

Lachlan laughed along with Artair.

"You two were perfect for each other from the start," Lachlan said. "We were just waiting for you both to realize it."

"Enough," Cavan ordered, annoyed by his brothers' teasing. "We need to focus on the mercenaries tonight and find out if they know anything about Ronan."

"Alyce says they don't," Lachlan reminded.

"That just means she hadn't seen or heard anything," Cavan said. "But what of before the mercenaries arrived in the area? Could they have seen our brother somewhere? Be alert and ask questions."

"There's one other thing I'd like to know," Lachlan said. "And that is who sent Septimus here to rescue Alyce?"

No one had a chance to respond. Their wives' jovial voices reached the men in the great hall before they entered, and Lachlan couldn't help but be struck senseless when he saw his wife.

She wore a deep green velvet gown gathered beneath her full breasts and falling in a swirl at her slipper-covered feet. Long sleeves fell at the wrists to gold-trimmed points, which also weaved through the velvet under her breasts. Her blond hair was piled high on her head with stray strands falling along her neck and a few short strands curling at the sides. Her cheeks were flushed pink and her full lips rosy. She was stunning.

He told her just that, though she objected.

"This is all," she said with a graceful swirl, "thanks to Zia and Honora. They worked magic."

Lachlan leaned close, whispering in her ear. "They had to have magic to work with from the start and you, my lovely wife, are a magical beauty."

Horns trumpeted the arrival of their guests, and Alyce gave her husband a quick kiss.

"Be good," she whispered.

"I thought I was," he teased with a nibble at her ear.

"I think perhaps," she said with a smile, "your charm will be tested tonight."

"Ye of little faith," he murmured.

"Ye, who knows her husband," Alyce laughed softly and took hold of his hand to tug him along to stand beside his brothers and greet the guests.

Lachlan bristled as soon as he caught sight of Septimus. He was ready to argue that the man wasn't as handsome as he, but damned if the mercenary hadn't caught the eye of every female servant who glanced at him. At one time their eyes would have held steady on Lachlan, but now their eyes were stuck on Septimus.

Cavan greeted the man with a firm handshake and welcomed him to the home of the clan Sinclare.

They soon were all seated at the table in front of the hearth, a few of Septimus's men occupying the other tables along with Cavan's warriors. Lachlan knew his brother had planned for any possibility and part of it was due to his wife's strategy skills.

Lachlan noticed his mother kept busy seeing to all her guests, though one rather large mercenary seemed to draw her attention the most, and he wondered if he was being a problem.

His wife's hand settled on his as they got comfortable at the table.

"That is Hagen and he a good man," she said with a nod in his direction.

He wasn't surprised that she noticed what he did, since she was always alert to everything going on around her.

Conversation was general at first with everyone being polite to a fault. Lachlan knew it wouldn't remain that way. Both sides sought answers and would eventually demand them.

A couple of hours later, with niceties and food done, Cavan said, "It is time to be truthful."

"I agree," Septimus said and looked directly at Lachlan. "I have come to rescue your wife."

"I've heard," Lachlan acknowledged, "though you've wasted your time. Alyce needs no rescuing."

"Isn't that for her to decide?" Septimus asked, though to Lachlan it sounded more like a challenge.

Lachlan ignored him and countered with another question. "Who sent you here?"

"What difference does it make?" Septimus said.

Before Lachlan could challenge him, Alyce spoke up.

"I'm curious myself, since it wouldn't have been anyone at Everagis; that would leave me to believe . . ." She stared at him.

Septimus nodded with a smile. "You knew since my arrival."

"I suspected," Alyce asked. "But why?"

"Explain," Cavan ordered curtly.

Septimus lost the smile. "My leader sent me here to see if Alyce remained of her own accord."

"Who is your leader?" Cavan asked.

"I cannot tell you that," Septimus said and offered no reason.

"Why?" Artair asked before anyone could.

"A command," Septimus said.

"It makes it seem as though you're hiding something," Lachlan accused.

"I expected your questions to center more on your brother Ronan," Septimus said. "And don't you search for a woman; your enemy's daughter who slipped away from you?"

"Perhaps all the answers tie together," Alyce suggested.

"You've suspected my leader's identity since the first night you entered our camp, haven't you?" Septimus asked.

"It seemed a logical assumption," Alyce admitted. "Your leader always remained in the shadows where he couldn't be seen. And when I demanded to meet with him you gave me an excuse and saw that it never happened. I asked myself why? Why did someone work so hard not to be seen? The answer was easy. He didn't want to be recognized, which meant I would recognize him, and why? He resembled Lachlan."

"So you assumed Ronan is our leader," Septimus said.

"Our brother wouldn't lead a band of mercenaries," Cavan said as if insulted by the mere suggestion.

"Why not?" Septimus asked just as insulted.

"He'd have no reason to," Artair explained. "He has a home to return to."

"Perhaps he has a good reason for not returning home," Septimus suggested.

"I don't believe that," Lachlan said. "Ronan would return home if he could, therefore, something is preventing him from coming home."

"I have to agree with Septimus on this," Alyce said

to everyone's surprise. "My father would have never believed that I would fake my death so I wouldn't have to return home."

Lachlan shook his head. "Not Ronan."

"You don't know that for sure," Alyce said. "You have no idea what has happened to him in the time he's been gone."

"It doesn't matter," Cavan agreed with Lachlan. "Ronan would come home if he could."

"Sometimes something happens to change people," Alyce said.

"Cavan changed," Honora said and looked with loving eyes at her husband, "but still he fought to get home. I believe Ronan would do the same."

"Any Sinclare would," Cavan said, his fist pounding the table. "I do not believe Ronan leads a band of mercenaries."

"What you mean is that you can't see your brother degrading himself that way," Septimus said and stood. "We're finished here."

Every one of his men got to their feet.

Cavan stood, though stilled his warriors with his raised hand. "I'll have an answer, Septimus."

"Don't you already have it?" Septimus challenged. "You don't believe your brother would lead a band of mercenaries like us." He motioned for his men to leave and they all filed out, except Dale and Hagen who waited for him near the door.

Septimus looked to Alyce. "I will wait one day. If you wish to return to Everagis join us and I will make certain you get home safely."

Lachlan stood and stepped toward him. "My wife isn't going anywhere."

"I came here to give her a choice, and I will see that she has it." Septimus turned and headed for the door, though he stopped just short of leaving and swerved around. "We would not want your brother Ronan part of us. He is a coward."

Chapter 34

L achlan and Artair went to go after Septimus, but Cavan's strong command stopped them.

"Let him go."

Reluctantly and angrily both brothers returned to the table.

Anger bubbled in Alyce and so she spoke without thinking. "You insulted him."

"You took his side before," Lachlan accused. "And you take it again?"

"I see the truth of the situation," she defended. "While you see what you want to see."

"What do you know of truth?" Lachlan asked sharply. "You believed that Ronan led the mercenaries and never shared that with me when you knew how important it was to me to find my brother."

His accusation felt like a slap to the face and it angered her all the more. "I wasn't certain. I assumed it could be your brother, since he hid his identity from me. Why else would he not speak with me face-to-face?"

"And you couldn't share it?"

"It wasn't my place?" she asked, hurrying off the bench to stand and glare in turn at each of them. "For whatever reason, your brother apparently doesn't want to be found. And Everagis needed the mercenaries' protection. You did as I expected upon meeting Septimus. You insulted and belittled him and expected him not to retaliate?"

"He called our brother a coward," Cavan said, his tone bitter.

"A generous admission," Alyce snapped.

Gasps circled the table, and it was Zia who spoke first.

"I know for certain Ronan is no coward. He suffered his wounds bravely while at my village."

"And he fought like a true warrior," Cavan said, his fist so tight at his side that his knuckles turned white.

"I cannot believe you side with Septimus and would believe our brother a coward," Lachlan said.

Alyce refused to give way to the tears that threatened. "You once promised me that nothing would hurt our friendship and that you would never judge or condemn me." She glared at her husband, her eyes heavy with unshed tears. "You lied to me."

Alyce ran from the room and up the stairs to the bedchamber. She shut the door behind her and let her annoying tears fall, swiping angrily at them now and again. She quickly slipped out of her dress and hurried into her skirt and blouse. She had little time if she planned to catch up with Septimus.

She ignored the ache in her heart and the voice that argued with her to calm down and see reason. She felt betrayed by her husband and nothing could make her see that any differently. If she couldn't trust him then she couldn't stay with him.

He loves you.

Alyce covered her ears and shook her head. "It doesn't matter."

Love does matter.

Damn, but she hated arguing with herself. And if love mattered so much where was her husband? Why hadn't he followed after her and continued arguing with her until they settled this? Didn't he care that he had hurt her?

She sat on the edge of the bed. She would give him a few more minutes. If he didn't barge through that door soon, then she would assume her decision a wise one and go home to Everagis.

Lachlan paced in front of the large fireplace in the great hall, his head and heart in turmoil. He would have never expected this from her "I can't believe she sided with Septimus."

"Don't be so harsh on her," Zia said. "I believe she was trying to help us in her own way."

"She went against her family," Cavan snapped.

"A family she has yet to feel safe with and a laird who has yet to fully trust her," Zia argued.

"Trust is earned," Cavan said curtly.

"Have I earned it yet?" Zia asked, her violet eyes challenging her brother-in-law.

Artair stepped between them. "Enough. I will not see family argue."

Cavan glared at him. "And who will you defend?"

"My wife," Artair said, stepping in front of his brother, "for she is my family as are you."

"You accuse me of not defending family?" Cavan asked, his dark eyes full of fury.

"Stop it!"

All eyes turned to Addie.

"I've heard enough."

Lachlan felt an instant repentance upon seeing the sadness in his mother's green eyes. That their arguing had hurt her was much too apparent. And he suddenly realized what he had done to his wife and how she must be feeling.

He had promised never to judge her and he had done just that. And oddly enough it was love that had driven him to it. Love for a brother he wanted desperately to return home. While he ignored the love he had for his wife and she had for him.

"Alyce was nothing but truthful," Addie said.

"But—"

"You are laird and I respect your position, Cavan," Addie said. "But you will remain silent while I have my say."

Lachlan saw that his mother waited for his reply, giving him the respect owed a laird.

Cavan nodded and Addie continued.

"Zia is right. Alyce tries to help us in her own way, while honoring her word. How can you fault her for that, when you yourselves would do the same? Don't you see that Alyce feels a kinship to your brother?"

Lachlan cringed at his own foolishness. He had allowed jealousy to interfere with reason. He didn't like that Septimus had come and, to him, threatened to take his wife away, and then he called his brother a coward, blinding Lachlan to any common sense.

"She thought Ronan needed protecting, from whom she wasn't certain and even if it proved to be family, she would have protected him. She honored her word at every turn and you condemn her for it."

Cavan could not hold his tongue. "She thought Septimus calling our brother a coward was a generous admission. Doesn't that upset you?"

Addie got teary-eyed. "It fills me with joy."

Lachlan felt like he had been hit by a charging horse, the realization was so sudden. "Good lord!"

"You understand what your wife was trying to tell you," Addie said, her smile touched by tears.

"Damn, I'm a fool," Lachlan said, shaking his head. "Why didn't I see it?"

"You and your brothers allowed your anger to get in the way," Addie said, "while Alyce remained a warrior and heard the truth of Septimus's words."

"What are you talking about?" Cavan demanded.

"I think I've got it," Artair said and his wife nodded as if she did too.

Honora placed her hand on her husband's arm. "How foolish of us."

"I must be deaf and blind," Cavan complained. "I don't know what any of you are saying."

"Alyce gave her word," Lachlan said. "Septimus

made it clear his tongue was sealed by command of his leader, and so if Ronan was somehow known to his leader, he could not say."

Cavan shut his eyes and shook his head. "And so he called him a coward."

"Which he couldn't have done," Addie said.

"Unless he had somehow known him," Lachlan finished. "And that is what my wife understood. That Septimus gave us a message even though his orders were otherwise."

"And he chose to call him a coward," Cavan said, "so that his men would not suspect that he divulged any pertinent information."

"He knew my wife would understand, damn it," Lachlan said, "while I couldn't wait to condemn her. She must feel as if I betrayed her as did her father when he abandoned her to the convent."

"We all did," Cavan said. "Go get your wife so that we may make amends."

Lachlan hugged his mother first and whispered, "Thank you for always believing in her."

"Alyce is trustworthy, brave, and true," Addie said. "I knew that when first I looked upon her. You must never forget it."

He felt chastised and so he should, for he had failed to believe in his wife when she needed him the most and if it took him the rest of his life, he would make it up to her. He hurried up the stone stairs and to his bedchamber.

He intended to grab hold of her and beg her forgiveness. While he didn't think she'd accept his apology easily, she eventually would, for she loved him and oddly enough he knew she would always forgive his foolishness.

He opened the door keeping a smile off his face, though he wanted to grin knowing that his wife would take great pleasure in making him plead his case.

He burst in the room and found it . . . empty.

Chapter 35

Alyce sniffled back tears.

Septimus laughed and shook his head. "Lachlan will come for you."

"No he won't." She sniffled again.

"He loves you."

"This is your fault," she said angrily and shook a fist at him.

"I just did what I was sent to do."

"Ruin my chances of a happy life?"

Septimus shook his head. "No, I give you a chance at a happy life. Your husband will come for you, and you will know beyond doubt that he wants you and loves you."

"This was your leader's intentions?"

"If I confide in you about my leader, you will be obliged to tell your husband and so I must remain silent," Septimus said.

"I understand. Can you tell me more about Ronan?"

"You intend to return home to your husband, don't you?"

Alyce nodded, her heart having grown heavier the further they traveled from Caithness. She couldn't bear the thought of never seeing her husband again, of never knowing his touch, his love and even his foolishness.

"I shouldn't have been so hasty to leave him. I should know by now all men are fools, and I should have given him a chance to make amends."

"I wouldn't be surprised if he was feeling the same way."

She brushed a tear from her face. "You think he realizes he's been a fool?"

"I know he loves you and that is enough."

"How do you know that?" she asked.

"He wears it proudly in his smile, in his eyes, in his actions for all to see," Septimus said. "The man has simply lost his heart to you and unless you return and forgive him, he will surely perish and die."

Alyce gasped. "He will not."

"Believe me," Septimus said with a hardened tone. "He will, for once true love is found and lost, life becomes meaningless."

Alyce sighed. "Oh my, you have lost a love."

"This is not about me," Septimus bristled. "I will send Hagen with you to make sure you return safely."

"It's not necessary."

"Don't argue. You won't win," he said. "Hagen goes with you."

Dale sped toward them reining in his horse at the last moment. "Trouble. A rogue band of warriors heads toward Caithness. They are clever, splitting up around sentries so it appears that two or three ride alone. I believe they will attack farms on the outskirts of Caithness."

"I will warn them," Alyce said, already turning her horse around.

"We will help," Septimus said.

Dale shook his head. "No. There is no time for us to reach them. If Alyce and Hagen take the trail our men used to scout Caithness they will reach the first farm in time to warn them."

"Surely the sentries will warn beforehand," Septimus said.

"The various sentries will alert the approach of two or three men, and soon enough understand what goes on," Dale said. "Time is of the essence here."

"I must go," Alyce said.

Septimus reached out and took hold of her arm. "First, let me tell you . . ." He leaned in close and whispered.

"The two of you needn't have come with me," Lachlan said to Cavan and Artair, who rode on either side of him. He then glanced over his shoulder. "And I don't believe we needed such a large contingent of men."

"It's simply a precaution in case Septimus should have other ideas," Cavan said. "Tactically, your wife would agree."

"I suppose she would," Lachlan said. "But I simply intend to collect my wife, after pleading what a fool I am, and return home with her."

Artair grinned. "That's a good start."

"I hope Alyce is all right," Lachlan said, having continually voiced his concern for her well-being since he had discovered her gone. He had gone mad with anger when he couldn't find her, which instantly turned to worry, and then he had been ready to jump on his horse and go after her as soon as he had realized that she had left for good, until Cavan had calmed him down and Artair had offered sensible advice.

They had waited until dawn, certain that the mercenaries would not leave until then, giving them time to reach their camp before or shortly after they left.

A scout rounded the bend and approached on a run. Breathless he said, "The camp was abandoned last night."

Alyce watched the band of rogue warriors gathered not far from the Connors farm from a safe place. They would attack them first, leaving suffering and grief behind, then move on to the next farm until someone stopped them.

She motioned for Hagen to follow her and when they were a safe distance, she ordered him to go to the keep and get help, and have them sound the alarm. She had hoped Lachlan had come after her and if he had, he might not be too far away to help her.

Alyce rode to the Connors farm as if she was going to pay a visit, calling out a lively greeting when she arrived. She kept a smile on her face until she entered their cottage and delivered the news.

"We'll have help soon enough," she encouraged when she watched Mary turn pale with fear.

Jake and his sons went into action, gathering weapons and pushing furniture aside to open the hiding spot he had fashioned for moments like this. He got upset when Alyce wouldn't join his wife and daughter.

"I won't hide from battle; I never have and I never will," Alyce said and took hold of one of the swords.

"You are pregnant," he said, clearly worried.

"My child is the son of two brave warriors," she said with a smile. "He knows better than to get in my way."

The blood-curdling scream outside announced the rogue band's arrival and had the two young men jumping in fright, but the sound of the horn from the keep denoting attack gave them courage.

"Word has been received," Alyce said joyfully. "Help will be here soon. Unfortunately, we can't remain inside for long. They will torch the cottage in their need to hurry their attack."

Lachlan urged his stallion to go faster but he was already going as fast as he could. As soon as he and his brothers had heard the attack horn sound, they hurried to the keep.

"It can't be Septimus," Lachlan called out to his brothers.

"We would have noticed that he reversed his tracks," Cavan said, keeping pace beside him. "Besides, Alyce would never have allowed it."

Lachlan was relieved to hear his brother say that, but he was damn frightened for his family's safety at the keep. At least he needn't worry about his wife; she was safe with Septimus.

Alyce took one warrior down with an arrow from the window and Peter, the youngest of the two Connor brothers, got another one. She quickly calculated that ten or more warriors remained and that was a hefty amount for her and Jake to fight on their own, but soon they would have no choice. The warriors were preparing torch arrows and she and Jake couldn't let them do that.

She turned to Peter and John. "You both keep as many warriors from descending as you can."

"No," John protested. "We'll join you."

Alyce shook her head. "You'll be more help to us in here with your arrows."

"Don't argue with us," Jake ordered his sons.

"We have to go now. They're almost ready to fire the first torch," Alyce said and looked to Peter. "Get him before he releases it. Get as many as you can."

The young lad nodded, though fear glazed his brown eyes.

The lad didn't disappoint them. He took the warrior down, and another, allowing his father and Alyce to make a hasty exit and surprise two warriors. Two more came at her and, while she was quick to wound one, the other sliced her shoulder before she landed a knife in his gut. Just then Hagen arrived, leading a group of Sinclare warriors.

He was off his horse and in front of her in seconds. She didn't protest since her shoulder burned and she didn't feel herself, though the babe remained calm. She was surprised to suddenly see Zia beside her and then she heard Honora's voice and not soon after Addie's. The clashing of swords continued around her, and she wasn't sure but she thought she saw a bow in Honora's hand and her shooting arrow after arrow, while it seemed that Addie, sword in hand, battled alongside Hagen who had left her side.

The whole scene seemed surreal and Alyce couldn't quite understand what Zia was saying to her. She staggered trying to remain standing. Then everything began spinning, and she heard shouts in the distance and the ground shook and just before everything went black, she saw her husband's face and felt his arms go around her.

Chapter 36

Lachlan sat by his wife's bedside waiting for her to wake up. He had so much to say to her and he was anxious to say it. When he had seen her collapsing, he had bolted off his horse and ran to her, leaving his brothers to protect him as he ran through the melee to his wife.

He had caught her just as her eyes fluttered closed, but he thought—he hoped—she had seen him, for he believed she had smiled at him before she passed out. Zia had tended her, assuring him the wound was nothing to worry about. And when she hadn't revived, Zia explained that it sometimes happened, but she would awaken soon enough. She suggested it would be good to get her back to the keep where she could rest in familiar surroundings.

He had followed her advice and had been sitting by her bed for over an hour now, worried that she wouldn't wake up, that he would never have the chance to tell her how sorry he was.

He took hold of her hand. It was warm and soft but also branded with a callous or two from hard work.

She always worked hard and never complained and she was always there for her friends and adopted family, and for him, though he was foolish enough to believe otherwise. He raised her hand to his lips and kissed the back and then the palm and then he gently nipped at each fingertip, a playfulness of his that never failed to delight her. He hoped and prayed it would rouse her from her sleep, but she didn't move.

He hung his head and gently brought her hand to rest against his chest over his heart.

"My heart belongs to you, Alyce," he said softly. "It always will. I wanted you to be happy. I wanted you to know you were free with me and what did I do? I failed you and why?"

"You're a fool."

His head shot up to see his wife's eyes open, and he smiled. "You're right."

She broke into a wide grin and tapped his chest. "But you're my fool."

He took hold of her hand, kissed it again, and then leaned over to gently kiss her lips. "I'm sorry."

She pressed her cheek to his. "I am too."

"You have no need to be."

"But I do," she said, taking hold of his arm to help her sit up.

He lifted her up with a supportive arm while his other hand stacked pillows behind her back.

She grabbed hold of his hand. "You're everything I wished for in a husband."

"You wanted a fool for a husband?" he teased.

She smiled and her blue eyes twinkled. "I wanted a good man with a good heart and I found him, only it took me awhile longer to realize just how good his heart truly is."

He shook his head. "I promised you I would never judge or—"

She pressed her fingers to his lips. "I should have told you my suspicions right away. I should have trusted your reaction."

He tried to disagree, she objected with a shake of her head, but he gently pried her fingers away. "How could you fully trust me when I never gave you a choice in marrying me?"

"It doesn't matter any—"

"It does matter," Lachlan insisted. "You had a right to that choice and if I had trusted our love enough, I would have given it to you. I feared you would deny me, yet I was confident I could make you see my decision was the best for us."

"It was best."

"Of course it was," he said with a smile.

"Then there is no need to discuss it any longer," she said. "What is done, is done. We start anew and bury the past—"

The door opened and Zia walked in along with Artair, Honora, and Cavan following soon after. Lachlan reluctantly gave them time to have their say, when he would have much preferred to continue talking with his wife.

He couldn't get her words out of his head.

Bury the past.

She was burying the past as she once buried her identity, to escape an unpleasant situation. He didn't want the past buried. He would rather resolve it so that it could never again hurt them.

A sprinkle of laughter broke through his musing and he was glad to see that all was well with his family again.

Addie rushed in breathless, her face smeared with sweat and dirt, a dirk sheathed at her waist and her green eyes bright. "Are you all right?" she asked, rushing over to Alyce.

"I'm fine," Alyce assured her.

"I knew you would be," Addie said proudly. "You're a Sinclare woman and today I finally remembered just what that meant. Bless you for reminding me, I finally feel alive again."

Lachlan could see the difference in his mother. She even looked younger than her fifty-three years. They all could see the difference, and it was good to see her . . . happy.

Zia finally chased everyone from the room, insisting that Alyce needed to rest, though she remained to speak with them.

"You suffered a minor wound that will barely scar, though I would recommend you curtail your strenuous activities from here on."

"Is there a problem?" Lachlan asked, taking hold of his wife's hand with worry.

"None that I foresee," Zia assured them both. "It's a precaution, after all your time is just two months away and I prefer you reserve your strength for that battle."

"I understand," Alyce said, "and will heed your advice."

"Good, then I will see you later for supper," she said and left.

Alyce yawned as Lachlan tucked the blanket around her. "There is something I must tell you, but I don't recall what it is."

"Don't worry," he said with a kiss. "You'll remember sooner or later. Now you must rest. We can talk later."

"You'll stay until I fall asleep?" she asked, reaching out to grab hold of his arm while her eyes started drifting closed.

"I'll stay as long as you want," he promised, pleased she wanted him there, though annoyed with himself for being the cause of her worries and injury. If he had kept his word and had not judged her, she would have never left with Septimus and she would have never been wounded.

He had to smile; knowing his wife she would have argued, telling him that the situation would have been worse since help would have come too late to the Connors. He was proud of his wife's courage and tenacity, both made her a remarkable woman . . . his woman, his love, his life.

He waited until she slept soundly and then he left. He had plans to make before she woke and he wanted everything perfect, since tonight his wife would finally have her chance to choose.

Alyce was famished and ate heartily, though no one knew she silently struggled to recall what it was she had to tell her husband. She knew it was important, very important and it troubled her that she could not recall it.

The great hall was filled with revelry, everyone celebrating the victory at the Connors farm and the news that the last of the rogue warrior band had been found and disposed of with haste. Caithness was safe once again and many paid homage to Alyce for her bravery.

She smiled and graciously accepted the many thanks bestowed on her and while Septimus's visit had stirred memories of her home and family, he had also made her appreciate her new home and family. She had been angry when she first arrived here and had little interest in the Sinclares, but she learned fast enough they were good and generous people, and it was hard not to like them.

A roar from the middle of the room got hers and everyone's attention. She was surprised to see her husband standing there and she smiled. He was devilishly handsome and she swelled with pride, for he belonged to her.

"I have something to say and I want all to hear me."

He walked toward his wife, his smile as charming as ever and his dark eyes aglow with what surprisingly looked like mischief. And Alyce smiled, prepared for whatever challenge he intended to throw at her.

However he startled her when he began with . . .

"Alyce Bunnock, I intended when the time was right to search for a wife, one that would fit my needs and plans for the future. I never considered love and then I met you and tasted true love for the first time. I knew from the start I didn't want to live life without you, and I knew one life would never be enough time for us to love, but it is what I have to offer you."

Alyce remained stunned when he took her hand in his.

"Alyce Bunnock. It sometimes frightens me how very much I love you, and how my world would crumble without you, but I give you a choice here and now. Marry me, Alyce. I love you and always will. If you choose not to accept my proposal, as hard as it would be for me, I will set you free."

Alyce struggled to get up and Lachlan quickly helped her stand. Tears glistened in her blue eyes and she shook her head.

"You don't wish to marry me?"

Loud gasps echoed in the great hall.

"No, you fool," she said aloud. "I just can't believe you offer me a choice. I can't believe you would free me from our vows."

"It is what I should have offered you from the beginning. And it is the only way we can ever truly be free to love one another."

"Good lord, I love you so much!"

"Does that mean you'll wed me?" he asked with an eager grin.

"Yes, yes, a thousand times yes! I will wed you," she cried and let her tears of joy flow.

Cavan stood and offered the first toast and told everyone to prepare for a wedding celebration to remember. Artair's toast followed and more after his.

"You truly mean to wed me all over again?" she whispered to her husband, surprised.

"Of course," he said. "I want it done right this time. We will be wed by a cleric, you will sign the document, and there will be a feast."

Alyce brushed her tears away. "You have given me what I always wanted. You have made my dreams come true."

He leaned close and whispered in her ear, "I will always make your dreams come true."

She pressed her cheek to his. "That you do whenever you kiss me, touch me, love me."

Addie's joyous voice broke them apart as they watched her raise her tankard. "I toast my daughters."

The three Sinclare brothers raised their goblets to their wives.

"To three strong, courageous, beautiful women I am proud to call my daughters and that my three sons were wise enough to love."

Alyce's loud gasp startled everyone.

"What's wrong?" Lachlan asked, dropping his tankard to the table when he saw his wife's hand grab her stomach.

"I remember," she said excited. "I remember what it is that was so important to tell you."

"What?" Lachlan asked anxiously.

Alyce smiled. "Ronan is on his way home."

Chapter 37

~~~⟨◯◯⟩~~~

Alyce was exhausted and the wedding festivities had just begun. Even though snow fell heavily outside, the whole village was warm and joyous as they helped celebrate the wedding of Lachlan and Alyce Sinclare.

It had taken a couple of months from Lachlan's proposal to arrange the exchange of vows and obtain new documents with the help of Bishop Aleatus, a close friend of the Sinclares, who had insisted on performing the ceremony. And all had hoped that Ronan would return before it and share in the grand day, but he still hadn't appeared.

Addie had seen to a feast fit for a king and queen while Honora and Zia had transformed the great hall into a magical woodland with winter greenery, pinecones, and berries everywhere; and numerous white candles flickered like dozens of bright stars throughout the room.

Her father even attended and gave his blessings and told her how proud he was that she did her duty like a true leader. It was enough to let Alyce know that in his own way he loved her.

She sighed, resting in a high-back chair that Zia had made certain to provide for her, insisting it would be much more comfortable than the usual bench. And she was glad she hadn't protested, since the chair helped ease the pain that had started in her back this morning.

Lachlan was busy talking with everyone, though he glanced her way often enough. He knew she was tired and he had wanted her to rest for an hour or so and then join the celebration, but she didn't want to miss a minute. It was all too exciting.

She watched with pleasure the younger children laughing while running after each other, and caressed her stomach thinking how in no time she and Lachlan's babe would be one of them. The twins certainly wanted to join in the revelry, one bouncing to get free from his mother's arms and the other trying to walk with his father's help, while Blythe sat contented in her father's arms.

She shook her head as she watched her father try desperately to gain Addie's favor, but surprisingly she spent much time with Hagen, who had yet to rejoin Septimus. There was a sparkle in both their eyes when they looked at each other, which was often. Whatever would her sons think?

A stabbing pain caused her to double over with a moan and Lachlan was at her side in a second, as was Zia. She could barely breathe let alone speak.

Addie appeared, Hagen at her side, and Alyce had

to smile, for if she were right about the pair, it would no doubt create a problem, though she would side with Addie.

"She's in labor?" Addie asked.

"I believe so," Zia said. "We need to get her upstairs."

Lachlan scooped her up and everyone cheered as he carried her out of the room and up the stairs.

Once Alyce was in bed, Zia attempted to chase Lachlan from the room.

"No, I won't leave her."

He turned when he heard his brother's laughter.

Cavan entered the room. "I recall saying the same, but you'll be coming with me just as I went with you, though I didn't want to."

"I'll be fine," Alyce assured him. "And if I should want you, I will send for you."

Lachlan nodded and kissed her cheek. "That's good enough for me, since I know nothing would stop you from getting me here even if you had to come get me yourself."

"You truly do know me," she laughed.

He nuzzled at her ear. "Every inch and breath of you, wife."

Alyce gasped startled, and Zia hurried over and with one look said, "The sack broke, the pains will be close soon enough."

Cavan rushed Lachlan out of the room and hurried him back to the festivities.

After an hour Lachlan snuck upstairs to check on his wife and his mother chased him away.

"She has no time for you now," she said, shutting the door in his face.

By the third time, Addie had stationed Hagen in front of the door with orders that Lachlan was not allowed to disturb them. Surprisingly, the large man was sympathetic to Lachlan's plight and took time to speak with him before convincing him it was better he waited downstairs.

It was just before midnight, the celebration worn down, a few stragglers remaining, mostly warriors with no women to go home to and a snowstorm raging outside.

"It could take the whole night," Artair said. "It's just the way of things."

"That makes me feel good," Lachlan said.

Cavan laughed. "He wasn't that reasonable when Zia gave birth."

Lachlan chuckled. "He wasn't?"

"Not a bit," Cavan said. "I remember that I had to hold him down from running to her near the end when her screams got bad."

Lachlan cringed. "Damn, why did you tell me that?"

"It's just the way of things," Artair insisted.

"I don't want to hear it," Lachlan said, covering his ears for a moment, though his eyes turned wide and his hands fell to his sides when he saw Hagen enter the hall.

"I was told to fetch you," he said to Lachlan.

Cavan stood. "Is there a problem?"

"Don't know," Hagen said. "Addie just told me to bring Lachlan."

Cavan placed a strong hand on Lachlan's shoulder.

"I haven't heard a scream from her," Lachlan said, worried as they climbed the stairs. "Why hasn't she screamed?"

Artair followed but offered no sensible advice and that worried Lachlan all the more. Something was wrong. Terribly wrong. Why hadn't he heard his wife scream while trying to deliver their child?

Hagen lead them down the hall to the bedchamber, Lachlan behind him and Cavan and Artair following. Hagen rapped on the door and when it opened he stepped aside.

Lachlan stood in the doorway afraid to enter, afraid to hear that he had lost his beloved wife or child or both.

"Mother?" he said as if begging her to tell him.

Addie broke into a grin. "Alyce delivered your son without so much as a peep."

Lachlan near cried out with relief and joy, and he hurried to his wife's side, stopping abruptly when he saw the bundle in her arms and peered over the blanket at his newborn son.

"He's handsome like you," Alyce said with pride. "And didn't give me a bit of trouble birthing, and he smiled just like you when Zia placed him in my arms."

"Just like you," Zia confirmed with a soft laugh.

Lachlan was speechless. His wife looked radiant, not at all weary, and his son was a good size with a thatch of dark hair just like his own. He felt blessed, so very blessed.

Alyce held the babe out to him. "Hold your son."

Lachlan didn't hesitate. He cradled the tiny bundle in his arms for all to see. "My son, Roark Sinclare." He announced proudly the name he and Alyce had decided upon.

Everyone took turns looking at the sleeping babe who in turn favored them with a smile just like his father's, and they all laughed claiming like father like son.

Once Alyce yawned, Zia chased everyone from the room and ordered her to rest for the babe would soon wake wanting to suckle.

Zia instructed Lachlan to fetch her if need be, even if it were just to ask a question.

Lachlan thanked her profusely as he walked her to the door.

"I've never seen such an easy birth," Zia said at the open door. "Your wife was remarkable, not a scream or a protest. She simply focused on her task and birthed her son so easily that she truly didn't need my help."

Lachlan swelled with pride. "Still, I'm glad you were here to help. It made me feel better."

Zia smiled. "Thank you. Now go to your wife and new son."

Lachlan closed the door as Zia walked into her husband's waiting arms.

He hurried over to his wife and son, slipped off his boots and quickly shed his shirt, though left his plaid on and crawled into bed to wrap his arms around Alyce and his son.

"This wasn't how I thought of our wedding night,

though it is so much more than I ever hoped or dreamed."

Alyce reached over and rested her hand to his cheek. "Thank you—"

"It is I who should thank you," he insisted. "You birthed our son."

"No, I want to thank you for having the patience to love me, for not giving up when I snapped at you or blamed you or shouted at you or ran away, or failed to realize just how deeply you loved me."

"Now you know," he said softly.

She yawned, her eyes fluttering closed. "And I will never forget."

He leaned over and kissed her cheek, then kissed his son's tiny red cheek and with a yawn snuggled around them and went to sleep.

Next month, don't miss these exciting new love stories only from Avon Books

One Reckless Summer by Toni Blake

Jenny Tolliver's been the good girl all her life, and it's gotten her nowhere. Now that her marriage has been busted up by her cheating ex, she's decided it's time to regroup and rediscover herself.

Led Astray by a Rake by Sara Bennett

Livy Monteith will simply not marry the proper young man her parents have chosen for her husband. And the man she desires is a shock to all—the sinful scoundrel Lord Dominic Lacey.

To Ruin the Duke by Debra Mullins

All of London is abuzz with the shocking exploits of Thornton Matherton, Duke of Wyldehaven, a man as sinful and wicked as his name. Miranda Fontaine will do whatever it takes to pin down the notorious duke . . . even if it means seducing him herself.

A Talent for Sin by Lavinia Kent

Violet, Lady Carrington has money, the freedom to make her own choices, and no husband to rule her. She also has a delightfully attentive young lover, Lord Peter St. Johns, to satisfy her every whim. But will Violet give him her hand in marriage?